A Royal Pain . . .

The illegitimate daughter of a prince and a notorious courtesan, Lucia has been confined to schools and convents for most of her life. But that hasn't stopped her from causing one scandal after another. Exasperated, her royal father decides that his exquisite hellion of a daughter must be married immediately. And Sir Ian Moore, Britain's most proper diplomat, is the perfect man to choose her a groom.

Diplomacy, not matchmaking, is Ian's forte, but he vows to get the chit married off as soon as possible so that he may return to more important duties. Yet, despite an abundance of very eager, worthwhile candidates, none is a match for Lucia's spirit and fire. And the more time Ian spends with the infuriating beauty, the more reluctant he is to marry her off. Could it be that he has already found Lucia the perfect husband . . . and it is Ian himself?

Laura Lee Guhrke

She's No Princess

An Avon Romantic Treasure

AVON BOOKS
An Imprint of HarperCollinsPublishers

This is a work of fiction. Names, characters, places, and incidents are products of the author's imagination or are used fictitiously and are not to be construed as real. Any resemblance to actual events, locales, organizations, or persons, living or dead, is entirely coincidental.

AVON BOOKS
An Imprint of HarperCollins*Publishers*
10 East 53rd Street
New York, New York 10022-5299

Copyright © 2006 by Laura Lee Guhrke
ISBN-13: 978-0-06-077474-5
ISBN-10: 0-06-077474-6
www.avonromance.com

First Avon Books paperback printing: June 2006

Avon Trademark Reg. U.S. Pat. Off. and in Other Countries, Marca Registrada, Hecho en U.S.A.
HarperCollins® is a registered trademark of HarperCollins Publishers Inc.

Printed in the U.S.A.

10 9 8 7 6 5 4 3 2 1

For Judy Guhrke.
You went the extra mile for me
in so many ways during
the writing of this book.
I love you, Mom.

Acknowledgments

My warmest thanks to fellow author Eloisa James and her husband, Alessandro Vettori. Their assistance with Italian language was invaluable to me during the writing of this book.

Prologue

Lucia had always been a good liar. Whether this was a good thing or a bad thing depended on one's point of view. Lucia thought it a very good thing indeed when she was facing a palace guard at midnight, with tobacco and money in her pocket and plans of temporary escape in her head.

"I couldn't sleep, so I wanted something to read," she said, and gestured to the book in her hand. A book, Lucia had learned long ago in her days at French finishing schools, was always a convenient explanation for nightly wanderings. And her father, Prince Cesare of Bolgheri, had one of the most extensive libraries in all of Europe. "I was on my way back to my rooms."

"Your rooms are that way," the guard explained, pointing in the opposite direction from where she'd been headed.

She glanced back over her shoulder, then returned her gaze to him. "They are?" she asked in pretended bewilderment. "I could have sworn they were the other way." She gestured to the long corridor in which they stood, a corridor of Siena marble, gold leaf, glittering mirrors, and dozens of doorways. "It's so confusing here, I always get lost. So many corridors . . ." Lucia let her voice trail off in a helpless fashion, then she smiled. Lucia had a smile that could melt a man of stone; she knew it, and she used it whenever necessary.

This guard was not made of stone. He softened at once. "Very understandable," he said, smiling back at her. "But you know we have orders from His Highness, Prince Cesare, that you are not allowed to wander about the palace at night."

Her father was a stranger to her and the Piazza di Bolgheri was a prison, but she had no intention of being locked up in some remote corner and forgotten. She was a woman grown, with every intention of doing as she pleased. She did not express these sentiments aloud, however. "I didn't mean to wander," she said, all meekness and contrition. "As I said, I couldn't sleep."

"I will be happy to escort you back to your rooms."

Not made of stone, but not stupid either. With a silent sigh of resignation, Lucia allowed herself to be led back to her suite, knowing this was only a temporary postponement of her plans. Tonight was the last night of Carnival in Bolgheri, and guards or no guards, she was not going to miss the festivities.

Back in her suite of rooms, she found that her maid was still gone. The magic of Carnival beckoned to everyone, and she had dismissed Margherita so that the girl might enjoy it. Lucia passed through the darkened rooms to the doors that led onto the terrace. She waited until the guard on patrol had passed her and turned the corner, then she slipped outside and took a different route to her intended destination.

Moonlight and fireworks lit the sky. The sounds of music and revelry beckoned to her, celebrations that would last only a few more hours.

Though she had been living in her father's palace a few months, Lucia had learned her way around in less than a week. She had already determined which places were the easiest points from which to escape, and she headed straight for one of them.

The bawdy noise of Carnival grew louder as she approached the edge of the palace grounds, but she had barely pulled the gardener's ladder from the shrubs where she'd hidden it earlier in the day and set it against the stone wall of Cesare's fruit garden before her night of adventure was interrupted once again.

The hand on her arm made her jump, but when she turned around expecting to face another palace guard, she instead found the last person she would have expected.

"Elena?" She stared at her half sister, amazed. "What are you doing out here?"

"I was looking out my window," Elena answered, out of breath. "I saw you crossing the lawn in the moonlight, and I ran down to follow you." The younger girl wrapped her night robe tighter around herself and glanced at the ladder, then looked back at her. "Are you running away?"

"Go back to bed."

"Don't run away!" the seventeen-year-old implored, her hand tightening on Lucia's arm. "Things have been so much fun since you came. Oh, Lucia, I couldn't bear it if you left."

"Don't be silly," she said as she pulled her arm free of her half sister's grasp. "I'm not running away. Although I will, the moment I can get enough money to do it. Tonight, I am just going out for Carnival."

"All by yourself?"

Lucia chuckled and opened her arms in a sweeping gesture. "Do you see anyone with me?"

"Papa would be furious if he found out."

Lucia gave Elena a stern look. "He isn't going to find out unless you tell him."

"I won't tell, I promise." Elena glanced again at the ladder, then back at her. "You do this all the time, don't you?"

The concept of sneaking out was one Elena was clearly not familiar with, but Lucia had known that long before she'd ever met her half sister. Elena was the good girl, the legitimate daughter, the true princess. Lucia was the wild one, Prince Cesare's bastard child and shameful secret. She was no princess, and nobody really expected her to be good. She wouldn't have traded places with Elena for anything.

"Go back to bed," she ordered, and turned toward the wall. "For heaven's sake, you're standing out here in your night robe."

"So are you."

"I have clothes on underneath."

"Are you wearing a costume?" Before Lucia could answer, Elena's hand closed around her arm again. "Take me with you."

"What?" Lucia stopped and shook her head. "Oh, no. Cesare would kill me. For me to sneak out and get into trouble is nothing. I've done it before, and they expect no better of me. It's different for you. You can't come."

"Oh, please. Antonio gets to go out and do whatever he pleases, but I only get to watch Carnival from the balcony. I want to wear a costume and go into the streets like everybody else does."

"No, you don't. It would shock you. It's crude, it's noisy. You'd hate it. You'd be horrified."

"I wouldn't. Please take me with you." Elena stared at her in the moonlight, looking for all the world like an adorable puppy who had been cruelly denied a walk. "They never let me go anywhere," she whispered, sounding so forlorn that Lucia's heart constricted with affection and pity.

Poor girl. Her older brother, Antonio, was allowed all the liberties the son of a prince could ask for, but Elena was destined from cradle to grave for a life of royal imprisonment, sheltered and pampered and married off in a few years for the sake of alliance, never having known the richness of life outside palace gates and golden carriages.

"Come along, then," she found herself saying before she could regain her common sense. "But stick close to me," she added, gesturing for her sister to precede her up the ladder. "The last thing I need is for you to get lost."

"You'll think I'm your shadow," Elena promised, and paused at the top of the wall, straddling it. "How do I get down?"

"Just sit there for a minute." Lucia moved the ladder over a few feet, climbed up, and hiked her skirts up above her knees to do as Elena had done. Then she hauled up the ladder and lowered it on the other side. After descending to the alley below, she beckoned to Elena to follow and stripped off her velvet night robe to reveal the peasant clothes she wore beneath.

"The first thing we have to do is get you a costume," she said as she unraveled her long braid of dark hair to let it hang down her back. "And a mask," she added, pulling a black-satin mask from her pocket and putting it across her eyes. She fastened the ties at the back of her head, wrapped a red kerchief around her hair, and started out of the alley. "Wait here."

With some of the money she'd been hoarding, Lucia was able to procure a costume and mask similar to her own for Elena from one of the many street vendors who provided such last-minute necessities to those unprepared for Carnival. True to her word, Elena stayed on her heels as they slipped out of the alley and began winding their way through the raucous streets of Bolgheri.

Carnival was always an impressive spectacle. The balconies and windows were swathed in colorful draperies, the carriages and wagons were laden with harlequins, dominoes, and jesters, boisterous crowds roamed the streets, and music, fireworks, and confetti filled the air. Lucia and Elena spent a few hours watching the entertainments of mimes, acrobats, minstrels, and jugglers. Street vendors tried to tempt them into games of chance, but Lucia refused, smiling. She wasn't such a fool to risk her few precious coins on games she knew she couldn't win.

Elena did not say much, but as she stared in wonder at the sights all around them, the smile of delight on her face spoke volumes. Her joy at being free, even if only for a night, was obvious and heartfelt, and Lucia was so glad she'd brought the younger girl along. When Elena was back inside the prison of the palace, she would have a memory that would always make her smile.

As they paused to watch a performance of the *Commedia dell'Arte* in the center of a square, Lucia noticed a cart and oxen pull up beside them. In the back were two young men dressed as Neapolitan harvesters. The driver braked the cart as the pair waved and called to them to gain their attention.

"Look, Elena, we have a pair of admirers."

Her half sister followed her glance, smiled shyly at the men, then looked away again. "How boldly they stare at us."

"They are tall and strong," Lucia said with approval. "A pity we cannot see their faces behind those masks to know if they are handsome. Ah, well." Lucia smiled at the pair of men and blew them a flirtatious kiss.

The taller one gestured to her to pull off her mask and kerchief. Still smiling, she shook her head in refusal and watched him put a hand over his heart as if devastated. Laughing, she waved good-bye and turned to Elena. "Come. I want a coffee."

Elena followed as Lucia merged into the midst of the crowded piazza, making her way toward the coffeehouses and bakeries on the opposite side. By the sheerest luck, they managed to gain a table at an outdoor café and ordered coffee. As they waited for it to be brought, Lucia pulled her tobacco and papers out of her pocket and began rolling a cigarette with the ease of long practice.

Elena stared at her in amazement. "You are going to smoke?"

"Don't look so horrified," Lucia answered, amused. "At least it's not hashish. Want one?"

"Women aren't supposed to smoke."

Lucia reached for the candle on their table.

"Exactly," she said, and lit her cigarette, then leaned back in her chair, smiling at Elena's shocked face.

In coloring, they were not unlike—both of them had the dark eyes and dark, curly hair of their father, but that was where the similarity ended. Elena was delicate, sweet, and painfully idealistic, everything Lucia was not. Perhaps that was why she had grown so fond of the girl during the three months she'd lived here. Though Elena participated in all royal functions and Lucia was kept out of sight at the opposite end of the palace, the two had managed to meet. Lonely and isolated from others, they had become secret friends.

"I didn't want to like you, you know," Lucia blurted out, blowing smoke into the air overhead.

"You didn't?"

"No. I came here fully prepared to hate you."

To her surprise, Elena began to laugh. "I didn't want to like you either," she confessed. "When we met, and you told me that you were Papa's bastard, I hated you. I didn't know he had any other daughter but me."

Lucia made a sound of derision. "That's no surprise. No one knows about me."

"I meant what I said before. I have had so much fun since you came. Hearing your stories, knowing all the outrageous things you've done, things I would never dare to do—"

"Listening to other people talk about life is no good, Elena," she interrupted. "Life is rich and sweet and very short. One has to live it, not watch it from a palace balcony."

Elena frowned, looking doubtful. But then she reached out her hand toward the cigarette. "Let me try this."

"If you've never smoked before, you won't like it," she said as she complied with the girl's request. "Just inhale a little bit," she added in warning, but it was too late.

In a fit of coughing, Elena waved away smoke and handed back the cigarette as quickly as possible. "That," she said with a shudder, "is one experience I am content to avoid. It's horrid!"

"It is rather," Lucia agreed.

"Why do you do it?"

"Because I'm not allowed to, I suppose."

"What else have you done that you're not allowed to do?"

"Nearly everything," she admitted, not sure if she should be proud of that fact or not.

"Doesn't your mother mind?"

"Mamma?" Lucia smiled, remembering Francesca's visits to her in boarding school, thinking of the dithery charm her mother possessed that captivated everyone. Lucia herself was not immune. She adored her mother. "It's hard to tell what Mamma really thinks about anything."

"Tell me more of the things you've done." Without waiting for an answer, she went on, "Have you ever kissed a man?"

"Of course."

Elena's eyes widened with all the eager curiosity

of any seventeen-year-old girl with no experience. "What was it like?"

Lucia told her the truth. "Wonderful. I can't explain why, but it is."

"Who did you kiss?" Elena asked. "Who was he?"

Lucia's mind flashed back to a summer three years before, and she was surprised to discover it no longer hurt to think of it. "His name was Armand. He was the blacksmith in the village by Madame Tournay's Academy. I was madly in love with him."

"A blacksmith? How did you meet him?"

"One day, I was in the village on an errand, and I saw him. He was standing over his anvil, pounding away. He had no shirt on, and sweat was running down his chest. I just stopped and stared at him. I'd never seen a man's bare chest before. He looked up and caught me staring. He smiled at me, and I fell in love with him. It was as simple as that. I started sneaking out at night to meet him. Armand made me feel beautiful and desirable for the first time in my life. It was the most glorious, wonderful thing that had ever happened to me."

Elena sighed and rested her elbow on the table, chin in her hand. "What happened?"

"Cesare found out, Armand married someone else, and I got sent to a convent."

"What?" Elena sat up in her chair, looking outraged. "I thought you were going to tell me some tragic tale of how he died of love for you."

"What romantic ideas you have, Elena."

"He was a cad! If he loved you, and . . . and kissed you, he should have married you, not some other girl!"

She could be philosophical about it now. "These things happen."

"I don't suppose you could have married a blacksmith anyway. Papa would never have consented."

Lucia knew she would have married Armand if he had loved her enough to defy her father. He'd taken Cesare's bribe of money and a merchant's daughter instead, and he'd broken her heart. That, she vowed, would never happen again. "When I wed," she told Elena, "it will be to a man who loves me so madly, so passionately, that nothing else matters to him. Otherwise, marriage is a trap, and a woman is a prisoner."

To her amazement, Elena nodded in agreement. "I am not yet married, but already I am trapped." Her pretty face took on an unhappy expression. "I have to wed some Austrian duke. His mother is English. It was all arranged by the British and Austrian ambassadors."

"I know. I heard all about it."

"I don't love him. I've never even met him, but I have to marry him. Papa insists on the match."

"Defy Cesare."

"I can't! It's all arranged. The treaties have been signed. Dowries paid. The Congress of Vienna will be preserved, we will have peace with Austria, and Bolgheri will have alliance with

England. There is nothing I can do to stop it. It is my duty."

Lucia wished there was something she could say to comfort her half sister, but there was nothing comforting about being forced to marry a man you did not love. She diverted the conversation. "At least when you feel trapped, you don't go off doing wild things and driving Cesare insane."

"Oh, I don't know," Elena said with a rueful smile. "I'm here with you, aren't I? Though I suppose it's the only time I'll ever have the chance to do something wild." She paused, and her expression became thoughtful as she studied Lucia. "Why do you always defy Papa? Do things that are forbidden?"

Lucia opened her mouth to answer, then realized she didn't know the answer. She fell silent, thinking it out before she spoke. "I like excitement, and there is a certain excitement in breaking the rules," she said after a moment. "Also, I love a challenge. Telling me what I can't do makes me want to do it."

"And when you break the rules, Papa has to remember you exist."

Lucia stiffened at her sister's words. For a sheltered, naive girl who didn't know much about life, Elena was very perceptive. "That, too," she admitted, and took a pull on her cigarette. Blowing out smoke, she added, "Why should he be allowed to pretend I was never born?"

"He shouldn't."

Lucia looked away from the compassion in her sister's face. That was ironic, since only a few hours earlier, it had been she pitying the younger girl. "It doesn't matter," she said, her voice brittle to her own ears. "I don't care."

"Yes, you do. But if it's any consolation to you, Papa forgets I exist most of the time. Antonio is allowed to do whatever he wants, but I cannot go anywhere, or do anything. Papa won't even let me attend a ball until I am eighteen. Before you came, there were times when I thought I'd go mad."

"I'm only in the palace because Cesare didn't know what else to do with me. His plan was for his palace guards to keep me under control." She paused to cast a meaningful glance around, then gave Elena a grin. "Do you think it's working?"

Elena grinned back at her. "I'm afraid not."

"I won't be controlled as if I am a puppet." Turning in her chair, she dropped the stub of her cigarette to the cobblestones. As she crushed it beneath her heel, Lucia spied the cart and oxen they'd seen earlier. It was circling the piazza, and the two men were standing in the back, scanning the crowd. "Don't turn your head," she ordered, "but I see those two men again. I think they are searching for us."

"Why should they be? They don't even know us."

"What does that matter? Men always want women, especially those who smile and laugh and flirt with them." She watched as the taller one turned in her direction. When he caught sight of her, he blew her a kiss, his answer to the one she'd given him, and she laughed, appreciating this sort of male attention for exactly what it was and enjoying it.

"They've seen us," she told Elena as her admirer turned to his companion and pointed in their direction. "They are coming this way."

"Oh!" Elena's eyes widened with excitement. "What if they want to talk to us?"

"Maybe we'll let them." Lucia leaned back in her chair with a casual air. "Or maybe," she added with a shrug, "we won't."

The cart pulled up beside the café where they sat, and a bouquet flew through the air to land in Lucia's lap. She looked down at the violets, then glanced at the man. After a moment, she picked up the bouquet and smiled at her admirer.

"What do the flowers mean?" Elena asked, glancing at the cart and back again.

"He wishes to make my acquaintance." The bouquet in her hand, she pushed back her chair and rose. "Let's go."

Without looking at the men, she turned and started in the opposite direction.

Elena hurried to catch up with her. "I don't understand. Don't you want to meet him?"

"I haven't decided."

"What if they lose us in the crowd?"

"Then I won't meet him, will I?"

"He'll think you don't like him, and he'll give up."

"He won't do that, I promise you."

As if to prove her words, the men's teasing voices called to them from close behind, indicating they had abandoned their cart and were following on foot. Within moments, they raced past Lucia and Elena, then turned to block their path through the crowd. Out of breath and laughing, Lucia's admirer dropped to one knee before her. "Sweet peasant," he said, "I beg you and your companion to let us walk with you a while."

"If we do," she answered, "you must first remove your masks, for I cannot walk with a man who keeps his face hidden from me."

He stood up. "If we show our faces, will you do the same? We know you must be beauties indeed behind those masks."

She considered that for a moment, then she consented with a nod. "But we must all unmask at the same time."

"Agreed."

Laughing, Lucia pulled off her kerchief and mask, then shook back the long, loose curls of her hair. She looked at the unmasked faces of their admirers and found the two men staring back at her and Elena in utter astonishment. As she studied their faces, Lucia realized their identity, and her laughter faded away.

"Sweet Gesù," she whispered, suddenly sick. She was staring at a pair of palace guards.

Chapter 1

It was a well-known fact among those in the British diplomatic corps that whenever His Majesty, King William IV, had a sticky situation on his hands, Sir Ian Moore would get the assignment. No one else had a chance.

It was true that Sir Ian, thirty-five years of age, had a successful, decade-long career as a diplomat. It was true that he was unmarried, unfettered, and willing to be a roving ambassador, able to go wherever duty to king and country sent him. Of course it was true that his loyalty and honor were beyond question. But during this time of peace in Europe, truly sticky situations where a diplomat could make his mark were rare, and many of Sir Ian's colleagues wished His Majesty's favorite ambassador would retire to his estate in Devonshire and give the rest of them a chance to shine.

The Turks and Greeks were a perfect example. Those people would test the mettle of any diplomat, so when a minor skirmish between those factions threatened to break into all-out war, no one was surprised when Sir Ian was sent to Anatolia. But everyone was surprised when scarcely a fortnight after his arrival in Constantinople, he was recalled to Gibraltar. Ambitious young diplomats crossed their fingers, hoping that somehow, some way, Ian Moore had finally blotted his copybook.

Ian knew his copybook was still quite satisfactory. As to the reason for his recall from the East, however, even Ian had to confess he was baffled.

"Why fetch me to Gibraltar?" he wondered aloud, sitting in his cabin aboard the *Mary Eliza*, one of His Britannic Majesty's finest and fastest ships of the line. As the ship carried him across the Mediterranean, Ian studied the map of Europe spread out on the table before him. "What could it mean?"

His valet, Harper, looked up from the shirt he was mending. "It must be very serious indeed for them to send for you so suddenly. Something big is happening."

"I cannot imagine what. The Turkish situation is the only thing of significance in this part of the world at present, and they intend to replace me in the middle of it. To what end?"

"All I know is it's a shame. There we were in

Constantinople, just settled in for a good, long stay, and then in the wink of an eye, there's a change of plan, and we're sailing off again." Harper shook his head with a sigh of regret. "Pity, that," he added. "Mighty fetching, those Turkish ladies looked in those trousers, and those veils of theirs ... makes a man wonder what's underneath. The sultan was going to give you one of his slave girls, you know."

"Harper, a true British gentleman would never own a slave girl. Barbaric practice."

"Maybe so, sir, but one of those Turkish girls would have worked on you like a tonic. Not to say you've been short-tempered of late, but—"

"That's absurd," Ian shot back, nettled. "I have not been short-tempered."

"If you say so, but you have been working hard for many months and haven't had any time for ladies." He paused, then added, "A man needs what he needs, you know."

Ian did not want to think about how long it had been since his needs in that particular area had been met. Too long. He shot a warning glance at the servant. "Harper, that's enough. Any more impudence from you, and I shall begin a search for a new valet."

The manservant, who had been valeting him since his fifteenth birthday, wasn't the least bit intimidated. The censure in Ian's voice slid off him like water off a duck. "Do you a world of good to loosen your cravat once in a while, sir, if you don't mind my saying so."

"I do mind." Ian drummed his fingers against the table, focusing his thoughts on important matters. "Why fetch me to Gibraltar?" he wondered again as he considered and rejected various possibilities. "Morocco is stable. Things in Spain are quiet. As for the French, well, our relations with them aren't good, but that's nothing new. I cannot imagine what the trouble is."

"Something to do with those Italians again, I say."

Ian hoped not. "I don't see how that is possible. The Italian situation is resolved. The Treaty of Bolgheri has been signed, the Congress of Vienna remains intact, and Princess Elena will be marrying the Duke of Ausberg when she reaches the age of twenty-one."

"Talk is, she doesn't want to marry him."

"She will do her duty. She has no choice."

Harper shrugged. "That's as may be, but girls are most unaccountable, sir. Especially the Italian ones," he added with feeling. "It's the temperament."

If there was anyone who ought to understand the Italian temperament, it was Ian. He'd spent a lot of time in that part of the world these past few years, pouring the soothing words of diplomacy over the Prince of Bolgheri and the Dukes of Venezia, Lombardy, and Tuscany, to preserve peace in the region and keep Italian nationalists from rebelling against the Austrian Empire, but despite his many trips to the region, he did not understand the Italians. He found their passions too dramatic and their moods too volatile for his fastidious British nature.

Ian gave up his speculations as a futile exercise and rolled up the map. Regardless of where they proposed to send him, he would do his duty. He always did. Nonetheless, when the *Mary Eliza* arrived at Gibraltar, and Ian presented himself at Government House, he could not help being surprised by his next assignment.

"You're sending me to London?"

"Not I, Sir Ian," Lord Stanton corrected him. "These orders are from the Prime Minister himself. You are to depart for home at once. I have dispatched Sir Gervase Humphrey to Constantinople to take your place and deal with the Turkish situation."

Sir Gervase hadn't enough experience. The Turks would make mincemeat of him. Ian, of course, refrained from expressing his opinion of his colleague. "What is the purpose of sending me to London?"

"This isn't any sort of demotion or reprimand. Quite the contrary, in fact. Consider this assignment a reward for all your hard work." Stanton clapped him on the shoulder, smiling. "You're going home, man. I'd have expected you to be overjoyed at the prospect. I'm going home myself in a couple months, and I'm delighted."

Ian wasn't delighted, and he was far more concerned with the reasons than the destination. "What diplomatic matter in London requires my attention?"

Stanton's expression became serious. "Sir Ian, you worked long and hard on the Italian situation, then there was that whole Dalmatian debacle, and then we sent you straight on to handle the Turks. You've only been home half a dozen times in the past four years and never for more than a few weeks. That's asking too much of any man, even you. So, the Prime Minister consulted with His Majesty, and they decided to send you back to England for a bit. It's almost June, the midst of the London season, you know. You'll have the chance for some pleasant company and good society. Think of it as a holiday."

"I don't need a holiday," Ian said, the sharp reply out of his mouth before he could stop it. Remembering the words of his valet, he pressed two fingers to his forehead until he regained his composure. It wasn't like him to be so testy. Perhaps he did need a rest, but that was hardly a reason to send him home.

He lifted his head and let his hand fall to his side. "William, we've known each other a long time. Between ourselves, could we stop doing the dance of diplomacy and come to the point? Why are they sending me home?"

"It's not a crisis by any means." Stanton pulled out a chair from the table and sat down. "But it is important. Prince Cesare of Bolgheri is coming for a three-month state visit in August, and they want you to handle the preparations. But this is really about Cesare's daughter."

The Italians again. Blast Harper for being right.

"Princess Elena is in London?" Ian also sat down, taking the chair opposite.

"No, not Elena. The other one."

"What other one?"

"Cesare's illegitimate daughter."

Ian raised an eyebrow. "Didn't know he had one."

"I'm sure he has a dozen, but this girl, Lucia, is a special case. Her mother was Cesare's favorite mistress. Seems he actually loved the woman. Years ago, of course."

"He fell in love with his mistress? Hard lines for a prince."

"He was quite a young man at the time—rash, hot-tempered, unmarried, and still sowing wild oats. A few years later, when he married Sophia of Tuscany, he set his mistress aside and sent the daughter off to live with her mother's relations in the countryside. He paid for her support, but he never publicly acknowledged her as his daughter."

"Cesare embarrassed over a bastard child?" Ian could not credit it. "Surely not."

"Not Cesare. The Duke of Tuscany demanded it during the negotiations of Sophia's marriage settlement. Later, Lucia was put in one of those academies for young ladies somewhere in Europe under her mother's name. She's been to half a dozen schools in Switzerland and France, but the girl's wild as a gypsy. Three years ago some scandal happened with a young man—a blacksmith—and right under the noses of the governesses at

Madame Something-or-Other's Academy outside Paris."

"How old is this girl?"

"Twenty-two. She was nineteen at the time. Anyway, nothing untoward happened to her, if you understand me." Stanton actually blushed. "The incident was all hushed up, Cesare got the young man married off to someone else and had Lucia locked up in a convent."

"To ensure there were no blacksmiths in the future."

"Exactly so. Problem was, the girl kept slipping out, doing God knows what. Cesare decided the only way to control her and avoid a public scandal was to have her right under his nose. He had her brought back to Bolgheri about six months ago and put her in an isolated wing of the palace until he could figure out what to do with her."

"And?"

For an answer, Stanton pulled a folded newspaper out of his dispatch case and tossed it across the table. It was clearly a scandal sheet. Ian scanned the article, quickly translating the Italian words, then he set the paper down without a change of expression. "So much for keeping the girl a secret. How accurate is this description of the incident?"

"They got their facts straight for the most part."

"What about Elena?"

"Nothing happened to either of the girls. They

wanted to go out for Carnival, just for a lark, you know. The guards, who were off duty at the time, escorted them back to the palace."

"They were not physically harmed?"

"No. Doctors examined them, and both girls are still . . ." His voice trailed off in acute embarrassment.

"Virgo intacta?" Ian supplied, Latin being the most tactful way of putting it.

Stanton gave a stiff nod. "Deuce of a mess if they hadn't been. Anyway, Cesare banished her, sending her off to live with cousins in Genoa, and he decided it was high time to find her a husband, one as far away from Bolgheri as possible."

"He acted for the best. The girl is clearly a bad influence on her sister." Ian fingered the edge of the three-month-old scandal sheet in front of him. "No success hushing up her indiscretions this time, however."

"Unfortunately not. Cesare was hoping to keep the incident quiet until he could get the girl married off, but as you can see, the story got out, along with rumors of her wild behavior. Like you, no one knew about this girl, and now word of her existence and this Carnival escapade is spreading throughout Italy. Prince Cesare finally admitted the girl was his own and granted her his surname of Valenti. His wife, Princess Sophia, is furious about it."

"Perhaps, but Cesare has no choice. His acknowledgment makes the girl better marriage material." Ian shoved the scandal sheet aside. "What about the Duke of Ausberg? Does he wish to back out of marriage to Elena for her part in this?"

"No, no. Elena is being seen as the victim of her half sister's influence. The marriage is going forward, and every aspect of the treaty remains intact."

"Then what is the problem?"

"Lucia wasn't in Genoa a month before she ran off. We have word she got herself to London and is living with her mother."

"Scandal sheets notwithstanding, if Elena suffered no harm from the incident, the Duke of Ausberg still wants to marry her, the treaty remains intact, Lucia's living with her mother, and all's well that ends well, where do I come in?"

"Cesare has a great deal of admiration for your diplomatic skills. He feels you are the perfect person to resolve the situation."

"What situation?"

"It's going to be tricky."

Ian leaned across the table, striving for patience. "What situation?" he repeated.

"While you are in London, you are to arrange a marriage for Lucia."

Ian stiffened in his chair. "You must be joking."

"You know I never joke about international relations. Cesare wants to get the girl married before she can cause the House of Bolgheri any further embarrassment. You are to find a suitable husband for her, make the diplomatic arrangements, and assist with negotiation of the marriage settlements."

"I have been removed from an important diplomatic mission in Anatolia to play matchmaker for some chit of a girl?"

"She is the daughter of a prince," Stanton reminded him. "And you played matchmaker for her sister."

"That was different. There was a treaty involved. The Congress of Vienna was at stake. Damn it, William—" Ian could feel his temper fraying, and that would never do. He bit back the frustrated words on the tip of his tongue and took a deep breath.

"Cesare does not want the girl back in Bolgheri for obvious reasons," Stanton went on. "Arranging a suitable marriage for her is the only alternative. Give her a strong-minded husband and a few children, and she'll settle down."

"And if she doesn't, she's her husband's problem?"

"Quite. Prince Cesare also desires to strengthen his alliance with us, and feels an English husband for her would be best. Catholic, though, of course. We have agreed to assist. She's already in London anyway. Get the girl launched into English society and find some suitable Catholic peer to marry her. Cesare gives you carte blanche. You will then assist his government's envoy and the groom's family in making the negotiations of the marriage settlement. They will be substantial, for the prince is providing an enormous dowry and income to get her off his hands. Before he goes home in October, Cesare expects a wedding. You will make that happen."

Lovely. A long and illustrious career of preventing wars, negotiating vital trade agreements, and preserving treaties had come to this. "Finding a husband for her could be handled by anyone in the diplomatic corps. She is rebellious and troublesome, I grant you. She's illegitimate, and her reputation has now been a bit damaged, but she does possess royal blood. The House of Medina isn't the richest principality in Europe, but it isn't the poorest either. Is she homely?"

"Quite the contrary. I'm told she's very pretty."

"Well, there you are. The girl's pretty, the father's a prince, there's plenty of money for a dowry. Despite her indiscretions, I'm sure there are prominent Catholic families in Britain who would be willing to connect with the House of Bolgheri through marriage. Especially with such a generous income from Cesare."

"Yes, but the prince insists that the girl's husband be a peer and possess substantial estates. No fortune hunters."

"I daresay, but surely there is someone already at Whitehall who could arrange all this. Why do you need me?"

"Cesare has asked for you specifically. He holds you in very high esteem and trusts your judgment. You are also well-respected by every peer in Britain, and you would facilitate matters nicely. Bolgheri is a desirable alliance for us, as you are well aware, and this marriage would further strengthen our influence on the Italian peninsula. We agreed to put your skills at Cesare's disposal. You do need a holiday, and you'll be in London anyway. It's perfect all round."

Perfect was not how Ian would have described it. "Ten years of faithful service to my country, and I am reduced to this."

"There's more." Stanton gave an apologetic little cough. "You won't like it."

"I am now a marriage broker for wayward girls," he muttered, jerking at his cravat. "I already don't like it."

"Her mother is Francesca."

"Good God. You mean to tell me that this girl's mother, Prince Cesare's former mistress, is England's most infamous courtesan?"

"Not quite so infamous nowadays. She's nearly fifty."

"She's been the toast of London for years. She has bedded more peers and ruined more fortunes than I can count. From what I hear, she's bankrupting Lord Chesterfield nowadays."

"All that's quite true, I'm afraid."

"Well, there you are." Ian tried to dredge up the discretion for which he was so well-known and the diplomatic finesse that had made him such a valuable asset to the British Empire, but for the life of him, he could not manage it at this moment. "What gentleman is going to want England's most notorious demimondaine for a mother-in-law, especially when the odds are he's bedded her himself? As to the daughter, from the way she's managed her life thus far, that scandal-ridden girl seems more suited to follow in her mother's footsteps than to become the wife of a British peer. At least that's what any gentleman I approach on her behalf is going to think. With a mother like Francesca, where am I going to find the daughter a titled husband with money, and a Catholic one, at that?"

"Cesare's orders are that the girl be removed from her mother's house and that there be no further contact with the woman. Seems the mother visited Lucia often when she was in those French finishing schools, and Cesare feels her influence is part of the reason the girl has turned out so wild."

"No doubt, but—"

"Lucia is to be placed with a suitable chaper-one and launched into English society while you search for an amenable groom and facilitate in-troductions."

"What of the girl? Does she have any say in the choice of her bridegroom?"

"No. His position, suitability, and willingness to marry her are what matter. Cesare trusts you to find the best match."

Ian was not flattered.

Stanton held out a sheaf of documents to him. "Here are your official orders from the Prime Minister, along with the specifics of Cesare's dower and a dossier of the girl's life."

"Such a coup for my diplomatic career," he

muttered with a tinge of bitterness as he took the documents.

"We have every confidence you will fulfill this assignment with your usual skill, Sir Ian." Stanton stood up with an air of finality. "We know you will do your duty."

Those words were a sharp reminder. Ian rose to his feet. He cleared his throat, straightened his cravat back to its original perfect knot, and with an effort, recovered his poise. "I always do my duty, Lord Stanton."

With a stiff bow, he departed, but his duty did not stop him from spending the journey from Gibraltar to London cursing troublesome Italian girls and international politics.

Lucia loved living with Francesca. They shopped and talked and spent countless hours together. Deprived of her mother for all but a few short visits each year throughout most of her life, she felt that she and Mamma were a real family at last.

Francesca was a charming hostess with a small, intimate circle of friends. Her current lover, Lord Chesterfield, a confirmed bachelor, won Lucia's approval at once because he was so obviously besotted with her mother. Being of the demimonde, Francesca cared little for the conventions of society. She also liked nothing better than scandalizing the respectable ladies of the ton.

For her part, Lucia was thoroughly enjoying herself. She was allowed to do what she liked and go where she wished, and she found that freedom lived up to all her expectations. Her mother gave her a generous allowance and all sorts of delightful suggestions on how to spend it. If anyone knew how to spend money, it was Francesca.

But one afternoon when Lucia had plans to go to Bond Street, she entered her mother's bedchamber to see if Francesca desired to accompany her and found the other woman already occupied. She was being fitted into a blue velvet riding habit by her modiste.

"I'm afraid I can't go with you today, darling. I have all sorts of plans. For one thing, my new riding habit has just arrived."

"So I see." Lucia studied her mother for a moment, appreciating how well the royal blue color complemented Francesca's dark auburn hair. She also noticed that the modiste was not simply fitting the riding habit, but was in fact stitching the pieces of it together right on Francesca's still-slender body, thereby achieving a skintight garment that would surely cause a scandal. "Are you wearing anything underneath that, Mamma?"

"Not a thing," Francesca answered, lifting her arm so that the modiste could stitch the side seam of the bodice into place over her bare skin. "Shocking, aren't I?"

Lucia walked over to the bed and fell back into the soft pillows lining the carved headboard. "Very shocking," she agreed in amusement. "But that won't stop the English ladies from rushing out to copy it. They'll all be getting stitched into their riding habits within a week."

"Exactly. But just as they begin to wear this fashion, I shall be on to something else."

Even at the age of forty-nine, no longer at the height of her beauty and with a few lights of silver in her hair, Francesca's daring but faultless fashion sense still held sway over the respectable ladies of the ton.

Lucia smiled. "I suppose you already have some new sensation in mind?"

"Of course," Francesca answered as a maid entered the boudoir with a calling card in her hand. "That carriage Chesterfield ordered for me will be here in less than a fortnight. It has mother-of-pearl inlaid on the doors and the ride—oh, Lucia, Chesterfield assures me it has the smoothest chassis you can imagine. I shall wear the fullest skirt I can find so that it billows all around me—a white skirt, I think—and I shall glide upon the Row like a swan glides upon the water. Not now, Parker," she added in English as the maid held out the calling card to her. "Heavens, can't you see I'm only half-dressed? I couldn't possibly see anyone now."

"The gentleman claims he is here on a matter of great importance," the maid replied. "He says that you were given to expect his arrival. Shall I have Mr. Fraser tell him you have gone out?"

Francesca shifted her position as the modiste moved to stitch up the other side of her bodice, then she glanced at the card. "Oh, dear, he's downstairs now? I've mixed things up, for I thought he was coming tomorrow—" She broke off and gave Lucia a rather furtive glance. "Tell him—umm—tell him I shall be down in a few minutes."

"Yes, ma'am." Parker set the man's card on the dressing table, curtsied, and departed.

"Who is he?" Lucia asked, her mother's odd glance at her a moment before making her curious.

"Oh, I don't know, darling," Francesca answered. "Go on to Bond Street and enjoy yourself." She tilted her head to look down at the modiste, who was on her knees stitching the gusset together under Francesca's arm. "Annabel, you must hurry. It doesn't do to keep a man waiting too long, especially when it's a matter of business. They get so impatient, poor dears."

"Yes, ma'am," Annabel murmured around a mouthful of pins.

"A matter of business?" Lucia repeated, more curious than ever. "Are you breaking with Chesterfield?"

"Not that sort of business." Francesca turned toward the mirror. "He wants to see me about some legal matter."

"What legal matter?"

"Oh, I don't know. Something deadly dull, I'm sure." She waved a hand toward the door. "Take the carriage to Bond Street. Since I'll be riding horseback to Hyde Park, I won't need it. Go on, now."

Lucia frowned, becoming suspicious. Her mother's manner was decidedly odd, almost eager to have her gone. She stood up and walked to the dressing table, taking the card before her mother could guess her intent and pick it up.

"Sir Ian Moore," she read aloud. "Ian Moore. I know that name." Her frown deepened as she tried to recall why it was familiar. When she looked at the card again and read his title, she knew. "He's the British ambassador who arranged for Elena to marry an Austrian duke. What is he doing here?"

"I told you, I don't know. A note came from someone at Whitehall that he would be coming to call, and I should expect him." She gestured to the card. "I can't refuse to see him. He is an ambassador."

"Elena's never even met that duke, and she's being forced to marry him to strengthen alliances. She's devastated about it."

"Indeed?" murmured Francesca as she picked up a blue velvet hat from the dressing table and put it on. "I wouldn't know anything about that. You know how bad I am about politics."

Lucia looked up and studied her mother's reflection in the mirror, watching as Francesca tipped her hat first one way and then another on her head, trying to determine the most flattering angle. It did not escape her notice that her mother would not meet her gaze in the mirror. With sudden clarity, Lucia knew exactly what that British ambassador was doing here.

"They're going to marry me off, aren't they? Just like they're doing with Elena." She could see the truth in her mother's face. "Aren't they?"

Francesca sighed, took off the hat, and tossed it over Annabel's head onto a nearby chair. "I didn't want you to know anything about it until after I had talked with him myself."

"That is why he's here, though, isn't it?" Lucia's blood began to boil.

"He is here about the possibility of a marriage for you, yes. Oh, darling," she added on a sigh as she studied her daughter's face, "you've always wanted a home of your own, marriage, and babies. When you were a little girl, I can't think how many times we used to plan your wedding, and dolls were the only toys you ever wanted to play with. Please don't say that episode with Armand has sworn you off love, and you intend to be a spinster, for I know you too well to believe it. Besides, I should hate not to have any grandchildren."

"Of course I want to get married, but I have no intention of letting Cesare arrange that marriage for me! I intend to choose my own husband, and I'm going to tell this oily little diplomat to pass that message along." Her fist tightening around his calling card, Lucia turned and started for the door.

"Don't do anything rash," her mother pleaded after her. "Moore is a powerful ambassador. He has enormous influence. Remember what I've always told you. Honey catches more flies than vinegar."

"Oh, I will be as sweet as honey," Lucia promised, "when I tell him to go to hell." Ignoring her mother's exasperated groan, Lucia started downstairs to the drawing room.

Ian would have thought that Francesca, the most notorious demirep in England, would possess a house in keeping with her flamboyant reputation. In this, he could not have been more wrong.

The home in which she lived was a quiet, discreet address in Cavendish Square, her butler was as dignified and impeccable as a servant could be, and her drawing room was an elegant, thoroughly English one of slate blue and willow green, with a painted porcelain shepherdess on the mantel, a landscape by Turner on the wall, and a beautiful Axminster carpet on the floor. Everything seemed designed for solid comfort, not for show. Of course, it was Chesterfield, Francesca's current protector, who paid the bills, and Chesterfield was a very conventional fellow.

The drawing room held a fine collection of books, and Ian was perusing their titles when the sound of footsteps caught his attention. He put a copy of Homer's *Iliad* back in its place and turned as a young woman came to a halt in the doorway.

No one could ever mistake her for an English girl, and Ian knew at once that standing before him was Lucia Valenti.

An image flashed through Ian's mind of this

young woman running across one of Italy's poppy-filled meadows, barefoot and laughing, with her skirts caught up in her hands and her coffee-black hair loosened from its combs to fly behind her in a thick, unruly mane. Odd, he thought, that his imagination should conjure such a vivid scene, for he was not a man given to flights of fancy. Still, there was a quality of barely restrained energy about her that made her seem vibrantly alive against the trappings of her conventional British surroundings.

She was tall for a woman, measuring about four inches beneath his own height. She had long legs, a small waist, and generous curves—curves that her low-necked, tightly corseted gown flaunted to full advantage. Her mother's influence, no doubt.

With eyes as dark as chocolate and skin like the soft froth on top of a cappuccino, there was nothing of conventional prettiness about her. She did not possess the required pink-rosebud mouth of a fashionable beauty, for her lips were wide, full, and as red as the flesh of a ripe cherry.

Staring at her delicious mouth, Ian knew no man who met her was going to care about the dictates of fashion. The ladies of the ton would shred her, but to any man with eyes, Lucia Valenti was a long, luscious armful of pure dessert.

Ian drew a deep breath. No wonder her father had locked her in a convent.

Chapter 2

⟋⟋⟋◯◯⟍⟍⟍

He wasn't at all what she had pictured. On her way downstairs, Lucia had imagined Ian Moore to be some oily, weasel-faced little fellow, oozing charm, who would couch his words in soothing, syrupy phrases that meant nothing. But when Lucia saw the British diplomat standing by the bookcase, his looks were so unlike the image in her mind that she came to an abrupt halt in the doorway.

He wasn't oily, and he certainly wasn't little. Lucia was taller than many men, but not this one. His wide shoulders and chest enhanced the impeccable fit of his striped waistcoat and buff-colored jacket. Dark blue trousers of an exact fit sheathed his lean hips and long legs. His linen shirt and silk neckcloth were snowy white. Looking at him, Lucia had an almost irresistible urge to muss his perfectly combed dark hair and untie his perfectly knotted cravat.

He probably wouldn't like that, she thought as she entered the room. This man had a hard line to his jaw and chin, showing resolution and discipline. He'd have no patience with that sort of teasing, which made the impulse to do so all the more tempting. Still, she had to concede that he was quite handsome for an Englishman, and her passionate Italian heart could only approve of such splendid masculinity, but when she looked into his eyes, her momentary feminine appreciation evaporated at once.

Though his lashes were thick and long, his eyes themselves were a tragedy. Cool, impersonal gray eyes that spoke of a frigid nature, eyes that studied her with such impassivity, she was almost insulted. What was she, a specimen under a microscope? A great pity that such a man as this should have eyes without a spark of passion in them.

"Sir Ian Moore," he said in well-bred accents. "How do you do, Miss Valenti?"

The mention of her name—the name her father had finally been forced to give her—was a forcible reminder of this man's purpose, and when he bowed, she responded with a curtsy that was little more than a dip of her knees. She moved to a settee of blue and ivory toile, sat down, and indicated for him to take the chair opposite her. "You came to see my mother, I understand, but she is unable to receive you at the moment. You will have to make do with me."

"I would not describe your company as making do," he said, oh-so-politely. "Though I regret your mother is unable to receive me. I had been given to understand she was expecting my arrival."

"She forgot about you," Lucia was delighted to inform him. "She is upstairs with her modiste being fitted for a new riding habit, and any thought of you went right out of her head."

"Perfectly understandable when a woman is with her modiste," he said with a charming smile that did not reach those cool eyes. "May we expect her to join us?"

"Hmm." Lucia tilted her head, pretending to think it over. "I could not say. The modiste is sewing the pieces of her riding habit onto her person. That is the only way to make it fit tightly enough to cause a sensation, you comprehend."

One corner of his mouth curved downward just a bit, the barest hint of his opinion on that. "I see."

That censure of her mamma, however slight it was, gave Lucia even more desire to needle him. "Dear me, I believe the gentleman disapproves," she murmured, affecting a British accent. She turned her head to the side as if speaking to a third party and went on, "Most improper for a woman to wear such a garment in public. She's the figure for it, I grant you, and that makes it even more indecent. D'you suppose she's any underclothes on?"

Turning the other way, she went on as if in answer, "Not possible. Naked as the day she was born underneath, I'll wager. What chemise and petticoat would fit under there?"

When Sir Ian did not respond to this raillery, she chose to forgo her imaginary companion and returned her attention to him. "Why did you wish to see my mother? The usual reason men visit her, I suppose?"

"I came to see both of you."

"Both of us? At once?" She gave him her most provoking smile. "No man has ever wanted *that* before. What a wicked man you are, Sir Ian, to make such an interesting suggestion."

He stiffened, a barely perceptible flex of his broad shoulders. "I hope you will find my suggestion interesting, once you stop making assumptions and learn what it is."

Lucia made a face. "Judging by your countenance, I doubt I want to. Tell me, are you always so haughty?"

"Are you always so impudent?"

"I'm afraid so," she said without apology. "Particularly to men who are haughty. Since you are not going to tell me why you came, I shall have to guess." She reached into the pocket of her skirt and pulled out his card. "Sir Ian Moore," she read. "G.C.M.G. Ambassador of—" She stopped and looked at him. "What do the letters mean?"

"His Majesty the King was gracious enough to

convey upon me a knighthood, the Knights Grand Cross, of the Most Distinguished Order of St. Michael and St. George."

"That sounds very grand. To warrant such a visitor, I must be more important to my father than I thought." She lifted the card again, and continued, "Ambassador of His Britannic Majesty, King William IV. Arranger of marital alliances that are none of his business, destroyer of the happiness of princesses, and person who solves the inconvenient problems of princes."

She gave him a wink and a mischievous smile. "I have no doubt," she continued as she tucked his card into the crevice between her breasts, "that I am Prince Cesare's most inconvenient problem. At least, I hope so." Leaving the tiniest corner of the card showing, she leaned back against the settee, watching for his reaction.

There was none. The impassive countenance of the diplomat did not change, but his disapproval of her pert manner toward him was plain enough. Ian Moore, she decided, had no sense of humor.

"From the fictional titles you have accorded to me," he said, "I can only conclude that you know my purpose in coming here is not to see your mother for the 'usual reason.' " Before she could answer, he went on, "Though you are correct that I have come at the request of your father, Prince Cesare. And also at the command of my government."

Now they were getting to the heart of the

matter. It was time to be serious. "Ah, the English meddle in this affair, too."

"Your father has decreed that you marry and has asked my government to assist him in finding a British husband for you. It is my assigned task to do so, and to negotiate the terms of your marriage settlement."

Lucia thought of all the times she'd been shuttled from one place to another. "*Si,*" she said with a nod. "Now that I can no longer be hidden away in some school or convent or palace, I must be married off."

"I regret that you see it in such an unfavorable light."

"But how else should I see it?" Before he could answer, she went on, "It is incomprehensible, I know, but I see no need to marry simply to save my father from embarrassment."

"Most young women are eager to marry."

"True," she agreed, "and most of us have the strange idea that we should choose our own spouses, not have them selected for us by diplomats."

"You are the daughter of a prince. Illegitimate, and therefore without title, but of the blood royal, nonetheless. Your father has publicly acknowledged you as his daughter—"

"Only because giving me his name makes him able to use me as a pawn in international politics. I am important enough now, it seems, to warrant my very own matchmaker."

"And that acknowledgment," he continued as

if she had not spoken, "places upon you certain duties. One of those duties is to marry well and appropriately."

Lucia bristled at that. "What of my father's duty to me? Cesare hid me away like a sordid secret, finally putting me in a convent. The nuns beat me. My room had no windows." She shuddered. "There were rats."

"Your father deeply regrets that action."

"I'll wager he does. Now that I am out of his reach."

Something stirred in those cool eyes, impatience perhaps. "Young woman, you are never out of his reach. The fact that I am here proves that. If Cesare asked my government to hand you over to him, we would do so at once, and men of the Scots Guard would be here to escort you to the nearest ship. But your father has decided that arranging a marriage for you is the best course and for the sake of alliance, he prefers a British gentleman."

"And if I do not share that preference?"

"I regret that my orders to find you a husband do not include a consideration of your preferences, Miss Valenti, although you may be reassured he will be a Catholic."

His religion wasn't what worried her. If her father and this diplomat thought she was going to marry a man of their choice and not her own, they were very much mistaken. She was not Elena, and she would not be bullied. "What a relief to know a man is in charge of my future," she murmured, pressing a hand to her forehead. "The pressure of choosing my own marriage partner might have proved too great a strain for my poor, muddled, feminine mind. Who is the fortunate bridegroom?"

"I do not have any specific one in mind as yet, but he will be a peer, a gentleman of breeding, with an impeccable background and connections. In addition—"

"What about love?"

He did not even blink. "It is my sincere hope you will develop a fondness for whichever gentleman is chosen for you."

It was such an absurd answer, she felt the desire to laugh, but the grave demeanor of the man opposite her made it clear that this was no laughing matter. "I did not ask about fondness," she said. "I asked about love."

"Real love takes time to develop, and we do not have that luxury. It is mid-June, and your father will be arriving in London for a state visit in August. My orders are to have a final marriage partner for you by the time of his arrival, based on his suitability for you and his desire to marry you."

Shocked, Lucia could only stare at him. "Six weeks? I am to meet a man and become betrothed to him in the next six weeks?"

"Given your situation, time is of the essence. Your father's wishes are clear. In addition, I have duties elsewhere, and you—"

"I am to be rushed into matrimony so that my father's schedule and your duties do not suffer?"

He met her gaze with eyes as cold and hard as steel. "No, you are being rushed into matrimony because of your own indiscreet behavior, which could have ruined not only you, but also your half sister."

That stung, mainly because she could not deny it. Lucia pressed her lips together and said nothing.

"The news of your exploit with Princess Elena has already appeared in an Italian scandal sheet," he went on. "It is inevitable that news will eventually reach here. It is hoped that your other past indiscretions, including your attachment to a French blacksmith, will not come to light."

Useless to explain to this man that she had loved Armand. He would not understand. She'd wager he had never been in love in his entire life. "And your point?"

"Rumors have an unfortunate tendency to grow and feed upon themselves until any shred of the truth is lost. The only way that will not matter is if you marry as soon as possible and marry well. Your father is offering an enormous dowry and annual income for you and your children, which helps. In addition, it is still the London season, so many suitable gentlemen will have the opportunity to meet you."

With each dispassionate word he spoke, Lucia could feel her ire rising. "I am to be paraded before an audience of men, and you are to choose one desperate enough and greedy enough to take me off my father's hands for the price of a dowry and income! I—" She broke off, anger and humiliation choking her. She swallowed hard, trying to regain her composure, but it was impossible. "I am not to be sold, nor even given away. No, a man must be *paid* to take me. No wonder you require only six weeks."

Not a muscle moved in the man's face. Lucia decided he wasn't quite human. Marble, perhaps, but definitely not human.

"I perceive your resentment," he said, "and it is understandable. However, you will not be paraded anywhere. Before consenting to an alliance, any man is going to want to spend some time with you and become acquainted. It is not uncommon for a young woman to bring a dowry and income to marriage. And as for the time frame, we have already discussed that. Your father's requirements are clear—"

"Cesare has never cared about me. I have seen my father half a dozen times in the whole of my life. Who is he to say I must marry? And who are you to be his minister of alliance? What gives either of you the right to dictate to me or control my life?"

Sir Ian looked at her with the patient expression of an adult tolerating the tantrum of a petulant child, which only enraged her more.

"While you are becoming acquainted with suitable gentlemen," he said with infuriating calm, "I will do what I can to contain the damage and prevent your reputation from becoming soiled here in Britain. However, I am no Hercules, and I have no desire to clean the Augean stables. From now on, you must be impeccable in your behavior. Given your illegitimacy, your mother, and your past, if you do anything further to damage your reputation, even I may not be able to save it."

"What a tragedy that would be."

Once again, a hint of impatience marred the diplomat's smooth, polished countenance. "Young woman, do you not understand the seriousness of your circumstances? Your reputation is teetering on the verge of collapse, casting shame upon yourself, your father's house, and your country. I advise you to behave yourself. Is that clear?"

Mother of God, here was one more person to order her, control her, mold her, restrict her. Could she not simply live her own life? "How could it not be clear?" she said with a mocking smile. "You explain it all so diplomatically."

Her sarcasm was ignored. "Good. Now, there is still the matter of your mother to be discussed."

Lucia's pasted-on smile vanished at once, and she tensed with foreboding, knowing she was about to hear more horrid pronouncements about her life and her future. As if what she'd heard already wasn't insulting enough. "What about my mother?"

"You cannot go on living with her. I will make arrangements for you to stay with suitable people—"

She sat bolt upright on the settee. "What?"

"You must realize you cannot continue to stay

under your mother's roof. This is an unacceptable environment for any young woman about to be launched in English society. I have no doubt your mother would agree with me. In any case, you will be severing all ties with your mother—"

"I will do no such thing!"

"You must. Your husband will require you to do so in any case."

"Any man who marries me accepts my mother. It is as simple as that."

"No, it is not as simple as that. Your devotion to your mother is admirable," he said, sounding anything but admiring, "but no British gentleman will tolerate it. Just the fact that you have been living with Francesca at all is bad enough, but every moment you continue to reside with her further damages your reputation."

Lucia wondered what would happen to her reputation if she slapped Britain's most famous ambassador across the face. She folded her arms, set her jaw, and said nothing.

He gave a heavy sigh, watching her. "Miss Valenti," he said in the wake of her silence, "it is highly inappropriate for me, as a gentleman, to speak of such matters to you, but I fear I must. Your mother is under the protection of Lord Chesterfield, a man to whom she is not married. It is he who pays for this house. Your mother is a demimondaine and is not accepted in good society. No gentleman is going to marry a young woman who keeps company with a courtesan, even if that courtesan is her mother."

"I will not marry a man who does not accept my mother," she said through clenched teeth. "I could never love such a man."

His sound of derision was the last straw. Lucia jumped to her feet. "Yes, love. It is such an inconvenient thing for fathers and diplomats, is it not? But it is so. He will love me enough to accept my mother, or I will not marry him."

He also stood up. "My orders are to have you removed from this house as soon as I can make suitable arrangements for you to stay elsewhere. As for love, we have already discussed that. Marrying for love is a luxury those of royal lineage can seldom afford. You certainly cannot."

"You are wrong. I *can* afford to marry for love. I can also afford to wait as long as I must to find that love. In the interim, I can live in reasonable comfort. My mother, that wicked *courtesan* of whom you speak so disparagingly, is good enough at her profession to support me quite well. I will make no loveless marriage for my father's sake or yours. And damn my reputation!"

"You cannot hope to defy your father. You must marry."

"I am perfectly willing to do so. Write to my father, Sir Ian, and tell him I shall marry when I find a man I love and who loves me. That is a task I am quite capable of managing without any help from you!"

With that, she turned and walked out of the room, slamming the door behind her. Ian Moore, a diplomat? If that hateful man was a diplomat, the world was in serious trouble.

Halfway up the stairs, Lucia turned on the landing and paused. From here, she could see the doorway to the drawing room reflected in the mirror on the wall, and she waited there until she saw Ian Moore go down the stairs to depart. Satisfied that the horrid man was finally gone, she went up to the second floor.

She encountered her mother halfway down the corridor as Francesca came out of her room, now completely sewn into her scandalously tight riding habit.

"Do not bother going down, Mamma," Lucia said as she passed. "He's gone."

"Without waiting to speak with me?" Francesca turned and followed her. "What did you say to him?"

"What any sensible woman would say," she said over her shoulder as she walked into her own room. "I appreciate your offer to find me a husband, but I can find him without your assistance, thank you very much. Now go away."

"Oh, Lucia!" Francesca groaned, closing the bedroom door behind them both. "I told you to be nice."

"Do not lecture me, Mamma. This is partly your fault. You should have told me he was coming here and why."

"I wanted to see him myself first and find out just what your father's plans are for you."

"Get married as soon as possible. That is all."

"And does your father have a particular man in mind?"

"No. This Sir Ian gets to choose. A gentleman, of course, a man of wealth and breeding, with an impeccable background and connections. Catholic, of course." Still seething, Lucia began to pace back and forth in front of her bed. "You should have heard him, Mamma. He talked as if finding a husband is like choosing a horse. Hmm . . . good teeth, strong and healthy, excellent breeding . . . yes, he'll do. Get the priest."

Francesca laughed. "Oh, my darling! I'm sure he didn't mean to imply anything of the kind."

"Oh, yes he did. Cesare comes in August, and I am to be engaged by then to whichever appropriate gentleman Sir Ian can find. Do I have a choice? Are my wishes considered? No! A man is being paid to take me. I have never felt so humiliated."

She stopped pacing and sat down on the edge of the bed. "Insufferable man. So cold, so haughty. So *English.*" She turned her head to look at her mother as the other woman sat down beside her. "He has orders from Cesare to move me out of this house, so that I can stay with *suitable* people."

"A perfectly understandable action. And a wise one."

"Not you, too? I won't go, Mamma."

"You cannot stay here forever." Francesca smiled a little and reached over to brush back a tendril of Lucia's hair. "My darling girl, ever since you arrived on my doorstep a month ago, I have been wondering what to do with you. When Cesare married and set me aside, I made him give me his solemn promise to take care of you because I would not be able to do so. You could not live with me then, and it is not good that you live with me now."

"But—"

"Listen to me, Lucia. I missed so much while you were growing up, only being able to see you at school in France a few times a year. I regret that I could not see you more."

"It wasn't your fault," Lucia said fiercely. "When I was a child, I could not live with you. I understand that. I always understood. But now—"

"It is no different now. It has been such a joy to have you here with me that I have been selfish, but the ambassador is right. Living here is hurting your reputation as a young lady."

"I don't care about that."

"I do. You are a grown woman, and a woman's reputation is everything. I know that from my own experience. My indiscretions put me beyond the pale, my parents disowned me, and I had to leave my home village. I went to Naples and became a woman on the town because I was ruined, and no man would marry me." She paused, then went on, "It grieves me to see you starting down the same path."

There was a hint of censure in her mother's voice, and it hurt. Lucia bit her lip and looked away.

"I understand you very well, Lucia," Francesca went on. "You chafe under rules, especially your father's rules. But what happened in Bolgheri could haunt you forever, unless Sir Ian can prevent it. If he can arrange for you to stay with respectable people and provide you with worthy connections, your past indiscretions will not matter."

She turned to meet her mother's gaze, dismayed. "You are making me go, then?"

"I won't force you." She gave Lucia a rueful smile. "If I were a good mother, I would, but I am not a good mother, for I am not strict, not of a serious turn of mind, and certainly not a good moral example."

"You are the most wonderful mother in the world." She watched Francesca shake her head, and she stifled any denial her mother might have made. "You are, Mamma. Do you know why? You are the only person who loves and accepts me just as I am."

"Of course I love you. That is why I advise you to go willingly. As I said, I won't force you, but Cesare could do so any time he likes. I would fight for you, but I would lose."

"They are going to force me to marry, and I have no say, no voice. I do not want my husband chosen for me!"

"There are ways around that. A woman can always choose. Make your choice and get Sir Ian and your father to think it was theirs."

"But I want a husband who loves me, Mamma.

How shall I find a man who loves me in only six weeks?"

Her mother smiled a little and caressed her cheek. "Any man who would not fall in love with you at first sight, my beautiful girl, is either blind or an idiot."

Lucia's lips twisted in a wry smile. "You are biased, Mamma."

"Perhaps, but I know men. You will have them lined up outside your door."

"Sir Ian says any English gentleman, whether he loves me or not, will demand that I sever all ties with you. I refused."

"My loyal daughter! No matter what happens, I would never disown you, Lucia, but I think you must disown me. At least for now. After you marry, we shall see."

"What if I do not like the people with whom I am to stay?" she asked, grasping at straws. "What if they are awful to me?"

"They could not be worse than the nuns."

Lucia started to argue further, but Francesca put a finger to her lips to stop her flow of protests. "I am asking you to make the most of this opportunity," her mother said. "Go to balls and parties, meet young men, make friends, enjoy the rest of the season with respectable people and enjoy yourself. Who knows what may happen?"

Lucia sighed. "I hate having no power over my own life."

"No power? What makes you think such a thing? My love, you have formidable weapons.

You have beauty and you have brains and you have a kind, loving heart. When a woman has those, it is the men who are powerless. The first thing you must do is get Sir Ian on your side. You have much charm, Lucia, much magnetism. Use it to persuade Sir Ian to allow you to make the choice of whom you marry."

The idea of charming Sir Ian was almost intolerable. Lucia groaned. "Is there no other way?"

"I'm afraid not."

She sighed and leaned her forehead against her mother's shoulder, resigning herself to the inevitable. "All right, Mamma. I'll go, if you wish it." She lifted her head and scowled, still compelled to stand by her convictions. "But I won't stay with people who are horrible to me or look down at me."

"I'm sure Sir Ian will agree to that."

"And I won't marry a man just to be respectable, ease Cesare's conscience, and fulfill Sir Ian's duty."

"Of course not."

"I will marry only if I am in love with a man, and he is in love with me."

"I understand."

"He'd better be enough in love with me," she added for good measure, "to acknowledge and respect my mother."

"I hope so."

"Hope is not a consideration, Mamma. That is how it's going to be. I just have to make Ian Moore see things my way."

Francesca rose. "Honey, not vinegar, darling. Remember."

"Mamma, I'll smother that man in honey. With any luck, he'll drown."

Chapter 3

"**M**arrying for love?" Ian shook his head in disbelief as he paced back and forth in front of the fireplace in his brother's library. "With the mess she's in, and only six weeks to find a husband, she expects to marry for love. I ask you, how absurd is that?"

"Very absurd indeed." Dylan Moore leaned back in his chair and took a sip of brandy from the snifter in his hand. "And most unreasonable of a young woman to expect it."

The hint of irony in his brother's voice did not escape his notice, and he flashed Dylan a glance of impatience as he paced. "It *is* unreasonable. She is the daughter of a prince, not the daughter of a shopkeeper. And her reputation is in serious jeopardy. Doesn't she understand that?"

"I'm sure you made her aware."

"For all the good it did." Ian turned and started back across the hearthrug yet again. "Does she really think Prince Cesare is going to put her romantic notions above international politics?"

"Most young ladies don't give a damn about international politics. Baffling, I know, but there it is."

"Given her past behavior, I suppose I should not have expected her to regard this matter with sense and judgment, but she is only hurting herself further by ignoring her position and her place in the world. Being illegitimate, she is not a princess, but she still has a duty to the House of Bolgheri. Prince Cesare is determined to get her married. She cannot hope to defy her father's wishes."

Dylan laughed. "Spoken like a man who has no daughters. If my Isabel is anything to go by, the wishes of fathers don't matter much."

Ian could not share his brother's amusement. "This isn't going to be easy, you know. British peers who are Catholic are a rare commodity."

"But so are worthy Catholic women to marry them," Dylan countered with breezy disregard for the difficulties.

"Wherever this girl goes, scandal follows," Ian went on. "And if her religion, her tainted reputation, and her defiance are not enough cause for concern, there's the matter of her mother."

With those words, he felt in need of a drink.

He stalked over to the liquor cabinet. "The House of Bolgheri is a valuable connection," he said, pouring himself a glass of port. "And she does bring an enormous income. Given that, I can convince a worthy Catholic peer with wealth of his own to marry Miss Valenti despite her past indiscretions, but the matter of her mother makes everything much more difficult. She would have to sever all contact with the woman, something she flatly refuses to do. In fact, she demands that her future husband agree to accept Francesca as part of his family. Accept a notorious demimondaine into the family? God, what a notion!"

"It would make things deuced awkward at family gatherings," Dylan agreed. "You're the one who knows all about proper protocol. Does a lord invite his demirep mother-in-law to the christenings of the children? Or not?"

Ian was in no frame of mind for his brother's sardonic wit. "Deuce take it, Dylan, can't you be serious for once?" He walked back over to the fireplace and resumed pacing, thinking out loud as he did so. "Once she is married, her husband will handle her and the matter of her mother as he sees fit. But until then, her relationship with Francesca is my problem. I don't wish to part the girl from her mother by force, but it seems I must."

"Not the most diplomatic thing to do."

"No, but given her defiance, I may not have a choice. Every moment she continues to live with her mother damages her further and makes my task harder. If I am to fulfill my duty, I must first see that she is accepted into good society, and that means she cannot remain in Francesca's household."

"So what are you going to do with her?"

"That's the crux of it. Taking on the job of chaperoning a young woman is a huge responsibility. Given the girl's past actions, it will take a great deal of persuasion for some matron to take it on. If the girl gets into trouble, her chaperone will come under criticism as well."

"You'll find someone, I'm sure."

"I daresay, but I don't have much time. And the girl is not in any frame of mind to cooperate."

"Do you blame her?"

"I expected her to face facts and be sensible. Instead, she was impertinent and demanding and rebellious by turns. It astonished me that a young lady of breeding would behave in such a way."

"Is it really so surprising, given how autocratic and high-handed you were about it all?"

"I was not autocratic. Nor high-handed." When he saw Dylan raise an eyebrow in disbelief, Ian went on, "As I told you, time is short, and I put the truth of her situation to her in a straightforward fashion. I got nothing but impudence and resentment leveled at me in return. At twenty-two years of age, she ought to have developed some seriousness of mind, but no. The girl has an unbelievably reckless disregard for her virtue, her position, her duty, and her future." He took another turn across the hearthrug. "Why?" he muttered to himself. "Why do the Italians always have to be such a problem?"

"It's not that she's Italian," Dylan said, sounding amused. "It's the fact that she's a woman that's got under your skin."

Those words brought Ian to an abrupt halt beside the fireplace, and the image of his card being tucked into the cleft of Miss Valenti's bodice flashed through his mind. He took another swallow of port. "I don't know what you mean."

"From what you described, you discussed this situation with her in your terms. International relations, political ramifications, duty, honor."

"And?"

"What does she care? From her point of view, here is some man she has never met, laying down the law on her father's behalf about her life and her future, talking to her as if she were an inconvenient problem to be dispensed with as quickly as possible. No wonder she was resentful. Any woman would be."

That was nothing but the truth, and Ian knew it. He looked at his younger brother, summoning his most dignified air. "It seems I made a slight diplomatic miscalculation."

"To say the least. What were you thinking?"

He hadn't been thinking, at least not about anything but getting this petty little problem off his plate. "I will not repeat my mistake, I assure you. When I meet with that young woman again, I intend to apply the first rule of diplomacy."

"Which is?"

"Get what I want, but make her think she's getting what she wants."

"Perfectly sound. Just remember you are not negotiating a trade agreement with Portugal." Dylan took a swallow of brandy. "If you want my advice—"

"I don't."

"Don't ever forget she's a woman."

The memory of Lucia Valenti's generous curves and cherry-red mouth were still quite vivid in Ian's mind. Forget she was a woman? He downed the last of his port. *Not bloody likely.*

The following morning, Lucia was not surprised to receive a note from Sir Ian, stating that he would call upon her that afternoon, that it would pain him to cause her any inconvenience, but expressing the fervent hope, as he put it, that she would be available to meet with him. A very diplomatic note, but dropped in the midst of all the polite phrases was the casual mention of a report he was writing to her father about her situation.

Lucia tapped the note against her palm, thinking over her own next move. She would cooperate with her father's plans, but on her own terms, and that meant finding a man who loved her. Love could not be forced, so her only choice was to take her mother's advice, stay with respectable people, go to parties, meet young men, and enjoy herself. Along the way, perhaps love would find her. One thing she was not going to do was stop seeing her mother. She intended to visit Mamma whenever she wished. That meant finding a chaperone she could get around. Sir Ian just had to see the situation her way.

He might be dictatorial, haughty, and cold-hearted, but he was still a man. *Sweet as honey*, she reminded herself that afternoon as his name was announced and he came into the drawing room. "Excellency," she greeted with a curtsy much more deferential than her last one. She sat down and indicated for him to sit opposite her.

"Miss Valenti," he said as he took the offered chair, "I fear that we got off to rather a bad start yesterday, and I would very much like to remedy that."

"As would I." A little flattery, she thought, a little bit of acting like the misguided but contrite girl, with a dash of making him feel important thrown into the mix, and she'd be in control of this whole situation. She smiled at him. "Sir Ian, I feel the same way. I cannot think what came over me yesterday. Surely you and I can find ways to compromise."

"I am certain we can." He paused, then said, "Perhaps we should begin with a discussion of where you are going to live for the remainder of the season. Have you given that any thought?"

Perfect, she thought. "Oh, yes. Upon reflection, I know that you were right in much of what you said. I realize my mother's house is not an appropriate place for me to be." She spread her hands wide in a gesture that asked for understanding. "I love my mother, and I have had little opportunity to visit with her over the years. I have a strong resistance to leaving her."

He leaned forward, eager to accept her point of view. "Of course. Your affection for your mother and your reluctance to be parted from her are understandable. You have a woman's tender heart."

Lucia pressed her hand to that tender heart, well aware of what such a gesture accentuated. After all, in the getting of her way, a woman had to use whatever weapons she had as effectively as possible. When Sir Ian's lashes lowered a fraction, she hoped he was appreciating two of her very best weapons.

"It pains me to leave Mamma and move in with strangers," she went on, "but I recognize that I must. The first step, then, is to determine with whom I might stay. I am sure you move in the finest circles of society. What is your opinion?"

He returned his gaze to her face. "There are several excellent possibilities. In our new spirit of compromise, perhaps I should outline them for you, and you choose which sounds most appealing?"

"That is so considerate of you." She gave him a look of gratitude. "Perhaps you might begin with your own preference?"

"It is your preference that matters, Miss Valenti."

The thought crossed her mind that if they kept up all this mutual consideration much longer, both of them would be nauseous. "You are too kind, Sir Ian, but guide me, if you would."

"The Countess of Snowden is one possibility you might consider. Her background is impeccable, and any young lady she chaperones would be accepted everywhere."

"What is she like?"

"A most sweet lady, and a most proper one. She speaks very slowly, and she's a bit deaf, but after all, she is nearly seventy. She doesn't attend many events in the evenings, but if you play piquet, she will adore you. Her home is several miles outside of London, but after I have chosen several suitable young men for you to meet, they can call upon Lady Snowden and yourself without too much trouble. Though she lives a bit far from any amusements, she has a fine barouche and would be happy to take you out in her carriage once or twice a week. I would be most amenable to leaving you in her hands."

"She sounds a most suitable chaperone," Lucia answered, thinking just the opposite. Her age was a good thing, but if the woman lived outside the city, there would be no way to get out and see Mamma without enormous risk. No, Lucia didn't think she'd be staying with Lady Snowden.

"Tell me about the others you have considered," she suggested. "After all, I must make a judicious choice."

"Of course. Lady Deane is another possibility. The baroness is a most hearty and invigorating woman. She has a strong constitution and believes in long walks in the fresh air every morning at sunrise. Exercise, she says, is most beneficial and wholesome. She's a rather stern taskmaster, but in my opinion, that develops one's character."

"I am sure my character is in need of some strengthening," Lucia said with a straight face. "My past behavior, I admit, has been rather . . . impulsive."

"Lady Deane would make certain you made no social faux pas, so you may put your mind at ease on that score. She would watch over you most carefully."

"I have no doubt. And I do adore waking at dawn." She paused, opened her eyes very wide, and bit her lip, hoping she looked like the weak and helpless female. "But I am hesitant about the taking of exercise. After all, it is men who should be the strong ones."

She tilted her head and let her gaze roam over the wide shoulders and chest of the man sitting before her, and she did not need to feign an appreciation for his physique. She hated to admit it, but his body was quite splendid. "Men of strength and power," she went on in a voice like butter, "men such as you, Sir Ian, are so appealing to the feminine . . . heart."

He glanced down again, shifted in his chair, and looked away. Lucia smiled, knowing that right now her heart was the last thing he was thinking about.

She heaved a sigh and shook her head as if coming out of an admiring reverie. "But I digress. Forgive me. Have you any other suggestions?"

He seemed to come out of rather a daze himself, and it took him a moment to answer. "There's Lady Monforth, of course. That would be a perfect situation for you. The marchioness is a most proper chaperone, and her daughter, Sarah, is only a few years older than you, so you would have a companion. Their London address is in the midst of Mayfair. Most fashionable."

And probably walking distance from her mother's house. Lucia felt a glimmer of relief. "That sounds most promising. What is the daughter like?"

"Lady Sarah is the loveliest young lady of my acquaintance," he answered, male admiration obvious in the sudden warmth of his voice. "A stunning beauty. Golden hair, deep blue eyes, and a perfect, milk-white complexion. The epitome of young English womanhood. I admire her greatly, but then, most men do."

Lucia repressed the urge to make gagging sounds.

"She is always surrounded by admirers," Sir Ian continued. "Through her, many suitable young men would have the opportunity to meet you. She isn't the most intelligent of companions, perhaps," he added with an indulgent smile, "but I am certain the two of you would be able to find things to talk about. Young ladies discuss all manner of things that we men do not comprehend. Fashions in sleeves and hair ribbon bows and such."

Lucia began to wonder how a man so dense had ever become such a widely respected diplomat. Did he really think she could be friends with a woman who was both beautiful *and* stupid? They should despise each other. "Are there any other choices?"

"I don't believe so . . ." He frowned, considering the matter.

Lucia waited, hoping he named someone, anyone, who sounded remotely in keeping with her needs for enjoyment and independence.

"There's my brother, I suppose," he said with doubt. "He and his wife live in Portman Square, which is right in the heart of things. And they are very good friends with the Duke and Duchess of Tremore. That's a valuable connection. But . . . no." He shook his head. "I couldn't even think of letting you stay there. My brother is outrageous, and as for his wife, well, I hardly think she would be an appropriate chaperone. She caused quite the scandal herself when she was a girl."

"She did?" Lucia's spirits began to rise. "What did she do? Tell me."

Sir Ian's face took on an expression of heavy disapproval. "She ran off to the Continent with some French painter when she was seventeen. She'd known the man a week. A week, mind you. And he didn't even marry her until two years later."

To Lucia's way of thinking, this woman sounded like a definite possibility. "What happened?"

"After her husband died, Grace came back to

England, but her reputation was in ruins. She became my brother's mistress. Needless to say, that didn't help her regain her respectability. My brother, Dylan, was quite the rake in his day, I'm ashamed to admit."

"Dylan?" Astonished, Lucia stared at him, unable to imagine this man with a brother whose reputation for outrageous behavior was so well-known. "Your brother is Dylan Moore, the composer?"

"Yes, I'm afraid so. I'm sure you can understand that staying with them would not be a good situation for you."

Oh, yes it would. She liked outrageous people. And Grace Moore, having done some scandalous things herself, would surely be a permissive chaperone. Lucia could go where she pleased, do what she wanted, and visit her mother any time she liked. She decided it was time for another layer of buttering up.

Lucia leaned forward in her chair, all wide-eyed and earnest. "But, Sir Ian, you are a member of their family. Given your impeccable reputation and influential position, your brother and his wife must therefore be considered respectable people."

"They are now." He smoothed his cravat, looking pleased with himself. "After I managed to salvage Grace's reputation."

"You did?" She gave him her most admiring gaze. "So I am not the first young lady to be saved by you? I am not at all surprised, given your diplomatic skills."

"It was not all due to me," he answered with an obvious attempt at modesty. "The Duchess of Tremore and her sister-in-law, Lady Hammond, were most helpful to my efforts. And, of course, Dylan has settled down to married life quite well. But still—" He hesitated, gray eyes narrowing on her with sternness. "Can I rely upon you to exercise the utmost self-restraint while in my brother's house?"

Lucia folded her hands in her lap, meek as a lamb. "I know I have made mistakes, but I am sure that if I had interesting companions, I would be very wise."

"I daresay, but I'm not certain the people you would meet through my brother's acquaintance would be of good character."

"But you would never choose a husband for me who was not of good character," she said with dulcet sweetness. "And if your brother and his wife are friends with a duke, that should provide many opportunities for me to meet people of the utmost breeding and suitability, thereby fortifying my reputation. I would so much like to stay with them. With your permission, of course."

Sir Ian sat back in his chair, folded his arms, and considered the matter. "It would be more amusing for you there, I suppose," he said with reluctance. "And I did give you your choice." Another long pause, then he nodded. "All right, Portman Square it is."

She gave a sigh of relief and satisfaction. "Thank you, Sir Ian. This shall be a new life for me, and it is so reassuring to know that I can rely upon you to advise me."

He smiled, looking as buttered up as a man could get. "No thanks are necessary, Miss Valenti. It is my pleasure to guide you in any way I can."

Lucia smiled back at him, looking grateful, feeling like a cat swimming in cream. Perhaps it was a terrible flaw in her character, but she did love getting her way.

Chapter 4

❧

Ian loved getting his way. There was nothing more exhilarating than a diplomatic negotiation concluded with success. He now had a second negotiation to undertake, and there was no predicting how it would turn out. His brother could be as contrary as springtime weather.

After leaving Francesca's house, he called at Portman Square, but he found that Dylan was out. Grace, however, was at home.

"Ian!" With a wide, delighted smile, his sister-in-law rose and came forward as he walked into the drawing room, her hands outstretched in greeting. "Dylan told me you were in London. I am so sorry I was out when you came to call last evening."

"I regret that as well. I so seldom get to see you." He took her hands and kissed her cheeks with warm affection. Grace was slender, blond, beautiful, and one of the most generous-hearted people Ian had ever met. She was certainly the best thing that had ever happened to his brother. She was also sensible, a quality Ian admired. Most people had no sense whatsoever.

"I would have written ahead that I was coming home," he went on as she sat down and he took the chair opposite her, "but there was no time to do so. This diplomatic mission cropped up rather suddenly."

"Would you care for tea?" When he nodded, she reached for the bellpull on the wall behind the chair where she sat, and a footman stepped into the drawing room. Grace ordered refreshments, and a few minutes later, she was pouring out a fragrant cup of China tea for each of them.

"So, are you allowed to discuss this diplomatic mission?" she asked, leaning back in her chair, cup and saucer in her hands. "Or is it a secret one this time?"

Ian also leaned back with his tea. "Quite the contrary. I wish to tell you all about it. In fact, my dear Grace, to accomplish this particular assignment, I am in need of your assistance."

The day after she and Sir Ian had come to agreement about her new living arrangements, trunks, satchels, and traveling cases were stacked in the foyer of the house in Cavendish Square to be transported to her new home. Lucia studied them as she waited with her mother for Sir Ian to arrive. "I had only one small satchel with me when I arrived on your doorstep, Mamma," she murmured. "I am departing with twenty times that much."

"We did keep Bond Street rather busy, didn't we?" Francesca agreed.

Lucia recognized the deliberate cheerfulness in her mother's voice, and she felt once again as if she were a little girl in boarding school. "This is a change, is it not?" she choked, blinking at the suddenly blurry pile of luggage. "This time, I am the one leaving you."

Francesca grasped her chin and turned her head to look her in the face. She gave her a frown that tried to be stern. It failed utterly, but it always did. Francesca was as stern as a kitten. "No tears now."

"No," she agreed, and forced herself to smile. "I intend to sneak out and see you whenever I can."

Francesca sighed. "You get that stubbornness from your father," she said, shaking her head, but without much disapproval. "I know you will not listen if I order you not to come, so I will not even attempt it. But if you do visit me, be careful how you manage it. Remember, in London society, discretion is all."

"Mamma," she said with a wobbly laugh, "if I can get past convent nuns and Cesare's guards, I can do anything."

At that moment, the carriage arrived, and Lucia was glad of it, for she knew all about good-byes and hated them. She turned away and started out of the house, but at the last minute, she ran back to her mother. "My birthday is only three weeks away," she said, inventing an excuse to stay another moment. "Don't forget, Mamma."

Her mother caressed her cheek. "Do I ever forget?"

"No. But you do forget things sometimes. I just . . . wanted to remind you."

"I promise I won't forget." Francesca kissed her forehead. "Go. Enjoy yourself and try not to worry about your future. Things will work out for the best."

This time, when Lucia turned away, she did not look back, and she cheered herself with the reminder that her new home was not all that far away.

Sir Ian was halfway to the front door when she emerged. He was impeccably dressed and had not a hair out of place. Of course, no speck of lint dared to dust his dark blue coat. He seemed more inhuman than ever.

He stopped on the walk as she approached. He bowed to her, then escorted her to the waiting carriage, where he assisted her to step up into the vehicle.

Someone else was inside, and when Lucia took her seat, she found herself sitting beside one of the loveliest women she had ever seen. Wheat-blond hair peeped out from beneath the woman's cream-colored bonnet, and her eyes were a clear, light green color, almost like peridot jewels. They made a striking contrast to her periwinkle blue dress and hat ribbons. Her golden beauty was so different from Lucia's own dark coloring that she could not help but stare in admiration, feeling as if she were looking at a painting by Bellini. When the woman spoke, her voice was warm and friendly.

"Miss Valenti, I am Grace Moore," she said, forgoing the formality of waiting for Sir Ian to enter the carriage and introduce them.

Not one to always mind her manners then, Lucia noted, remembering the story Sir Ian had told her of the woman's scandalous elopement. Given her angelic looks, it was hard to credit. "How do you do?"

Grace Moore studied her for a moment, then she gave Lucia a wide smile. "Ian did not tell me what a lovely young woman you are."

"I was thinking the same thing about you. You look a bit like a Bellini Madonna."

"But not as pious, I hope! I find pious people tiring, don't you? One is always conscious of not living up to their standards. It wears one out."

"You have nothing to fear from me," Lucia assured her. "I lived in a convent for nearly a year, and I was always exhausted."

They both laughed at that as Sir Ian entered the carriage. "It seems the pair of you are already friends," he commented as he sat down beside his sister-in-law.

"We are going to get on famously," Grace told him as the carriage jerked into motion and started down the street.

Lucia was inclined to agree with her. Perhaps she was going to enjoy her new situation after all. She hoped so, after all the tricky maneuvering she'd done to arrange it.

Lucia's optimistic hope about her new life was reinforced once she arrived at Portman Square and a maid showed her into her bedchamber. The room had two big windows and was done up in golden yellow and creamy white, with simple walnut furnishings and vases filled with daffodils and hyacinth. She found the room very pleasing, for it was simple, not ostentatious, and she liked that. She'd had enough of gilded chairs and marble floors in her father's palace. Falling back into the plush luxury of her bed's thick mattress, she thought of the hard beds and windowless cells of the convent and laughed aloud. She did like things simple, but she also liked comfort. Here she had both.

"You seem pleased with your room," a voice commented, and Lucia sat up to find Sir Ian in the corridor, watching her through the open doorway.

"*Si*," she answered, giving him a smile as she leaned back on her elbows. "Yellow is my favorite color, so I do like this room. And the bed is most comfortable." She gave him a flirtatious smile, just to see how he would react. "I like comfortable beds."

"Excellent." With a bow, he turned away from the doorway and started down the corridor.

Lucia gave a sigh and fell back into the pillows. Flirtation was a waste on that man, and it was a crime, for he was quite handsome. Still, she was feeling a bit less hostile toward him, probably because she'd managed to wrap him around her finger yesterday.

"I shall see you at dinner," his voice echoed back to her from farther down the corridor.

She frowned and sat up, uncertain she'd heard him right. "What do you mean?" she called after him as she rose from the bed and started toward the door. When he reappeared in the doorway, she came to a halt. "What do you mean?" she repeated. "Are you coming to dinner here this evening?"

He gave her a look of surprise. "Of course, and most other evenings as well. After all, I do live here."

"What?"

"Yes." Sir Ian gestured down the corridor. "My room is right next to yours. Did I not tell you that yesterday?"

"No," she said, feeling dismay sinking in. "You failed to mention it."

He brushed an imaginary speck of lint from his sleeve. "How remiss of me. My apologies."

"You did this on purpose," she accused, folding her arms and glaring at him. "You lied to me."

He put his hand on his heart. "Miss Valenti,

you wound me with such an accusation. Even I, as—how did you put it?" He paused a second. "Ah, yes. As strong and powerful a man as I am, I also have some sensibilities. I do not lie."

Lucia's eyes narrowed. He had maneuvered her with his talk of other chaperones, pretending to consider her wishes and give her a choice when he'd had her presence here in mind all along. Like a fool, she had fallen right into his trap. "Tricked me, then," she amended. "Do you like that accusation better?"

"For what purpose would I trick you into living here as opposed to somewhere else?"

"So that you can make certain I behave myself, of course."

"What an excellent notion." He smiled, not at all ashamed of his deception, and it was a smile so galling, so self-satisfied, Lucia couldn't stand it.

"Of all the devious things to do. You, you . . . oh, you—" She broke off, trying to think of what to say to him that was satisfying enough. Though she spoke four languages, only one of them was sufficient to describe her opinion of him at this moment, and Lucia lapsed into Italian. *"Tu furbo bastardo manipolatore!"*

"I must protest. Clever and manipulating I may be, but I assure you my parents were married for an entire year before I was born." He leaned into the room, reaching for the handle of the door. "Dinner is at seven o'clock. Since my ten-year-old niece will be joining us, I suggest you wear something a bit less—" His cool gray eyes dipped to her bodice without a spark of masculine interest. "Less revealing."

Before she could say another word, he closed the door between them.

"Oh!" Lucia stared at the door, outraged that insufferable man had gotten the best of her and the underhanded way he had done it.

She had escaped schools, relatives, palaces, and convents only to find herself saddled with Ian Moore. If that man was dogging her heels at every waking moment, she wouldn't have any freedom.

Accidenti! They all wanted her to get married, didn't they? How on earth was she ever going to find the right man to marry with Ian Moore hovering nearby all the time, ready to remind her and every man she met of the proprieties? No couple could fall in love properly under such circumstances.

And what about her mother? Lucia stopped in front of one window of her room, lifted the sash, and leaned out for a look. Not a tree in sight. No sneaking out that way. Thoroughly vexed, she closed the window and stalked about the room.

"Furbo bastardo," she muttered, and proceeded to vent her frustration by coming up with more unflattering descriptions of Ian Moore in Italian. It was only when she ran out of names to call him that she stopped pacing.

She glanced up and caught sight of her own reflection in the mirror of the dressing table, and it was only then, looking into her own eyes, that she admitted the true reason for her frustration. She had underestimated that Englishman, and she was angry at herself for making such a foolish mistake.

She told herself it did not matter where she stayed. She had not come all the way to England only to be denied her mother's company. And she would wear what she liked and go where she wished. And by heaven, she wasn't going to let anyone, especially that man, choose her husband for her.

Her gaze moved past her own reflection to that of the closed door. She just had to be more clever than Sir Ian Moore.

After Ian had changed into evening clothes and returned to the drawing room, he found that Dylan had arrived home. Since Miss Valenti had not yet come down to join them before dinner, talk of her was the subject of their conversation.

"I hope she likes it here." Grace looked at her brother-in-law, her green eyes anxious. "After all, we are strangers to her."

"She liked you well enough, and I am certain she will grow accustomed to living here." Ian sat down in a chair facing the couple opposite him on the settee. "Miss Valenti has a rather adventurous streak in her character, and I have imbued her with the notion that living with people who have scandalous pasts is going to be exciting."

"You've always been rather a devious fellow," Dylan remarked.

He thought of Miss Valenti's words a short time ago. "So I have been told." He leaned back, smiling. "Grace is helping me to play up the scandal a bit."

"Yes," Grace agreed. "I did not mention to Miss Valenti that we are now highly respectable members of society."

Dylan laughed and turned his head to kiss his wife's hair. "You and I respectable," he murmured. "Who would ever have thought it?"

Ian gave his sister-in-law a look of gratitude. "Thank you for taking on the job of chaperoning the girl. I realize what an enormous responsibility it is for you."

"No thanks are necessary, Ian," she assured him. "It is the least I can do after you saved my reputation."

"Salvaging the reputations of young ladies seems to have become my lot in life," Ian said wryly. "But Grace, I hope you do not come to regret this. Chaperoning Miss Valenti will not be easy. I hope you can manage her."

"Managing her will be no great problem for my wife." Dylan stretched his arm across the back of the settee behind his wife. "She manages me quite well, and Isabel, too, for that matter. I doubt Miss Valenti will give her much trouble."

"You had best meet the young lady before you come to that conclusion," Ian answered. "I assure you, dear brother, Miss Valenti is capable of creating more chaos than you ever could."

"I shall look forward to meeting her, then. I adore chaos. Shall you stay to dinner?"

Surprised, Ian glanced at Grace. "Didn't you tell him?"

Grace lifted one hand in a gesture of futility. "He's been gone all day and just arrived home. I barely had the opportunity to explain about Miss Valenti and my role as her chaperone before you came in. I haven't had the chance to tell him the rest."

Dylan looked from his wife to his brother and back again. "The rest of what?"

It was Ian who answered. "As long as Miss Valenti is living here, I am living here as well."

"What?" Dylan gave a groan of despair that Ian hoped was in jest. "Ye gods, must you?"

"Yes, I must. I know you and I don't always get on, Dylan, but I cannot allow Grace to bear the full responsibility for Miss Valenti's conduct. It would be too great a burden. With her total wont of propriety, it would be easy for some fortune-hunting scoundrel to maneuver her into a compromising situation and take advantage of it. Until she is safely married off, I intend to watch over that young woman like a hawk."

Dylan grinned. "What, afraid she'll go sneaking off with some unsuitable young man for a few kisses in the back garden?"

That was exactly what he was afraid of. He looked at his brother with grim determination.

"She isn't going to be sneaking out anywhere."

"Poor Miss Valenti," Dylan murmured. "With you hovering over her, she won't be able to have any fun."

Ian thought of her flirtatious dark eyes, mischievous laugh, and shapely body. "I believe Lucia Valenti has already had enough fun to last a lifetime."

Ian was not surprised when Miss Valenti paid no mind to his instructions about her dress. When she came down for dinner, she was wearing a gown of pristine white, but there was nothing pristine about the neckline. It was low enough that any man would have to be blind not to notice what it accentuated. Ian did not miss how Dylan raised an eyebrow at the sight of such perfect assets so splendidly displayed nor the mocking smile his younger brother sent in his direction. Dylan had always had a most irritating sense of humor.

As for Isabel, the child took one look at Miss Valenti, pronounced her dress "absolutely smashing," and declared that when she grew up she'd have one just like it, only in red. Dylan's expression changed at once to a frown of fatherly disapproval, and it was Ian's turn to grin. Isabel was going to give Dylan hell when she grew up, and after years of watching his younger brother break every rule under the sun, Ian was going to enjoy that.

Grace, being a woman of serene temperament

and tact, conveyed no opinion of Miss Valenti's dress by either word or expression and informed Isabel that until she grew up and was a married woman, pastel shades for her gowns were the order of the day.

Isabel protested, but the ongoing battle over the child's favorite color was cut off by the announcement of Dylan's butler, Osgoode, that dinner was served.

After they were seated in the dining room, Grace turned the conversation to social topics. "Dylan and I received an invitation from Lady Kettering to attend her amateur concert on Thursday next," she told them. "I was going to decline, but perhaps I should accept. Ian and Miss Valenti could come with us."

"An amateur concert would be a good way to introduce Miss Valenti into society," Ian agreed.

"Lady Kettering and I had planned to shop the day after tomorrow in Bond Street and take tea. If you are agreeable, Miss Valenti," she said with a glance at Lucia, "I shall bring you along and explain how I am chaperoning you for the season. Knowing that, she will be sure to extend the concert invitation to include you." She returned her attention to her brother-in-law. "I shall also explain your unexpected arrival from the East, Ian. She will include you as well."

Dylan groaned. "I hate those amateur concerts. They are an assault to one's ears. Young ladies with little musical talent playing their instruments with great enthusiasm. Most of the time, when they play something of mine, I cringe. Must we go?"

"Miss Valenti might enjoy it." Grace turned to Lucia. "Do you like music?"

"I do," Lucia answered. "I like it very much."

"Do you play an instrument yourself?"

"I learned the Spanish guitar as a girl."

Isabel spoke up. Turning to Lucia, who sat beside her, she asked, "But are you any good?"

"Isabel!" Grace reproved, but Lucia only laughed.

"Good enough that your papa would not cringe, I promise you," she answered the child's question. "But I have heard that you are a most excellent musician. And a composer, too, like your papa."

The child's face lit up like a candle. "You've heard that about me? Uncle Ian must have told you."

"No, no. I heard about you before I ever came here. Your father is very famous, you see, so of course, people have talked of you and your talent as well. I hope you will consent to play the pianoforte for me?"

"Oh, yes!" Isabel cried, delighted. "After dinner."

"Not tonight," Grace put in. "Your bedtime is nine o'clock. You can play for Miss Valenti another time."

Isabel's protests to this were in vain. After dessert, she was marched off to bed by her nanny, Molly Knight. Grace took Lucia into the drawing room for coffee while Ian and Dylan remained in the dining room for port and brandy.

After a few minutes of polite interest in Ian's work with the Turks and Greeks, Dylan just had to turn the conversation to their houseguest. And of course, he had to do so with his usual sardonic amusement. "You didn't tell me how pretty she was. She'll have every young man in London panting over her before you've finished the introductions." He swirled the brandy in his glass with a grin. "I don't know what you are worried about. You'll have her engaged in a month."

"We shall see. Attraction is all very well, but a man's love seems to be her primary consideration, and that is not something I can control."

"I thought you said her preferences do not matter."

"They don't." Ian gave his brother a wry glance over the top of his glass of port. "But this entire business would be much easier to manage if love were involved. What I need," he added and took a drink, "is a good love potion."

Dylan laughed. "That young woman *is* a love potion."

A true enough observation. Ian, however, didn't know if that fact made things better or worse. Probably worse, he concluded with resignation.

Chapter 5

L ucia and Grace had barely sat down to their
coffee in the drawing room when an inter-
ruption occurred. Isabel's nanny came in and informed Grace that the child was refusing to go to
sleep.

"She wants the next chapter of her story,
ma'am," Miss Knight said. "She's not closing her
eyes without it, she says."

"Heavens, with Miss Valenti's arrival, I forgot."
Grace set down her cup and saucer, giving Lucia
an apologetic look. "Dylan and I always tuck Isabel into bed at night and read with her before she
goes to sleep. We are in the midst of Victor Hu-
go's *Hunchback of Notre Dame*. Do you mind if I
leave you for a short while?"

"Of course not."

Grace departed with the nanny, and Lucia was alone in the drawing room. She sat back in her chair with her tea, thinking over her new situation.

Despite the fact that Sir Ian had maneuvered her into this house, she did have to admit she liked his family. Dylan Moore was as wickedly charming as his reputation would suggest, his wife was as nice as she was beautiful, and Isabel's impatience with proprieties rather reminded her of herself, especially at that age. Isabel was a fortunate girl, she reflected, to have two parents there to tuck her in and read with her every night.

Suddenly restless, Lucia set her cup aside, rose from her chair, and took a turn about the drawing room, shoving aside any feelings of self-pity about her own upbringing before they could surface. Instead, she turned her mind to a much more intriguing occupation: how to get around Ian Moore.

All her efforts yesterday had been wasted. She might have a permissive chaperone, but she was also stuck with him, and she had the feeling he would be anything but permissive. He'd be worse than Cesare, given half a chance.

Lucia came to a halt beside a chess table, staring down at the black-and-white-marble game pieces, thinking of their conversation the day before. He had been devilishly ingenious, maneuvering her around like a chess piece, all the while letting her think she was in control of the situation. She could not afford to underestimate him again.

She was determined to have control over her own destiny, and Sir Ian was the key to achieving that goal. Cesare respected him and trusted him enough to put him in charge of her future. Lucia knew her mother was right. She had to get Sir Ian on her side, persuade him to let her choose her own mate. But how?

Idly, she picked up a knight from the table and ran her thumb along the intricate carving of the piece, thinking out her own next move. *Use your charm and your magnetism*, Francesca had said. That was all very well, she thought with a hint of exasperation, but Ian Moore was proving rather impervious to both, a most frustrating circumstance and one she'd not often encountered in her life. Without being unduly conceited, Lucia had known from the time she was sixteen that she had a potent effect on the opposite sex, but her feminine appeal had been useless with Sir Ian so far. On the other hand, it was early days yet, and she refused to be discouraged. Ian Moore might be haughty and proper and terribly stuffy, but he was still just a man, with all a man's vulnerabilities.

"Do you play chess?"

Lucia turned her head to find the subject of her thoughts beside her. She gave him her prettiest smile. Smiling at a man went a long way and cost a woman nothing. "I do. I like the game."

His eyes narrowed a bit in assessment as he studied her. "I daresay, but—to quote my niece—are you any good?"

"I am very good," she answered at once. "I am a chess player most excellent."

One corner of his mouth curved upward in what might have been a hint of a smile. "You certainly don't hide any of your lights under a bushel, do you?"

"A bushel?" she repeated in bewilderment. "What a strange question! I do not understand this hiding of lights."

"It's an idiom, an expression," he explained. "I was really commenting that you make no effort to downplay your talents and abilities."

"Of course not." She was astonished. "Why should I?"

"Some would consider modesty about one's accomplishments a virtue."

"The English are extraordinary." She shook her head, confounded by these Anglo-Saxon notions of modesty. "It is no virtue to hide one's abilities. If one has been blessed by God with a certain talent and can do a thing well, why not be proud of it? Besides, a woman has little enough power in the world." With deliberate intent, she ran her fingertips along her bare collarbone. Her move succeeded in drawing his attention downward, and any hint of a smile on his face vanished.

"Whatever appealing qualities she has," Lucia went on, "she should make certain men are aware of them and appreciate them. That way, your sex never takes mine for granted."

"Any man who takes you for granted," he said, lifting his impassive gaze to her face, "is a fool."

Encouraged by the tenseness of his voice, if not his countenance, she moved closer to him. "Are you a fool, Sir Ian?"

He remained rigidly still beside her, hands clasped behind his back, his expression implacable. "No, Miss Valenti, I am not. So whatever schemes you are hatching in that clever brain of yours, set them aside and stop flirting with me."

She made a face at him and moved a step away. "I do not know why I make the effort. You do not flirt back, so flirting with you is not amusing. Not fun."

"I am devastated to hear it." He made an openhanded gesture to the chessboard in front of them. "Are we going to play or not?"

She hesitated, looking at him as she pretended to think it over. "I am not certain I wish to play chess with you," she said after a moment. Setting the knight back on the board, she turned the predominant question of the evening back on him. "Are *you* any good?"

That got a full and genuine grin from him. "Deuce take it, you're a saucy creature, aren't you?"

Despite the fact that she had succeeded in making him smile, Lucia felt compelled to protest his words. "I am no creature. *Ma insomma!* What an extraordinary thing to say. Creature? You speak as if I am a dragon or a . . . a sea monster."

"Again, it is an expression. It is not meant to be taken literally." He pulled out the chair in front of the white chessmen and gave her an inquiring glance.

She hesitated a moment longer, then took the offered chair. He circled the table to the opposite side, pulled off his evening coat, and draped it over the back of his chair. "I never meant to imply anything insulting toward you," he said as he sat down.

"I should hope not. Being a diplomat, you should choose your words with more care." She paused with her hand poised over her queen's pawn. "Compliments, for example," she said with a pointed glance at him, "are always appreciated."

"Indeed?" He lowered his gaze to the board. "I shall keep that in mind next time I meet with the Turks."

Lucia gave a heavy sigh and slid the pawn two spaces forward in the opening move of the game. "Your lack of skill at flirtation is a thing to make pity."

He moved his knight. "Is it?"

"Yes." Lucia did not look at him. Instead, she kept her gaze on the game. "A handsome man should always know how to flirt with women. If he does not, it is a waste of his looks."

"So I am handsome now, am I?" He sounded

amused. "And to think a few hours ago, I was a clever, manipulating bastard."

"You are still that," she assured him, and moved another pawn, "so do not get conceited just because I find you handsome." She stuck her nose in the air and turned her face away. "Besides, I am still angry at the way you tricked me."

"Were you not attempting to trick me?"

Lucia returned her gaze to his. "That is different."

"Ah, one set of rules for me and a different one for you. Not very fair." He slid his bishop across the board, the exact move she had expected. He was a good player, she concluded, but not very imaginative.

She slid her own bishop into place. "I am fighting for my happiness, my life, my future. I do not care about what is fair."

"And I am doing my duty," he countered, taking her pawn just as she had expected him to do. "My duty is just as important to me as your happiness is to you."

"Nothing is more important than love."

"I know women always think love and happiness are inevitably tied together, but that is not true."

"It is true, and it compels me to warn you. In the choosing of my husband, I will do whatever I have to do to ensure my happiness. Your duty is your own affair."

"I am warned, then." With those words, he seemed inclined to settle into the game rather than converse, and she followed his lead. They each concentrated on their strategies, Lucia forming hers on his conservative, rather predictable style of play. The game slowed to a crawl, for he took far longer to make his moves than she did hers. That might or might not be an indication he was in over his head; but sometimes, he made haphazard moves that seemed without purpose, indicating that he could be floundering. She was quick to take advantage of those moments to further her own bold plan of attack.

She lounged back in her chair between moves, studying him. The lamplight caught the glints of lighter brown in his dark hair as he studied the board between them. His nose had been broken at some point in his life, she noted. There was a faint white scar at the edge of his jaw and another over his brow. Given this man's smooth, polished demeanor, she could not see him engaging in fisticuffs with anyone. Her gaze lowered to roam over what she could see of his body above the table, and her mind imagined the muscle and sinew beneath his immaculate white linen and moss green waistcoat. If he ever had engaged in fighting to gain those scars and that broken nose, he had probably won. It was tragic beyond belief that a man so finely made was such a dry stick.

As they played, the music of Dylan Moore's piano floated to them from the music room across the foyer, along with the sound of his wife's violin in accompaniment, but after a few hours, the music stopped, and the house became silent. Servants turned down lamps and blew out candles, leaving Lucia and Sir Ian the only ones still awake in the quiet house.

"I have been thinking of your words from earlier this evening," he said as he reached out to move one of his remaining pawns. "The dictates of my conscience cannot ignore how important happiness in marriage is to you."

Startled, she looked up, searching his face as he leaned back in his chair. Was the marble statue beginning to soften already? Surely not. She returned her attention to the game.

"I can only hope," he went on as she reached out to make her next move, "that of the men on my list, one will satisfy your need for that happiness."

Lucia caught her breath and paused, her hand poised over the board. "You have an actual list? Already?"

"Of course. I told you time is short, and your situation requires an alliance, not a courtship. I shall be contacting each of the gentlemen during the next few days, and arrange for them to meet you. Lady Kettering's concert might be a good start in that regard."

He said nothing more. Impatient, Lucia pulled her hand back and stirred in her chair. "Who is on this list?" she asked. "What are these men like?"

"I cannot discuss them with you until I have determined which ones are amenable to alliance with your father's house. It wouldn't be right." He gestured to the board. "Your move," he reminded her.

"You are the most provoking man!" Lucia accused, and shoved her knight into a new position, taking his. "First you bring up the subject of my future husband, then refuse to discuss the possible candidates. You tease me cruelly."

He lifted his gaze from the board, looking affronted. "I do not tease, Miss Valenti," he said with mild reproof. "It is not in my nature."

Sir Ian returned his attention to the game without another word. They played chess in silence for some minutes, but Lucia's mind was on another game. Between moves, she watched him, trying to determine how she could get around this man's impossible, bewildering sense of ethics. She wanted to know about these men, and damn it all, she deserved to know. It was her future he was toying with.

Lucia smoothed her hair, bit her lips to deepen their color, and straightened in her chair, leaning forward to present herself in the way most favorable to a man. "Sir Ian?"

He didn't even look up. "Hmm?"

His arm was stretched out along the side of the board, and she touched his hand to gain his attention. "Your sense of honor and fair play are admirable," she said, letting the tip of her finger linger on his hand for a moment before she pulled back.

His lips twisted in that hint of a smile. "Pouring

the butter on me again, I see," he murmured and reached out to take her bishop with his knight. "Your turn."

She moved a pawn, uninterested. Very few of his moves so far had surprised her, her strategy was unaltered, and she was reasonably confident of victory. The chess game was not as challenging to her as the other game they were playing at this moment. "It is no wonder my father admires you so. You are a most excellent diplomat. So discreet."

He looked up. "What do you want, Miss Valenti?"

"Your discretion does you much credit, but my feminine curiosity overwhelms me. Could you not tell me something about these men? Not their names, of course," she added at once, "for I would not dream of asking you to violate your sense of propriety." She gave him a wicked little smile. "Although I'd love it if you would."

"No doubt." He studied her for a moment, then he said, "I have several peers in mind. Your father, I am sure, would prefer the gentleman of highest rank."

That information told her absolutely nothing. "But what are they like?"

He frowned, uncomprehending. "Like?"

"Yes. Are they young? Handsome?"

He lifted a fist to his mouth and gave an uncomfortable little cough. "I am no judge of what women find attractive, Miss Valenti. You will have to meet them and see for yourself."

"But are they tall? Strong like you?" She paused to give Sir Ian's shoulders and chest another glance, and she had no need to feign her show of appreciation. "That is important. I like men who are strong and tall because I am so tall myself, you see."

Sir Ian cast a doubtful look at her in return, not even appearing to notice the obvious admiration she had just given his own physique. "Do you not want to know about their character?"

She dismissed character with a wave of her hand. "I have no need to fear about that. You would never choose for me a man who was not of good character."

Sir Ian shook his head. "Miss Valenti, I am confused. You have insisted to me that happiness in marriage is what you seek."

"And?"

He returned his attention to the board. "Since happiness in marriage is not determined by physical appearance, there is no reason to discuss how these men look."

Mother of God. She stared at Sir Ian in horror. *All of them are ugly.*

As the man opposite her concentrated on the chess game, Lucia began envisioning a lifetime of being chained to a husband who came up to her chin. What if he was old? Or had a big belly? Or bad teeth? It didn't bear thinking about such awful possibilities, especially in regard to the physical side of marriage. She wanted lots of babies, and she didn't want to make them with a man who had bad teeth. She *had* to be allowed to choose her own mate.

It was time, she decided with renewed resolve, to pull out the heavy guns.

As they played chess, she managed to remove some of her hairpins without his notice. She stuck them in her pocket. After he made his next move, she stood up with a delicate, ladylike yawn.

Always the perfect gentleman, Sir Ian rose as well. "Do you wish to retire for the night and continue our game another time?"

"Oh, no," she assured him. "I just wish to take a turn about the room and stretch a bit."

In furtherance of that seemingly innocent endeavor, Lucia spread her arms wide and arched her back, drawing out that stretch as long as she could, then she gave a little moan of relief and lowered her arms. With another yawn, she shook her head, and, thanks to those missing hairpins, she succeeded in bringing down a few locks of her hair. Pushing them out of her face, she gave him a sleepy smile, then turned and walked away.

Sure he was watching, she put a subtle but deliberate sway in her hips as she walked to the flagon of wine and glasses on a table at the opposite end of the room. "Would you like a glass of *porto*?" she asked.

"Yes, thank you."

She poured for both of them. Glasses in hand, she turned around, only to find he had left the table as well and had moved to the opposite side of the room. He was standing with his back to her, studying one of the paintings on the wall. She had given him her best walk, and he was looking at a painting?

With a sigh, she brought both glasses to where he stood. He glanced at her just long enough to take his glass from her hand, then he returned his attention to the painting before him. Lucia looked at it as well. Much to her aggravation, she found that the picture in which he displayed such interest was a dark, rather dreary portrait of a wizened old woman in a black dress and a hideous cap.

Accidenti! He was looking at that when he ought to be looking at her? Lucia lifted her eyes heavenward, shook her head, and turned away. What could a woman do with such a man?

She strolled about the drawing room for several minutes, watching him out of the corner of her eye, but he kept his back to her the entire time and never even glanced in her direction. Finally, she gave it up and resumed her seat at the chess table. "Sir Ian?"

"Yes, Miss Valenti?" he said without turning around.

"Are you ready to continue?" She sat down.

There was a long pause. Then he took a sip of wine, gave a brisk tug to the hem of his waistcoat with his free hand, and turned around. "Yes, I believe I am."

They resumed the game. Lucia refused to be daunted by his lack of appreciation for her physical attributes, and after considering the situation for several minutes, she changed tactics. "Sir Ian," she began, "I have been thinking."

"Uh-oh," he murmured. "That's dangerous."

She ignored that. "If I recall our first conversation on the topic of my marriage, you said my father had very strict requirements for my future husband, but you did not outline them in any sort of detail. May I ask what those requirements are?"

He moved his rook right into the path of her bishop, and looked up. "Prince Cesare requires a British gentleman. He offers a sizable dowry, but only to a man already possessed of considerable wealth, for he has no desire to support some impecunious, debt-ridden fellow with his treasury."

She nodded with approval, for she wanted no fortune hunter for a husband. "So he must be rich. What else?"

"He must be a Catholic, of course. And he must be landed aristocracy with substantial estates. In other words, a titled peer or his eldest son, the higher the better."

"Understandable. My father has much pride." She paused long enough to capture Sir Ian's rook. Setting the chess piece at the side of the board, she said, "I confess, I like what I hear. Titled, many estates, and rich. *Magnifico!* I do love to shop."

"I believe there was also some mention of a man of strong will who would make you behave yourself. If you overspend, such a man won't blindly give you more."

She laughed, causing him to raise an eyebrow. "You find that amusing, Miss Valenti?"

"I find it delightful. I told you, I love strong men. I should walk all over a weak one."

He raked a glance over her, but she could read nothing in his face, and when he spoke, his voice was bland. "I have no doubt of that whatsoever."

"You are a strong man," she murmured with a dreamy sigh. "Such a great pity I cannot marry you."

That implacable expression did not falter. "Miss Valenti, marrying me would be out of the question. I have no title, only a knighthood. I have but one estate, and though it is prosperous, it is hardly worthy of mention. Your father would never consent to such a match."

Per Diana! she thought, almost at the point of despair, *the man is hopeless.*

"I know. You are right, of course." She reached out, put her hand over his. "It is so reassuring to know I have a man such as yourself to guide me, a man on whom I can rely."

He turned his head, his attention diverted from the chessboard to her hand over his, then he looked up and met her gaze. His eyes were like polished steel. With deliberate slowness, he pulled his hand away. "Quite."

Lucia knew a forthright approach was all she had left. Explained in the most effective way possible, of course. "Sir Ian, I shall be frank with you."

"That would be a refreshing change." He moved a chess piece.

"I wish to choose my own husband."

"That goes against your father's specific orders. I am to choose."

"All right, then. I should like to choose my own suitors. Make my own list from the men I meet. You can then approach them."

"That would not be wise," he said, his attention still fixed on the game. "You have a predilection for blacksmiths."

"You would not choose for me a blacksmith, nor would Cesare allow me to marry him. Once I am in your English society for a bit, I shall meet young men and begin to have preferences. What would be the harm in allowing me to make my own list? Men you would find suitable, of course. Men of whom my father would approve. But also men I find attractive."

"As I said, it would not be wise."

Lucia made a sound of thorough exasperation and raked her fingers through her hair, scattering her remaining hairpins. The rest of her hair came tumbling down around her face and shoulders. How, she wondered, shoving hair out her face, could she make him understand?

"Sir Ian, I am Italian," she said in a low, sultry voice. "I am young, and I am passionate."

That did the trick. He looked up.

She gazed at him without blinking and chose her words with deliberate care, words that defied all his British proprieties. "I want a strong, handsome, virile husband who can love me with a passion equal to my own."

She shook back her hair, smoldering at this man's unreasonable refusal to compromise with her. "That man," she said, "will never have need of courtesans. That man will sleep in no bed but mine. That man I will treat like a king, and I will be the light that brightens his day. That man will give me many children. That man will wake up in my arms every morning with a smile on his face, and he will be in love with me every single day of his life until they put him in the ground. It cannot be left to you or my father to decide who that man is."

Sir Ian said nothing. He simply looked at her, and she could read nothing in his face. Absolutely nothing.

After a long moment of silence, she said, "I want to make my own list."

"No." His features might have been carved in granite.

"But—"

"No." He made a gesture to the board. "It's your move."

She wanted to scream with frustration. This man was impossible to reason with, and he must truly have no heart at all. There was no fire in him. No understanding of passion. Damn all the English. If she ever married a man as cold as this one, she would go mad.

Telling him all that, however, would not help her get her way. Nor would pushing the matter any further at this moment. Forever the optimist, Lucia decided it would be best to make a strategic retreat and hope for better opportunities later. She looked down at the board and tried to return her attention to chess.

He had moved his knight. Lucia knew she had maneuvered him into a corner some time ago, and his play since then had not extricated him. Only one more move to make before she had him hopelessly trapped.

She started to reach out her hand, then hesitated and drew back. The thought crossed her mind that it was not too late to lose on purpose. It might help her cause. On the other hand, letting a man win at games had never been an appealing tactic to her. Besides, his curt, peremptory manner and the futility of all her efforts to make him see reason aggravated her beyond bearing. She made her move. "Check."

He leaned forward at once and made a move of his own. "Checkmate."

Her lips parted in astonishment. She studied the chessmen that remained on the board and realized that he had, indeed, checkmated her, and she had never seen it coming.

Lucia's mind flashed back over the past few hours, and only now could she comprehend the strategy behind his seemingly predictable play and the genius of his occasional haphazard moves. Once again, he had laid a trap for her, and she had fallen into it. A brilliant trap, she had to admit. In hindsight, it was crystal clear. Why had she not seen it sooner?

"No one defeats me at chess," she murmured, still unable to quite believe it. "No one."

"Don't frown so fiercely. I first learned to play chess when I was a boy of eight. I've been playing this game longer than you have been alive."

She did not find that comforting, and he must have sensed it. "You are an excellent player," he told her, "and you have the imagination to defeat anyone, even players of greater skill than yourself. But, if I might be so bold as to venture advice, do not become overconfident and take your victory for granted too soon."

"You distracted me in the midst of the game by bringing up that damnable list of yours."

He smiled, shaking his head. "Excuses, excuses."

"It is the truth." But there was another truth, and she was fair enough to admit it. "Still, I have only myself to blame. My mind became preoccupied with trying to beguile you into seeing things my way, and I stopped concentrating on the chess."

"So you did."

Lucia slumped in her chair, discouraged all around. Resting her elbow on the table and her cheek in her hand, she stared at the board and watched his hands as he began putting chessmen back in their places. "And it did not even work," she added dismally, her feminine pride stung. "My charms are wasted on you."

His hands stilled. "I would not say that."

The sudden intensity in his voice startled her, and she looked up to find him watching her. In the lamplight, his face was as smooth and unreadable as ever, yet there was something in those gray eyes, something more of hot molten silver than of cool, polished steel, and she caught her breath. "You are human after all," she whispered in amazement.

"Flesh and blood, like any other man." He resumed sorting chess pieces. "And just as susceptible, it seems, to the charms of a beautiful woman."

Her spirits brightened at those words. She leaned forward in her chair, quick to take advantage of the moment. "So, does that mean I can make my own list?"

He didn't even hesitate. "Not a chance."

Chapter 6

Relentless. The woman was relentless. Ian leaned back in his carriage and rubbed a hand over his tired eyes, wishing he'd gotten even a few minutes of sleep the night before. But no, he'd lain in bed for hours, taunted by Miss Valenti's provocative maneuverings. Giving up on any possibility of sleep, he'd gotten out of bed and gone into Dylan's library.

Thank heaven his brother actually possessed a current copy of *Burke's Peerage*. Ian had spent the night poring over names, making a list of potential marriage partners for Miss Valenti. He'd only mentioned having an actual list in the futile hope that discussing her future husband would keep his mind on his duty.

He had confirmed with Grace this morning which of the men on his list were in town at present, and which ones might be seeking wives. Women like Lucia Valenti caused kings to abdicate and warlords to invade their neighbors; but perhaps some of the peers on his list would consider marrying Italy's version of Helen of Troy. If so, he intended to make sure at least some of those poor, clueless sods attended Lady Kettering's amateur concert three days hence. Perhaps one of the men who met her would be strong enough, handsome enough, *virile* enough to get her off his hands. Then Ian could go back to his own life.

It would not have cost him to let her have her way last night, to let her make her own list, choose her own possible marriage partners. As long as the man met Cesare's requirements and wanted to marry her, he could let her pick any fellow she wished. But she had angered him with her soft sighs and her bold gazes over his body, with her oh-so-innocent stretching and her hip-swaying walk. Thank God he'd had the presence of mind to go look at stupid paintings until he'd gotten his baser nature under control.

That woman was a cock-tease, and she knew it, too. It was beyond his understanding how she had managed to keep her innocence this long. Amazing that some tormented devil hadn't deprived her of it long ago.

It was only after all her attempts to manipulate him had failed that she'd tried a direct approach.

And when Lucia Valenti decided to be direct, she did it with a vengeance.

The carriage came to a stop, breaking into his thoughts. Ian looked out the window and stared at the front door of Lord Blair's London residence as he waited for his driver to open the carriage door. Blair, an earl in his own right, was also the cousin and heir of the Marquess of Monforth. Blair met every one of Prince Cesare's requirements. When it came to the expectations of Cesare's daughter, however, Ian was less certain.

In his mind's eye, he could still see her, a sultry hellion of a woman, sitting before him with her hair coming down and her dark eyes smoldering as she'd told him what sort of man he was supposed to find for her. Listening to that brazen speech of hers had played merry hell with his reason, for all he'd been able to think about at that moment was shoving aside the table and giving her a taste of what male virility really meant.

The carriage door opened, causing Ian to remember where he was and why. He straightened his cravat, cooled his blood, and thought of his duty. It was fortunate for Miss Valenti that he was a civilized man.

There had to be a way to bring Sir Ian around to her way of thinking.

Lucia pondered her situation as she sat sipping tea and eating iced lemon cake with Lady Kettering, Grace, and several young ladies who had stopped to join them in the tea shop. As the others discussed the latest fashions, she thought over various strategies for how to deal with her present problem, a tall, dark-haired, very obstinate problem.

Women's voices eddied all around her, but the feminine voice Lucia heard in her mind was that of her mother.

Get Sir Ian on your side.

Her mother's suggestion to use her charm and magnetism hadn't helped her gain the man's cooperation last night. Perhaps she just needed to be more patient. Lucia sighed. Patience had never been one of her strengths. Besides, she only had six weeks. Patience was not something she could afford.

"Don't you agree, Miss Valenti?"

"Hmm?" She came out of her reverie with a start and looked at the young woman who sat with two other young ladies on the opposite side of the table. Lady Sarah Monforth, seated between her companions, was gazing at Lucia over the top of her teacup in inquiry.

Realizing she had just been asked a question, and with no knowledge of what that question had been, Lucia said the only thing she could think of. "I am so sorry. My mind was preoccupied. I was thinking of . . . of the . . . um . . . the current fashion in . . . um . . . necklines."

"Necklines?" Lady Sarah smiled, but her big blue eyes narrowed a fraction, making her smile as artificial as the soft pink blush in her white cheeks. Golden lashes lowered, then lifted. "It comes as no surprise that your thoughts are on that topic." She turned to glance at the companions on either side of her. "Does it, ladies?"

As if on cue, Lady Wellburn spoke. "Indeed not. The neckline is clearly Miss Valenti's favorite part of a gown."

Lucia stiffened at the stifled giggling of several young women at the table, and she did not miss the flash of satisfaction in Lady Sarah's eyes. For a moment, she felt as if she were back in finishing school, being teased by the girls who did not like her. Lucia bit back her desire to make a meowing sound in Sarah's direction. She smiled instead, her sweetest, prettiest smile.

"And that is as it should be," Grace said, and turned to Lucia. "If I had as splendid a figure as you, my dear friend, I should make my necklines very daring." She gestured to her own bosom with a sigh of regret. "Alas, I am not so fortunate."

Lucia gave her a look of gratitude. "I think you are lovely," she said, and meant it.

"I have heard the fashions in Italy are much more daring than they are here," Lady Kettering said, and diverted the conversation by gesturing to the waiter who stood beside her holding a silver teapot. "More tea, anyone?"

"I must apologize," Grace told Lucia as their carriage took them back toward Portman Square. "I should never have subjected you to Lady Sarah and her friends."

"They happened by, and Lady Kettering invited them to join us. Do not apologize for what is not your fault. For their opinion, I care nothing." That wasn't completely true, for it still stung to know she was being laughed at. "On the other hand, I should not wish to be unfashionable. Do you think I should have different gowns?"

"Lucia, do not let Lady Sarah and her friends bother you. The latest fashions are the only thing they know anything about. Frivolous idiots, all of them."

"Perhaps, but Lady Sarah has something her friends do not. She has cunning, that one. She arranges for others to say what she wants said. It is a talent, that."

"A malicious talent, but you are right. She does have her following. We are not among her set, however, so I hope we can succeed in avoiding them most of the time."

"I hope so as well. But—" She hesitated, still feeling a hint of self-doubt. "Do you think I should change my gowns?"

"Again, no, I do not. I meant every word of what I said. If I had your figure, I should flaunt it shamelessly. Besides, the off-shoulder necklines and shawl collars so prevalent now would not suit you. To look well in them, you would need to bind your bosom, and what a waste that would be. Terribly uncomfortable, too, I imagine."

"It is painful. When I first went away to school, I was a girl of only twelve, and though I was younger, I was far bigger than the other girls, and they teased me all the time. So, I started binding my breasts with linen, very tight, to make them flatter. It hurt, but I did not want to be teased. The next time my mother came to see me, she was horrified. She told me to stop doing that. She said she loved me just as I was, I did not need to change for anyone, and I should be happy with myself as the good God made me."

"Very sensible advice."

Lucia smiled. "To some, my mamma seems to have a brain of feathers, for she is always late, forgets engagements, and spends money like water; but underneath all of that, she is of the most sensible."

"You love her very much, don't you?"

"Yes." Lucia stopped smiling. "I wish I could see her."

"Are you asking my permission to do so?"

"If I did, would you give it?"

"I cannot." Grace looked at her with compassion. "Please believe that I understand your feelings. When my mother died, I had been separated from her for years, and I will always regret that. But Ian has given me strict instructions not to allow you to see Francesca, and even though I know how hard it is for you to be separated from your mother, I must accede to Ian's wishes. He has done more for me than I can ever repay."

"I understand." She paused. "Sir Ian says I shall always have to be separated from my mother. That my association with her will be unacceptable to any gentleman because of what she is."

"I fear that may be true."

"I refuse to believe it." She met the other woman's sympathetic gaze. "Since I must marry, I must find a man who loves me. If he loves me enough, he will accept my mother when we are married and give me his permission to see her. I will persuade him."

"That may also be true." Grace was silent for a moment, then she gave a little laugh. "We find our conversation back where it started, I think."

Lucia frowned in puzzlement. "What do you mean?"

"You are supposed to be getting a husband, and men, heaven bless them, care nothing for women's fashions. I find most men are far more susceptible to a full bosom and a low neckline."

Lucia laughed. "My thoughts exactly."

Sir Ian, however, was not most men. Though he had admitted to a hint of susceptibility where she was concerned, Lucia had the feeling that wasn't enough to bring him around to her way of thinking. It was clear he intended to carry out her father's wishes to the letter, and none of her persuasive tactics the night before had served to change his mind. She had to get him on her side, but how?

At dinner, she studied him as a general about to engage in a battle campaign would study a map, trying to determine what method of attack to employ next, but it wasn't until late in the evening that she had a new plan in mind.

While others in the house were preparing for bed, Lucia went in search of her quarry. She found him in the library, which was perfect for her purposes. Peeking around the open doorway, she saw him seated at his brother's desk, his head bent over a letter he was writing. If this was a battle, the first step was to know the enemy. She intended to do just that.

He glanced up as she entered the room and immediately rose to his feet with a bow.

"I came in search of a book," she said. "I hope I am not disturbing you?"

"Not at all."

She moved toward the bookshelves at the other end of the room and began to peruse the titles there as he resumed his seat and his work.

Lucia waited, pretending vast interest in her task, trying to be patient, hoping he would open conversation. He finally did.

"Are you looking for a particular type of book to read?" he asked.

She glanced at him and found he was still writing his letter. "No, I do not think so," she answered. "There are so many here, it will be hard to choose one."

She ran her fingertips lightly over the spines of volumes closest to her. "There are several etiquette books here. Are they for Isabel?"

"Yes, I believe so." He set down his quill and sprinkled blotting powder over the document before him, then blew it off and reached for sealing wax. "Though I doubt she's read any of them."

"Why should she? Etiquette books are dull."

"You would say something like that."

She smiled. "Do not mistake my meaning, Sir Ian. I find etiquette books very useful."

He set his finished letter aside and looked at her. "Do you, indeed?" His voice was skeptical.

She smiled. "They are most excellent for propping doors open."

That got an answering smile from him, but if she thought that would cause him to give her his full attention, she was mistaken. He reached for a fresh sheet of paper, dipped his quill in the inkwell, and began again.

She moved a bit farther down the shelves, trying to think of a way to keep the conversation going, but he did it for her. "I am writing a report to your father," he said. "Is there anything you would like me to say on your behalf?"

"That I wish to choose my own husband?"

"Your father's mind is not going to be changed on that point, I fear, regardless of what I may say."

"Yes, he buys a man for me instead."

"I will do what I can to make certain the man I recommend is not merely a fortune hunter. But you have to understand that when you are launched into society, you will be the victim of everyone's scrutiny. Possible suitors and their relations will insist upon knowing your background. They will gossip, and word will spread. That is something I cannot prevent. Given your illegitimacy, your mother's identity, and the incident at

Carnival, any gentlemen not after your money will have legitimate reservations about marrying you."

"You are telling these men what happened in Bolgheri?"

"Yes. I am phrasing it as diplomatically as possible, of course."

"Would it not be easier to find me a husband if you did not tell them?"

"It is not a question of what is easier. The news of what happened in Bolgheri is already spreading over Europe. It is bound to arrive here. I do not want any serious suitor to have an unpleasant shock, so I am defusing the damage early."

"I see." She moved further along the shelves, studying the books. "Your brother's collection of books is very fine," she said, veering the subject away from herself.

"Yes. I have often envied Dylan that."

"You have?" She turned to look at him. "But why? Surely you could have a set of books just as fine."

"There would be no point, for I should never be able to enjoy them." He gestured to documents spread all around him. "I am away from home most of the time, and it is impractical to carry one's book collection all over the globe."

"True." She leaned back against the bookshelves behind her. "Is your profession the reason you have never married?"

"I am gone all the time, usually never staying in one place for more than a few months. I should have to leave a wife and children at home, or cart them about from place to place. It would not be right."

She tilted her head, studying him. "Do you always do what is right?"

"I try to, yes."

She smiled. "I don't."

That got a wry smile from him in return. "So I've noticed," he said, and returned his attention to his work.

"To never marry, to never have children, to travel all about and never settle at home must be lonely."

The quill stopped moving, but only for the barest second. "It can be," he said, and resumed writing.

"Your work is very important to you, isn't it?"

"Yes."

"Why?"

That garnered his full attention. He stopped writing and rested his elbows on the desk. Rolling the quill in his palms, he thought about it for a moment before he spoke. "Britain is the most powerful nation in the world, and I believe such a position carries enormous responsibility. I do what I can to ensure my nation uses its power wisely."

Lucia thought about that for a moment, then she shook her head. "That may be true, but it is not the reason."

She straightened away from the bookshelf and walked over to a place beside his chair. Facing him, she sat on top of the desk, oblivious to the papers spread across its surface.

"There are chairs in the room," he pointed out.

She settled herself more comfortably where she was, rustling the papers beneath her. "It is all very noble, what you say about your country's power and responsibility, but that is not the main reason you do what you do."

He turned his head to look up at her. "You are sitting on a very important trade agreement with the Dutch."

She waved aside the Dutch. "No, you are a diplomat because you like to be the one who has the power in any situation."

"That, too," he admitted.

"And," she went on, "because you are so good at hiding how you feel, you always have the power. You always have the upper hand. Is that not how you see it?"

"Yes. You would not agree, I daresay, for you wear your feelings on your sleeve, and those feelings change from moment to moment."

Lucia was not bothered by that assessment. "I am capricious, it is true. I am a person of strong emotions, and I do not hide them."

"But it robs you of control over a given situation."

"Perhaps." She slanted him a knowing look, her mouth curving upward at the corners. "Perhaps not."

He made no reaction. How she would love to

shake this man's iron discipline. Her blood stirred with a hint of excitement, and she could not resist the temptation to try. She leaned a little closer to him. "There is more than one way to have power, Sir Ian," she said in her silkiest way. "And being out of control is not always a bad thing."

He did not move. "Is that supposed to persuade me to hand over control of your situation to you?"

Lucia leaned back and admitted it. "I hope so."

"Why do you want it so much?"

She smiled sweetly. "Because I cannot have it."

Sir Ian expelled a harsh breath that was almost a laugh. "That I believe."

"Sir Ian, I shall be serious with you. Getting married is the most important thing a woman does in her life. It must be a choice. My choice and his, made with mutual respect and love."

He stirred in his chair as if impatient, but she pushed on. "Cesare says I shall not have the choice of whom to marry, but he only says that to punish me, for he is angry. Sir Ian, please do not do me this injustice. Giving me the choice of whom I marry costs you nothing, and it is the right thing to do. You said yourself that you always do what is right."

Sir Ian shoved back his chair and stood up. Afraid he was leaving, Lucia jumped off the desk and put a hand on his arm. "My father offers much money for some man to marry me, but if I do not have that man's love and respect, I shall be under his boot, and that would make me unhappy all my days."

He stiffened, and Lucia felt a pang of disappointment. She let her hand fall to her side. "I should have known you would not understand."

She turned away, but his next words brought her up short. "On the contrary, Miss Valenti, I do understand."

"You do?" She stopped and faced him again. Hope flickered to life.

"Yes. I recognize that you have a profound need to control your own destiny, and a deep desire for love. You are not in the same position as your sister, and treaties are not at stake. Your preferences in this matter should have been considered from the beginning." He clasped his hands behind his back. "In that regard, I was . . . I was . . ."

"Wrong?" she supplied.

"Hasty."

"Of course," she agreed at once, allowing him that description. "What happens now?"

He gave the hem of his waistcoat a tug. "A compromise seems in order. I agree to allow your preference to be the deciding factor. However, I insist upon certain conditions."

Lucia gave a sigh of relief. "What conditions?"

"Each and every man you meet must have my approval before you are to have anything further to do with him. And you may be sure that Grace will be well aware of what sort of men I would find acceptable. No blacksmiths. No poets, no painters, no rakes, or scoundrels of any kind."

She feigned disappointment. "A pity. Always, I have wanted a rake to fall in love with me. It is every woman's dream."

"And women wonder why we men find your sex utterly baffling."

"I assure you, I shall not fall in love with a rake. No, no." She gave a dreamy, tongue-in-cheek sigh. "But it would be so exciting if he fell in love with me."

"To my mind, you've had enough excitement in your life."

"You really are impossible to tease," she told him with an exasperated sigh. "What other conditions do you have?"

"Obviously, the man in question must be willing to marry you," he said, and began gathering the papers on his desk. "In addition, all Cesare's requirements must be met: a Catholic peer with a title, estates, fortune, and respected connections. And the schedule remains the same. Your father arrives less than six weeks from now. You have until then to find a man acceptable to us both."

"But—"

"Six weeks." He dropped his sheaf of documents into the leather dispatch case that lay open on the desk and looked at her, his expression hard and resolute. "If you have not chosen a particular man from among your suitors by then, I will choose one for you."

She did not know if that amount of time would be sufficient to find the man she wanted, but she knew she could push him no further at this point. "I agree to your conditions."

"Excellent. Now, as it is very late, I believe I shall go to bed." He closed his dispatch case. Grasping it by the handles, he bowed, then moved past her and left the room. It was probably fortunate for both of them that he did not hear her next words.

"I agree," she repeated in a whisper toward the open doorway. "For now."

Chapter 7

~~~~~~~~~~~~~~~~~~~~~~~~~~

Rosehill, Lord and Lady Kettering's residence during the London season, had the advantage of being north of Hyde Park, in Bayswater. Though only a short distance from Town, it was considered to be in the country, Grace explained to Lucia as they rode with Dylan and Ian to that destination.

The estate was possessed of generous grounds and splendid gardens, and Lady Kettering's annual amateur concert was held in the manner of a garden party, unreliable English weather permitting, of course. On the lawn, Lucia was told, there would be an enormous marquee, and beneath it, a stage would provide the means by which accomplished young ladies could show off their talents, or as Dylan had pointed out, their lack thereof. Facing the stage would be plenty of seats for the hopefully appreciative audience. After the young ladies had finished playing, an octet of professional musicians would take over. Guests could then partake of refreshments and visit with friends at the tables on the lawn or stroll through the grounds.

As beautiful as the setting proved to be, if Lucia had any hopes of meeting men such as those she had described to Sir Ian, those hopes went unfulfilled. She had now been given the ability to choose, but it hardly mattered. Not a single man at Lady Kettering's event made her pulses rise one tiny bit. Some of the men were nice, some were handsome, all were polite, but none proved appealing enough or interesting enough to attract her.

Nonetheless, Lucia did like to be liked, and she was determined to make a good impression. So, she sat on a chair under the marquee, fanning herself in the warm spring afternoon, smiling at people until her jaw ached. She flirted with the men delicately and complimented them shamelessly. She laughed at their jokes and listened to their stories. She did everything she could to give each man she met her utmost attention. There were times, such as this moment, when that was an uphill struggle.

"Of course, it's all in the pollination, my dear Miss Valenti," Lord Walford said, leaning forward in his chair to explain in detail. "And that is a tricky business. You see, once the anthers ripen and the pollen is released . . ."

Lucia stared at Walford, trying to conceal her bafflement. She did not understand how a man who was sitting with a young woman he might decide to marry could wish to discuss rose pollination. Englishmen, she decided, were incomprehensible. She liked pretty flowers as well as the next girl, but she did not need an hour-long dissertation on how to breed them.

She somehow managed to extricate herself from Lord Walford, only to be introduced to some other man. With each introduction, with each discussion of the weather and each polite inquiry about her health, Lucia felt her future happiness moving further and further out of reach. By sunset, she could take no more. She whispered to Grace that she needed to be alone for a short while. Slipping away, she went for a walk.

After strolling along a graveled path, she found a charming, quiet little grotto with a fountain. Breathing a sigh of relief that she was alone at last, and no gentleman was going to offer to fetch her yet another glass of punch or give her his assessment of the beautiful day, she sat down on a stone bench. Leaning forward, she rested one elbow on her knee and her chin in her hand. She stared into the lily pond nearby, discouraged and confused.

She did not understand the English. Truly, she did not. How could she ever fall in love and marry one of them? She was accustomed to torrid

Frenchmen and volatile Italian men. These Englishmen, with their civility and restraint and lack of romance, seemed so dull by comparison. Where was the passion? The fire?

A pair of gray eyes came into her mind. There was fire there. She had seen it lurking beneath that polished, polite veneer the other night.

Or she might have just imagined it. Today, Sir Ian was scrupulously polite, his address was impeccable, and his occasional conversations with her were just as trivial as those of all the other men with whom she had spoken.

Perhaps she had expected too much from this first outing. After all, this was her first foray into English society, and it had been unrealistic to think that the man of her dreams was going to appear as easily as that. But he was out there, she knew it, and she was going to find him. She had to.

Lucia closed her eyes and said a little prayer to God that by the time her father arrived, she found a man—not one she was forced to marry, but one she wanted to marry—a man who could make her pulse race and her breath catch, a man she could talk to and laugh with, a man she could love for a lifetime. Lucia didn't think that was too much to ask.

From the look of things, Ian could only conclude that Miss Valenti had suitors eating out of her hand, because at any given time, half a dozen of them were following her around like little puppies hoping for treats. It was not until late in the afternoon when the party was almost over that Ian managed to catch her alone, sitting on a stone bench in a grotto, gazing into a lily pond. She looked up as he approached.

Ian glanced around. "No flock of admirers following you?"

"Not at the moment, no." She glanced around and put a finger to her lips. "I am hiding," she confided in a whisper. "They have exhausted me."

This did not sound promising. Ian sat down beside her on the bench and decided to take the gentlemen in question one by one, starting with the most eligible parti. "What did you think of Lord Blair?"

She thought it over for a long moment before she spoke. "He is a good man, I think. But his cousin—" She broke off and made a sound of contempt.

"You wouldn't be marrying his cousin," Ian pointed out.

"You should," she countered. "After all, Lady Sarah is the loveliest young woman of your acquaintance. A stunning beauty, if I recall your opinion."

Ian remembered their conversation about Lady Sarah, and he couldn't help smiling at the asperity in her voice. "I did rather embellish her attributes, didn't I? But," he couldn't help adding, "she is lovely to look at."

She gestured to their surroundings. "So is a garden. But one cannot have a conversation with it."

Ian gave her an innocent look. "Is conversation important?"

"Not to a man, I suppose, though I should have thought better of you than that. However, if you wish to admire a woman as dim as a firefly and as malicious as a wasp, Sir Ian, that is your affair."

"Perhaps you do not like Lady Sarah because she has as many admirers here today as you do."

Lucia made a sound of derision, and Ian decided it would be best to leave off further discussion of Lady Sarah Monforth. "Lord Blair is the eldest son of a marquess. The family is one of the finest and wealthiest in Britain. He seems to like you very much."

She considered for a moment before she spoke. "He has one fatal flaw. He is too nice."

"That is a flaw?"

She looked at him as if he were as hopelessly brain deficient as Lady Sarah. "I told you what sort of man I want. Do you not remember?"

How could he forget?

"I could twist Lord Blair around my little finger," she went on. "He would be one of those husbands whose favorite words are, 'Yes, my dear,' and, 'Of course, my dear.' I want to be happy with my husband, and I want him to be happy with me." She thought it over for a moment, then she said, "I do not believe Lord Blair is right for me. We should not make each other happy."

Ian gave up on Blair for the moment. "What of Lord Montrose?"

"Ah," she said, nodding with what might have been approval. "He made me laugh, that one. And he is handsome."

Ian had no time to be encouraged by that comment, for she immediately went on, "Yes, very handsome, indeed. And he knows it, too. The entire time I spoke with him, he was preening for me and strutting like a peacock. I do not think I want to marry a peacock."

So much for that hint of approval. Ian tried again. "Lord Haye?"

Miss Valenti shook her head. "Weak chin."

"You would dismiss a man for something as trivial as a weak chin?"

"But I hate a man with a weak chin."

"One is too nice, one is too handsome, one has a weak chin," he said with a hint of irritation. "Good God, are you going to dismiss every man you meet on such trivialities as these?"

"A weak chin is not trivial. I do not want sons with weak chins."

It was then that he perceived the smile curving the corners of her mouth.

"Think of the family portraits," she went on.

Impudent baggage, he thought, striving not to laugh, for it would only encourage her. "Do be serious and give an honest opinion, if you please. Haye is an earl. He has a fine estate in Sussex with very beautiful grounds. His sisters, I can assure you, are very fine young ladies and are not at all like Lady Sarah. I know Haye personally, Miss Valenti, and despite his chin, I know him to be a sound man. Do you truly dislike him?"

She became serious again. "I did not dislike him," she said with a sigh. "Dislike would have been preferable."

"I do not understand what you mean."

"I felt nothing when I looked at him, when I talked with him." She lifted her hands, fingers pressed to thumbs in a purely Italian gesture of exasperation as she tried to explain. "Nothing. No excitement, no spark."

"A first meeting can be deceiving. You might change your mind once you know him better."

She considered that. After a moment, she nodded. "Very well," she said, but her voice was doubtful. "You believe Haye is a good man, so I shall not be too quick to judge. We shall keep him on our list and see. As you say, perhaps I shall change my mind about him if I get to know him better."

Ian did not want to trust Miss Valenti's unpredictable moods. Haye could not be the only possible candidate. "What did you think of Lord Walford?"

She frowned. "Which one was he again?"

"He was the one in the marquee with you. You seemed rather taken with him."

"Oh, that one!" she cried in a tone that did not bode well for Walford's chances. "He cornered me to tell me all about this new rose he is breeding. How could you think I was taken with him?"

"How could I not? You spent an hour talking with him."

"It took me an hour to get away, for I did not want to be rude and hurt his feelings." She made a sound of exasperation and stood up. "If he corners me again, Sir Ian, please come to my rescue. Save me from another lecture on rose pollination."

Ian grinned as he stood up and followed her. "I see your point," he said, falling in step beside her on the gravel path. "The man is, perhaps, a bit dull."

"Dull?" she repeated. "That is not the word I would use." She halted and looked at him. "Sir Ian, I ask you this: When a pretty woman—and I like to think I am pretty enough—when a pretty woman is sitting in front of a man, why would he be talking about the breeding of roses?"

Ian looked at her mouth, with its cupid's-bow upper lip and pouty lower one, and conceded himself equally baffled. Realizing he was headed into dangerous territory with thoughts like that, he returned his attention to the subject at hand. Being a diplomat, he tried to be diplomatic. "Perhaps Walford was so overwhelmed by your beauty, it was the only thing he could think of to talk about."

She was not mollified. "Then he should have complimented me, do you not think, instead of his newest flower creation?"

"So that is what you want of a suitor?" he asked, genuinely curious. "Compliments?"

"Better a discussion of my hips," she countered, "than a discussion of rose hips!"

She walked away. Ian stood back, studying her figure for a moment, and he could not disagree with her about that. "Walford is, I take it, out of contention?" he asked, and started to follow her.

"It wasn't only him. All of them were the same. What is it about you Englishmen?" she demanded, lifting her hands in exasperation. "Have you no passion?"

She halted and turned around so abruptly he cannoned into her. Without thinking, he brought his hands up on either side of her hips to prevent her from falling. Beneath his palms, he felt the shape and curve of her, and all that passion Englishmen supposedly lacked flared up inside him with the quickness of a lit match. They were standing so close, he could smell the fragrance of her hair. Apple blossoms, he realized, inhaling deeply. His hands tightened their grip, and he wanted to pull her that last bit closer, but this lascivious intent had barely crossed his mind before he was jerking his hands away. He took a step back and clasped his hands behind him, reminding himself that he was a gentleman and cursing himself because such a reminder should not have been necessary.

"We may not demonstrate it, Miss Valenti," he said, fighting to regain his control, "but Englishmen are capable of the deepest passions, believe me."

He could hear the harshness in his own voice.

She heard it, too, for she leaned back to look up into his face. "I am sorry if I have offended you," she murmured, her eyes wide as she stared into his.

Ian turned away. "We'd best return to the party," he said as he started back toward the marquee. He didn't look behind him to see if she was following. There was only so much temptation a man could endure.

Lucia soon discovered that Sir Ian's strategy for finding her a husband seemed akin to throwing mud against a wall. Some would have to stick. The mud, alas, was not the sort her lusty Italian heart was hoping for.

During the fortnight following Lady Kettering's concert, Lord Haye, Lord Montrose, Lord Blair, Lord Walford, and about a dozen other possible suitors frequently found their way to Portman Square. Lucia was not inclined toward any of them, and though Grace assured her that familiarity often changed one's mind in matters of the heart, two weeks of calls by these gentlemen did not change Lucia's.

She was inundated with enough male attention to satisfy any woman, but as much as Lucia enjoyed flirtation, she began to refrain from it. She did not want to encourage any of these men or hurt them. She tried to be more aloof and distant, but it was an aggravating truth about men that the less interest a woman displayed in them, the more enamored they became.

Even more aggravating to Lucia was the fact that the man responsible for this bachelor parade was nowhere in the vicinity. Telling Grace he had important diplomatic matters to handle, he gave over full charge of Lucia's launch into society to his sister-in-law. When she did chance to see him, he was so aloof and stuffy that she became certain any spark of fire in that man's eyes had been a trick of the light or her imagination.

Despite the admiration she received from many bachelors of London society, the ladies were not so generous, a fact that those two weeks made painfully obvious. Though some invitations came their way, and she was included in those invitations along with the Moore family, Lucia felt the coolness of other women everywhere she went. She did not want to admit how much it hurt to be ostracized, but she found herself confiding her feelings to Isabel one evening over a chess game.

"Why should you care what they think?" Isabel asked.

"It would be nice to have female friends in this country, since I am going to live here for the rest of my life."

"They are just jealous." Isabel moved a knight to take Lucia's bishop. "You are prettier than any of them. And much more fun."

"*Grazie*, Isabel." Lucia made her next chess play, fully aware that it was an unwise move that put her in danger. She smiled at her petite defender across the table. "That is the nicest compliment I have ever received."

"From my daughter, it is high praise," Dylan said from his place at the writing desk where he was composing a letter. "She is very chary of granting her good opinion to anyone. It took me forever to gain it. Grace, too. And Ian."

"Mr. Moore, I suspect it is my ability to teach her the Spanish guitar that is at the heart of her liking for me."

"Not true!" Isabel protested. "I do like you, really. You're not silly like most ladies. You don't twitter or fuss or say mean things behind other people's backs. Lady Sarah is the worst of the lot."

"Isabel!" Grace said, lowering the embroidery in her hands with a laugh. "You mustn't say such things. It isn't proper."

"My niece is misbehaving again?" Sir Ian entered the drawing room, a sheaf of papers in his hand. He smiled at the little girl as he crossed the room to Dylan's side. "Why am I not surprised?"

"I'm not misbehaving, Uncle Ian, honestly. It's just that the ladies are being mean to Lucia, and it's not right."

"Mean?" He paused beside Dylan's chair and looked at Lucia. "What are they doing?"

"It's nothing," she answered. "Isabel exaggerates."

He took her at her word and turned to his brother, handing him the papers. "Dylan, take a look at these expenditures from Plumfield. Are they comparable to what you are paying at Nightingale's Gate, or do they seem high to you?"

While Dylan complied, Ian returned his

attention to his niece. "Are you exaggerating about this, Isabel?"

"No! They are mean." She moved her bishop, just as Lucia had known she would. "Checkmate!"

"What?" Lucia stared down at the board in pretended amazement. "How did you manage that?"

Laughing, the child turned toward the man on the other side of the room. "Look, Uncle Ian. I beat Lucia at chess. I never beat you, but I beat her, and she's good. Really good."

He gave Lucia what might have been a glance of puzzlement, but it was gone before she could be sure. "Yes, Miss Valenti is very skilled," he agreed. "If you defeated her, Isabel, that is quite an accomplishment."

Lucia returned her attention to the child opposite her. "I could swear I had you trapped."

"Not for a second."

"You distracted me," Lucia accused her. "We started talking about the ladies, and you distracted me from the game."

"I didn't!" Isabel grinned, clearly delighted with her victory. "I beat you fair and square. Didn't I? Admit it."

She sighed, slumping in her chair. "You did," she confessed in her best discouraged fashion. "And I never saw it coming. I should have paid better attention."

"Got distracted during the game, did you, Miss Valenti?" Ian's voice once again entered their conversation. "You seem to let that happen often."

"I am afraid I do," she agreed mildly, biting her lip.

His frown deepened. He started in their direction as if to study the board, and Lucia felt a pang of alarm. He might start asking questions about the way play had gone, and Isabel would realize the truth. He hadn't taken more than one step toward them, however, before Dylan spoke. Ian returned his attention to his brother, and with a silent sigh of relief, Lucia began rearranging the chess pieces to hide the evidence of her deliberate loss.

"These expenses seem reasonable to me," Dylan told him. "Prices have been rising these past few years."

"I need to come home more often, it seems." Ian once again started toward the chess table, but when he saw that Lucia had already returned the chess pieces to their original places, he turned to his sister-in-law instead. "Grace, perhaps you should tell me what is going on with the ladies of the ton."

Grace looked up from her needlework, but she hesitated before replying. With a glance at Lucia, she returned her attention to Ian, and said, "Perhaps we should discuss this another time."

Knowing it was her presence that caused Grace to hesitate, Lucia spoke. "I want to know. Why do they dislike me?"

"Jealous cats," Isabel pronounced.

"Isabel," Grace said, "I want you to go upstairs and tell Molly it's time for your bath."

The child started to protest, but Grace cut her off. "Dinner is in an hour. Go."

Isabel slid out of her chair. "I never hear any of the good gossip," she mumbled as she headed out of the room.

Grace waited until she could be sure Isabel was upstairs before she spoke. "Dylan and I usually receive numerous invitations during the season, but matrons are not issuing very many to us at present." She shot Lucia a look of apology. "So there is a lack of acceptance. Some of it is due to Miss Valenti's position."

"That I am illegitimate?" Lucia's chin lifted. "Or that I am Francesca's daughter?"

"Both, I'm sorry to say. I also agree with Isabel's point about jealousy. It is somewhat understandable. They resent that Lucia, a foreign girl with a courtesan mother, has had so many gentlemen callers, and that she is admired by them. Everywhere we go—bookstores, parks, the art galleries—men express the wish for an introduction to her."

Her husband groaned. "And those are the ones who haven't met her. Grace, my darling, the men who have already been introduced accost me in Brooks's to talk about Miss Valenti."

"They do?" Lucia asked. "What do they say?"

"They ask me questions about you," Dylan replied, turning in his chair to look at her. "What flowers you like and who your favorite poets are—as if I know any of these things! I suggest they ask you. Or, if they can't work up the nerve for that, to make these inquiries of Grace. They rhapsodize, Miss Valenti, about your beauty and your wit and your delightful accent. If I hear one more description of your chocolate eyes and your cherry-red lips, I shall be forced to retreat to the country."

"They are saying things like that?" Ian asked, his voice sharp.

"All the time. Stop working long enough to get about town, and you would hear it for yourself." He paused, looking up at his brother. "I'd have thought you'd be happy about this, Ian."

"So I am."

"Then why are you frowning like thunder?"

He took a moment to answer. "The situation of the matrons concerns me," he finally said. "It must be resolved. But I am pleased to hear Miss Valenti has so many suitors." His frown vanished, and he gave her a nod as he walked by her chair. "It bodes well."

Lucia frowned at his back as he walked away. Being inundated with men would only bode well if she had a speck of desire for any of them. And did Sir Ian have to be so pleased about it? Really, she thought, aggrieved, a man with any passion in him would have been just a little bit jealous.

Ian paused at the door and turned. "Grace, to entrench Miss Valenti into the ton, she must have the good opinion of the matrons, don't you agree?"

"Yes."

He tapped the sheaf of papers in his hand against his palm, lost in thought. Lucia wondered what scheme he was coming up with now, but she was not kept in suspense long. "Dylan, I believe that, for once, you have given me sound advice."

"I always give you sound advice. You just don't listen very often."

He ignored that. "I do need to get about town more. I believe it might be time for me to call upon some of the matrons and start mentioning Miss Valenti's half brother."

"Antonio?" Lucia stared at him, bewildered. "What could be the purpose of mentioning him?"

"Prince Antonio is a very important man. He is the future ruler of Bolgheri, and a grandson to the King of the Two Sicilies. He has always wished to come to London, of course."

"Antonio is coming to London?" Lucia asked in surprise.

Sir Ian raised an eyebrow. "Did I say so?"

She saw a tiny smile at one corner of his mouth, and she suddenly understood. "You are clever, just as I said," she accused, but with a hint of admiration. "I see what it is you do."

"I don't," Grace said. "What does your half brother have to do with any of this?"

Lucia looked at the other woman. "Antonio," she explained, "is not yet married. He is also most handsome."

"Ah." Dylan began to laugh. "I can just see you, Ian, in the drawing rooms of all the matrons with marriageable daughters and sisters, sipping tea and hinting that Prince Antonio is looking about for an English bride. No doubt you'll be mentioning how much affection he has for his dear half sister, Lucia."

"I will say only what is true," Ian said with dignity. "I cannot help it if others allow their imaginations to fill in missing details."

"What other strategies do you have in mind for Miss Valenti's acceptance into society?" Dylan asked with lively curiosity.

"Something not so subtle, dear brother. I intend to pull out the heavy guns." Ian studied Lucia across the room for a moment. "Grace, I hear the Duchess of Tremore has finally arrived in town. I think Miss Valenti should meet her."

Chapter 8

I t was clear that Sir Ian intended to waste no
time in implementing his plans, for the following afternoon, the Duchess of Tremore came
to call.

He had referred to her as the "heavy guns,"
but in looks at least, the duchess did not fit that
description at all. Lucia had envisioned a stout,
middle-aged matron, but in reality, the duchess
was a young and slender woman, with a warm
smile and lovely violet-blue eyes behind gold-
rimmed spectacles. Lucia did not see how such a
mild-mannered woman was going to force society to accept her, but she had also come to appreciate that when it came to strategy, Sir Ian knew
what he was doing.

147

The duchess was obviously on terms of great intimacy and friendship with Grace, for when she entered the room, the two women embraced like sisters.

"Daphne, how are you feeling?" Grace asked her. "And how is the baby? The last time I saw Anthony, he told me your recovery has been difficult, but your letters to me make no mention of illness."

"Because there has been nothing to mention. I suffered a cold right after the birth—a bad cold, yes, but nothing more than that. You know how Anthony fusses about these things. He was even refusing to go to London and take his seat in the House until I was well enough to come with him, but I refused to let him do such a thing. Honestly, he was hovering over me every minute and making me so insane, I told him if he did not go to Town and leave me to recover in peace, I was going to shoot him."

"And how is little Rosalind?"

"Not so little now. She may have been a month early and only five pounds when she was born, but in the two months since then, she's become fat as a ball of butter." She glanced at Lucia. "But Grace, you must introduce me to your new friend."

"This is Miss Valenti," Grace said. "Lucia, may I present the Duchess of Tremore."

"Your Grace." Lucia gave a deep curtsy.

"When Sir Ian came to call on me this morning,"

the duchess said, "he told me all about your situation, Miss Valenti."

Lucia gave the duchess a rueful smile. "I fear I have become Sir Ian's greatest inconvenience."

"He did not say so. I believe he thinks it is the ladies of the ton who are being inconvenient." She sat down in the nearest chair and waited until Grace and Lucia had seated themselves as well before she spoke again.

"Grace, you and Ian have no call to be worried about this." She looked at Lucia. "Gaining the acceptance of the ladies for you, Miss Valenti, is going to be a very simple matter."

"I take it you have a plan, Daphne?" Grace asked.

"I do. Ian suspects that several prominent ladies will be calling on you this afternoon, because he has been spreading word of Miss Valenti's handsome half brother to everyone. I suggest the three of us spend a long, leisurely afternoon right here, visiting."

"I'll ring for tea," Grace said, pulling the bell. "I take it your carriage is out front?"

"Of course, where any lady who comes by can see the Tremore insignia." She turned to Lucia. "During the next few days, the three of us shall make calls together. Of course, we shall also take rides in my carriage, shop in Bond Street, all that sort of thing. It is important that you be seen, Miss Valenti."

"Will your aid and this business of Prince Antonio be enough?" Grace asked. "There's the issue of Lucia's mother, and you know how spiteful ladies can be about that sort of thing."

The duchess did not seem troubled. "While we are making calls and such, I shall drop a few hints about your half brother, Miss Valenti, just as Ian is doing. I shall also make casual mention of my upcoming parties." She settled back in her chair with a complacent expression. "Ian has asked me to give a country house party for you at Tremore Hall at the end of July when the season is over, but we must do something before then. I believe I shall have a water party. Tremore's new yacht, *The Cleopatra*, is docked at Chelsea, you know."

Lucia did not quite understand what sailing had to do with gaining her acceptance into society, but it was obvious Grace comprehended at once, for she began to laugh. "And your husband has been most exclusive in his choice of who is allowed to sail upon his yacht. Thus far, his few invitations have been for only his closest friends. His *male* friends, I might add. Even I have not been allowed on board as yet, though Dylan has gone out with him twice."

"Such a shame I have been in the country," the duchess said, "and such a frustration to the ladies. You see," she added, turning to Lucia, "my husband has informed me that the most absurd rumors are circulating about *The Cleopatra*. The ladies are dying to know if it really has naughty Roman frescoes in the master cabin and if I did indeed have a pink-marble bath installed. I think it is time to have a water party and satisfy their curiosity. Miss Valenti, I hope you do not get sea-sick?"

That night, Lucia ensconced herself in the library with a book, but she found it impossible to read. Her attention kept drifting away from the novel in her lap to the events of the afternoon and the man who had brought them about.

Sir Ian had spent a busy day, for while the Duchess of Tremore was at Portman Square, many other people had come to call as well. Lord Haye paid a visit, which was not unusual, for he called nearly every day, but on this visit he was accompanied by his two sisters. Lord Blair also came to call, and unfortunately, Lady Sarah came, too. Lord Montrose brought his mother and his sister.

It was fortunate that Lucia had a talent for acting, since she had spent most of her afternoon expressing murmurs of affection for her dear half brother, whom she had only spoken with twice in her life.

Yes, everything was going just as Sir Ian had anticipated. With that thought came an acute sense of loneliness, a feeling so sudden that it startled her. Those women were not interested in being her friends. They did not like her. They wanted her brother, the prince.

As for the men, it was nice to be admired, but admiration was not enough. And if any of them did profess love, how could she ever be sure that it was her and not her money they loved? As for her own feelings, she was no fonder of Haye, Montrose, Blair, Walford, or any other of the suitors who called upon her than she had been upon meeting them. They all seemed to lack the thing she craved most.

Englishmen are capable of the deepest passions, believe me.

Absurd, she thought in vexation, that she should have half a dozen admirers, yet only be able to think about a man who did not admire her much at all.

She returned her book to its place and began perusing the shelves for something interesting enough to change the direction of her thoughts and preoccupy her mind, but it was useless.

She stared at the rows of books in front of her, but in her mind's eye, it was Sir Ian she saw in front of her as he had looked in Lady Kettering's garden. So rigid he was, so controlled, and yet she sensed the passion there, seething beneath the surface. It was rather like the hot lava of a volcano.

"Looking for a book again?"

The sound of his voice was so unexpected, she jumped. *"Per Bacco!"* she cried, whirling around. "How you startled me."

"My apologies."

"Did you come in here to work?" she asked, noting the leather case in his hand as he crossed the room to the desk.

"Yes, although, I have already been working this entire day." He circled the desk and set his case on top, then removed his dark blue evening coat and slung it over the back of his chair. "I spent a very productive afternoon."

"Yes, I know. We have had a barrage of callers. The ladies are beginning to accept me, it seems."

He paused in the act of removing documents from his dispatch case. "You do not seem happy about it. What's wrong? I thought you wanted the ladies to like you."

She shrugged. "It is not me they like. They pretend because they want to meet Antonio and impress the duchess. I want to be liked for myself."

"Give it time, Miss Valenti. You will make genuine friends. Acceptance comes first."

She sighed and turned to lean back against the bookcase. "Patience has never been one of my talents."

That got a smile from him. "What did you think of the duchess?"

"She was very nice to me. I liked her. She is planning what you call a water party."

"Ah, yes, Tremore's new yacht. Excellent. I expect you shall be receiving many such invitations from now on."

"I think so, too. I was right about you all along, Sir Ian. We are all your chess pieces, and you move us all around."

"Odd, since I have been feeling that I am the one being manipulated." He paused a moment, but before she could ask what he meant by that, he spoke again. "Did Isabel really defeat you at chess last night?"

She turned away and resumed her search for a book. "You saw for yourself."

"Isabel, though a good player for her age, is no match for a player of your skill."

"I got distracted."

"Distracted, my eye," he muttered. "You let her win, didn't you?"

She looked at him. "If I did, what of it? She and I are now the best of friends."

"Is that why you did it? To gain her friendship?"

Lucia shrugged and returned her attention to the books. "Allowing her to win pleased her and cost me nothing."

"Did you let *me* win?"

She turned in amazement, prepared to emphatically deny it, only to find him watching her with a frown, hands on hips, eyes narrowed. She caught back her hasty denial and turned away, thinking things over.

He believed she might have lost to him on purpose, and he didn't like it. He didn't like it at all.

"Did you?" he asked again, more insistent this time. When she remained silent, he started across the room toward her, and she moved farther along the bookshelves toward the far end of the room.

"I want to know," he said, following her as she circled the billiard table. "The night we played chess, I thought you got distracted in the midst of the game, but was it just a show for my benefit?"

He sounded almost angry at the possibility she

had lost deliberately. Lucia decided this opportunity to needle him was just too good to pass up, for she might see that fire in his eyes again. She paused beside the billiard table. Staring down at the green felt surface, she let several more seconds pass before she spoke. "Why would I let you win on purpose?"

"To please me, charm me, get me on your side. To get your way."

"If that was my motive," she said, glancing up at him long enough to smile, "it worked, did it not? I am now allowed to choose my husband."

"With my approval," he reminded her. "I could change my mind about that."

"You will not change your mind. It would not be right, and you always do what is right. You told me so."

As if that were an end to the matter, she changed the subject. "I have always wanted to learn to play this game," she said, idly pushing billiard balls around with her fingers. She grabbed the red one off the table and turned to face him. "Will you teach me?"

The determination in his face made it clear he was unimpressed by her diversionary tactics. "Forget about billiards," he said, taking the ball out of her hand and putting it back on the table. "I want to know about the chess. Did you lose our game on purpose?"

"I only lose to people I want to like me."

That puzzled him. His brows drew together. "You don't want me to like you?"

"I have deemed you a lost cause. You will never like me."

His dark lashes lowered a fraction as he looked at her mouth. "Never, Miss Valenti, is a long time."

Something in his voice and the way he looked at her mouth made her insides begin to quiver with excitement, and when he looked up, there it was. That spark, flaring up as quick and breathtaking as a flash of lightning, making those gray eyes like silvery fire and smoke, his gaze so intense that she felt hot and shivery all at once.

How, she wondered in a daze, could she have ever thought his eyes were cold? Never again would she make that mistake. Never again would she deem that look to be a trick of light or a fancy of her imagination.

She remembered how he'd put his hands on her hips that day in Lady Kettering's garden to keep her from falling, of how he had jerked back, minding his manners, ever the gentleman. What would it take to bring this man's tightly leashed passions to the surface? It would be a dangerous game, that.

"Stop prevaricating," he ordered, interrupting her delicious speculations, "and answer my question."

"Why should I?" she countered. "No matter what I say, you will not believe it."

"Convince me. God knows," he added, his voice harsh, "you could convince a man of anything."

"Not you."

"Even me." He leaned closer, and his hand cupped her cheek. Wildly, she wondered if he was going to kiss her. If he did, she wouldn't kiss him back, she decided as she closed her eyes. He didn't deserve it. But when his thumb brushed back and forth across her mouth, she began changing her mind about that. Maybe she'd kiss him back. Her lips parted. Maybe.

"But," he went on, as his thumb caressed her mouth, "you would have no scruples about losing on purpose if you thought it would get you something." With startling suddenness, he let her go and stepped back. "I want a rematch."

She opened her eyes and fought to come to her senses. "What?"

"I want a rematch." He folded his arms across his chest, looking grim. "It's the only way I'm going to know."

Lucia felt a ridiculous sense of disappointment. He hadn't even tried to kiss her. *Accidenti!* It was an insult, that. The least he could have done was *try*. "No," she said, taking great satisfaction in refusing. "I am not giving you a rematch."

"Your unwillingness tells me I defeated you fairly, and you don't want to lose to me a second time."

"Have it your own way." Pretending indifference, she gave a huge yawn and patted her mouth with her fingers. "I am very tired, so if you don't mind, I am going to bed.

"After all," she added as she stepped around

him and walked away, "it's exhausting to have so many men clamoring for my attention all the time. Good night."

If she thought he would let her refusal to play chess with him again pass without consequences, she was mistaken. She got as far as the door before he spoke.

"A rematch, Miss Valenti. Or I shall take my revenge."

She stopped and turned. "What sort of revenge?"

"Ugly men." He smiled. "Old, ugly men."

"But we agreed that I shall be allowed to choose from among my suitors."

"With my approval. Awful for you if any suitor under sixty got crossed off the list." He tilted his head as if struck by a sudden thought. "Of course, we could keep Walford. He's only thirty-nine, but he's short."

"You are being impossible! What does a chess game matter compared to my future life?"

"Was that a yes or no answer?"

"Men! You are so childish about these things!"

"Calling me names won't help you."

She could never read him. He might be bluffing, he might be serious. Lucia took a deep breath. *Think,* she told herself. *Employ strategy. Feminine strategy.*

Glancing past him, she caught sight of the billiard table. With sudden inspiration, she envisioned what playing billiards with him would be like. She'd have to lean over the table, wouldn't she? He'd have to show her how to hold the stick, wouldn't he? The possibility of igniting that passion inside him was an irresistible challenge. Besides, he was being thoroughly unreasonable over a silly chess game.

"All right," she said, lifting her hands as if in capitulation. "You win. I will give you your rematch at chess. But—" She paused, and it was her turn to smile. "I have one condition."

"What condition?"

"You will teach me billiards first."

He stiffened, looking uncomfortable. "I do not think that would be wise," he said, and tugged at his cravat, setting it askew.

Lucia watched him and realized he was thinking the same thing she was, and it unnerved him. How delightful. There was hope for him yet. "Teach me billiards, Englishman," she said, "and I will give you your rematch at chess. Otherwise, no, and you may send all the ugly men you please. I have many suitors already who are not ugly." With her sweetest smile, she added, "I am sure one of them would be happy to teach me billiards."

Before he could reply, she vanished out the door.

The Cleopatra was a three-masted yacht with a crew of sixteen. Its master cabin had no naughty frescoes, much to the disappointment of the ladies, but they were gratified by the fact that there was indeed a pink marble bath. The yacht also possessed a dining room where a vast array of refreshments had been laid out for the fortunate few invited to the water party hosted by the Duke and Duchess of Tremore. At their leisure, guests could partake of cold duck and ham, exotic fruit from the duke's famous conservatory, chilled champagne, and tiny chocolates. They could also stroll along the wide promenade decks or mingle and talk. They could dance on the quarterdeck to the music of the string quartet.

Lucia participated in all of these delights and thoroughly enjoyed them, but at sunset, she wandered back to the stern of the ship on her own, leaning over the rail to watch the final rays of the sun disappear beyond the horizon as the ship glided eastward along the Thames, back toward London.

The duke and duchess were gracious hosts, the weather had been beautiful all day, and the party had been deemed a smashing success by all the guests, with the exception of Sir Ian, who could make no judgment about it. He did not attend. In fact, since she had issued her challenge to him three days before, Lucia had not even seen him. He was avoiding her, no doubt. Obviously, he did not find teaching her how to play billiards an appealing notion.

Lucia felt rather depressed.

"Miss Valenti, why are you back here all alone?"

She turned at the sound of Lord Haye's voice. "I am fond of sunsets."

"It is a beautiful one." He came to stand beside her. "A fine day all around, wonderful for a water party."

"Yes." The weather, she thought dully, was a fine topic.

"Why do you like sunsets?" he asked.

The unexpected question surprised her. "Because they are beautiful. Warm, vibrant, full of vivid color."

"I like them for the same reasons." He turned toward her. "That is why I like you."

She opened her mouth to make a glib reply, but when she looked at him, she found that he was gazing at her in sincere, genuine admiration. "Thank you, my lord," she said. "That is one of the loveliest compliments I have ever received."

She turned again toward the sunset, and so did he. Both of them fell silent as they watched the sun disappear and twilight descend over the water. In the fading light, she cast surreptitious sideways glances at his profile, studying him as he looked out over the water. Despite her initial impression of his chin, he was not an unattractive man. The same height as she, Haye had sandy hair, hazel eyes, and a nice face. In fact, everything about him was nice. *Nice*, she thought wistfully, *is a good thing. Isn't it?*

"We seem to be alone," Haye said, breaking into her thoughts.

She glanced around and found that there wasn't another person in sight. "Yes," she agreed. "We seem to be the only ones who like sunsets."

"Miss Valenti," he said in a brisk voice and turned toward her again, "I have been waiting for such a moment, and I must seize it. You must know that I admire you tremendously."

To Lucia's astonishment, he took up her hand. "My lord," she murmured, taking another look around. She tried to pull her hand away, but he held it fast.

"I know I should not be so bold," he went on, "but I cannot help it. Your vivacity and your charm have . . . have quite captivated me. You must know it."

Lucia looked up at him, tried to see if there was any passion in him. "Do you like billiards, my lord?"

He blinked. "I beg your pardon?"

"Do you like billiards?"

"Why, yes. Yes, I do."

"You would teach me to play, wouldn't you? Help me hold the stick?"

"Cue," he corrected. "Yes, of course."

She smiled and moved a little closer to him. "You would stand behind me and guide my hand to hit the ball?"

"Of course I would, if you like." The erotic aspects of such a situation obviously did not occur to him, for his face bore a hint of bewilderment that she was talking about billiards at such a moment but nothing more. She couldn't quite tell in the dim evening light, but she had the sinking feeling there was no spark of heat in his eyes.

"Miss Valenti, I realize that we have only

known each other three weeks, but your situation demands a hasty courtship and an even more hasty engagement. Sir Ian has already informed me of what happened in Bolgheri with Princess Elena, and I assure you that I regard the incident as nothing more than a minor indiscretion. I also want to say that in these three weeks, I have developed a deep, heartfelt regard for you. As to your dowry and income, all I can do is assure you it is not those which motivate my feelings. I have a substantial fortune and could secure your future and that of our children very well without your dowry."

He was proposing. Lucia shoved aside her surprise and forced herself to consider the matter objectively, trying to decide if she could learn to love this man. She was right about his chin, but he had attractive eyes. If she married him, he would treat her well. He might even be persuaded to let her see her mother from time to time. She had no doubt his admiration for her was genuine. It might grow into love.

This wasn't quite what she'd been hoping for, but perhaps it was time to think realistically, not romantically. She had to marry somebody. She had no illusions about her situation. August was three short weeks away. If she did not have a groom by then, Sir Ian would pick one. If she refused to wed, her father would drag her to the altar.

Nonetheless, there was one thing she needed to know before she could even consider the possibility of marrying Lord Haye. Lucia took a deep breath, put her free hand behind her back, and crossed her fingers. Then she kissed him.

That kiss, alas, told her everything she needed to know. So much for thinking realistically.

Chapter 9

It was just a chess game, Ian reminded himself for perhaps the hundredth time. Stupid to be bothered by the notion that Miss Valenti had deliberately lost in some calculated attempt to curry his favor. During the game, he'd thought her to be a skilled but overly reckless player. Now, he wondered if the entire time she'd been playing him.

What a galling notion, to think he'd been outmaneuvered. And by a tantalizing, temperamental tease of a woman.

Even more galling was the idea of some besotted suitor teaching her billiards, and how that image kept distracting him from his work. During the past three days, he had left Miss Valenti in the capable hands of Grace and the Duchess of Tremore and had filled his own schedule with international matters, including preparations for Prince Cesare's state visit, but he had only managed to keep half his attention on those tasks. He attended meetings at Whitehall and dined with Italian envoys and Prussian ambassadors, but throughout it all, his mind kept taunting him with images of Lord Haye or Lord Montrose showing Miss Valenti how to hold a billiard cue, touching her hand, leaning against her. He knew what they'd be thinking, feeling, wanting. Oh, yes, he knew damn well.

He had tried to keep his time occupied every waking hour with his duties, but tonight Ian found himself with a free evening. The Spanish minister, he was informed, had a cold. His dinner plans canceled, Ian returned to Portman Square quite early, but no one else was home. Dylan, Grace, and Miss Valenti had gone to Tremore's water party on the Thames.

Ian handed over his cloak and hat, then went upstairs to the library and tried to work. A diplomat always had stacks of correspondence to address, and over the next few hours he attempted to deal with it, but he made little progress. His gaze kept straying to the billiard table across the room.

The only reason she wanted him to teach her billiards was because he was refusing. And also because she was a tease who used that perfect body of hers to torment men just for the hell of it.

Ian forced his attention back to his work, but he had just managed to refocus his thoughts on the letter he was composing when he was interrupted, and by the very person he'd been trying the past few days to forget.

"Has anyone ever told you that you work too hard?"

He did not look up. "Good evening, Miss Valenti," he said as he continued to write. "Did you enjoy the duchess's water party?"

"Yes. I like the yachting."

"I am glad to hear it. Dylan and Grace return with you?"

"Yes, but only to bring me home." She came into the library and closed the door behind her. "They have gone on to another party."

"You did not wish to accompany them?"

"No. Lady Sarah was also invited, and I do not like her."

"Lady Sarah is invited to many parties. Even if you do not wish to marry Lord Blair, you will not be able to avoid his cousin all the time."

"I know." She paused, then said, "Lord Haye's sisters came with him to the water party today. You were right about him, Sir Ian. He is a good man, very nice."

Ian stopped writing at the mention of Haye, and his hand tightened around his quill. "Excellent," he said and tried to continue his letter, but he could not remember where he had left off. He paused to glance through the last paragraph. "And therefore, Sir Gervase," he murmured, and resumed writing.

Of course, she had to come sit on his desk again. It really was becoming a most distracting habit of hers. He found it impossible to work with the scent of apple blossoms wafting past. "Miss Valenti," he said without pausing in his task, "would you mind moving off my desk? I need to refer to the letter you are sitting on."

She did not do as he requested. Instead, she tilted onto one hip as if he was supposed to pull the document from underneath. Ian glanced up, expecting that she was being a tease again, but he was mistaken. She was staring past him into space, her thoughts clearly elsewhere. Ian reached for Sir Gervase's letter from Anatolia, and though he was careful not to touch her, the back of his hand brushed the fabric of her dress, and heat rushed through his body. He jerked the letter away as if he'd been burned.

The sound of rustling paper seemed to draw her attention back to him. "What are you writing?" she asked. "Or is it a secret?"

His work seemed a safe enough topic. "I am composing a letter to Sir Gervase Humphrey. He is the ambassador who was sent to Constantinople in my place so that I could come here, and he has written to tell me the Turks are being troublesome. Since I have worked with them before, he seeks my advice."

"And what advice do you give him?"

"I am telling him that bullying the Turks won't work. I have suggested that since he is a diplomat, he should try something else."

"What?"

"Diplomacy."

She laughed. "You do not like Sir Gervase, do you?"

"No." Ian signed his name and reached for blotting powder. "He is a fool."

She was silent as he folded and sealed his letter. It wasn't until he had set the letter aside and was reaching for another sheet of paper that she spoke again. "Do not be too hard on him. He is attempting to measure up to you, and that would be difficult for anyone."

"Nonsense."

"It is not nonsense. Your brother feels it, I think, for he is younger than you. You are the good son, he is the wild one. That is why you and he do not always get along."

Ian dipped his quill in the inkwell. "Dylan is a composer. He has an artistic temperament. He and I see life very differently." With that, he began to address a letter to the Prince of Sweden.

His reserve did not discourage her in the least. "It is true that the two of you are like the oil and the water," she agreed. "He is fun. You are stuffy. Have you always been this way?"

He took exception to that description. "I am not stuffy," he protested. "As for Dylan, he was always rebellious, he did what he pleased and, somehow, he always got away with it. I never had that luxury."

"Your father expected more of you, no doubt, since you were the older son. It is a burden, the expectations of others."

Unbidden, a memory from long ago sprang into his mind, and he stopped writing.

How could you disgrace the family with such a failure? Where is your pride? Where is your honor toward your family name? God, Ian, I despair of you. I truly do.

"It can be a burden," he admitted, his father's voice echoing in his ears. He set down his quill and leaned back in his chair. "I remember one year at Cambridge I failed my examinations," he found himself saying, "and my father was so disappointed in me and so incensed at my lack of attention to my studies that he did not speak to me or write to me for a year."

"A year? That is a cruel punishment."

"It took that long for me to take my examinations again."

Lucia leaned back on his desk, palms flattened on the desk, her weight on her arms. "What caused your lack of attention to your studies? Gambling? Drinking?"

"A very pretty bedmaker."

"I do not understand. What is a bedmaker?"

Ian shook his head, coming out of the past. "This is a most unsuitable topic for conversation. I should not have said anything about it." With that, he picked up his quill and resumed his work. Of course she could not let it go.

"You say pretty, so a bedmaker must be a girl. Was she your mistress?" When he did not answer, she leaned forward, scooting sideways on his desk until she was practically sitting on his letter to the Swedish prince. "You can tell me."

He shifted in his chair. "It would not be appropriate."

Lucia leaned forward, bringing her face closer to his. "I won't tell anyone," she promised in a teasing whisper, tilting her head and trying to look into his eyes. "It shall be our secret. Was she your mistress?"

"No. Bedmakers are maids for the lads at Cambridge. They make the beds."

"And unmake them, no?" She did not wait for confirmation of this, but immediately asked another question. "Were you in love with her?"

A pair of laughing hazel eyes and a radiant smile flashed through Ian's mind. "That is none of your business."

"Did you want to marry her?"

He drew a deep breath, thinking of Gretna Green and the impossible dreams of sixteen years ago. "I am a gentleman, Tess was a maid. It would not have done."

"That is not an answer to my question. Did you want to marry her?"

"My father never gave me the opportunity. He paid her off with a handsome sum, and she married someone else. She was quite happy to do so." With a hint of anger, he asked, "Does that satisfy your curiosity?"

"It is like me with my blacksmith," she said softly. "You loved this Tess very much, I think."

Damn her. She could worm secrets out of stone. "I must finish this letter," he said, "and you are now sitting on it. Please move."

She jumped off the desk and walked away, but if he thought the topic of his past was closed, he was mistaken. From the other side of the room, she spoke again. "Is that girl, Tess, the real reason you have never married?"

The quill slipped in his fingers, ink bled all over the word beneath the nib, ruining the letter. He would have to begin again. Completely frustrated, he tossed down his quill and stood up. "God, you ask the most improper questions! With all the time you spent in French finishing schools, did they never teach you manners?"

She looked at him, eyes wide with surprise at his outburst. After a moment, she spoke. "You are very impressive when you are angry. Did you know that?" Without waiting for an answer, she went on, "You should get angry more often. You would be less stuffy if you—" She broke off, waving one hand in the air as if searching for the right words. "How do you English say it? If you let off the steam."

"I do not need to let off steam, and I am not stuffy. I merely observe the manners of good society, which means I do not probe into people's private lives." He shot her a pointed glance across the room. "Unlike some people."

"Dry as a stick," she went on, assessing his character with blithe disregard for his protests or his censure. "You do not enjoy life enough."

"That is absurd."

"Is it?" She pulled a billiard cue off the rack on the wall and held it out in front of her as if studying its straightness. "You obey all the rules," she went on, "and you do all the right things." She stood the cue on the floor beside her and pressed the fist of her free hand to her heart. "You keep all your feelings knotted up here. It is not good, that. Do you never have fun?"

"Of course I do."

"I have not seen it. You work all the time. You never play." She lifted the cue in her hands again. "I have to use the stick to hit the ball, no?" Without waiting for an answer, she experimented with the cue in an awkward manner, trying to figure out the proper method of holding it.

Ian watched as she faced the table between them and leaned over. *Provocative minx,* he thought, his throat dry as he stared at the view.

She pushed the cue hard through her fingers to take a shot and managed to hit the white cue ball, but instead of gliding over the felt, the ball jumped the bumper and went flying off the table, barely missing Grace's favorite vase of French porcelain. It landed on the carpet with a thud.

"Keep that up," he said, "and you're going to break something."

She came around the table and picked up the ball. "Not if you teach me the correct way."

He shouldn't. But he was going to. Deep down, he'd known that all along. He began walking toward her, feeling as if he were headed for the edge of a cliff, yet he was unable to stop. "Do I get my rematch at chess?"

"Of course. I always keep to a bargain."

Ian came to her side at the billiard table and took the cue and ball from her. He demonstrated how to hold the cue in the correct manner, then gave it back to her and watched as she tried to duplicate what he had done. After a moment, it was clear that in this, at least, she was not acting. She had never held a billiard cue in her life.

"No," he said and stepped closer. Even as he reminded himself that it was highly inappropriate for him to be touching her, he put his hand on hers and moved her index finger over the top of the cue. "Hold it like that."

Her skin was like warm satin. "And make sure the cue stays centered on top of your thumb," he added, manipulating her hand with his. "Like so. And over your middle finger as well."

Ian forced himself to pull his hand back, and she tapped the ball with the cue. It hit the red, and both rolled about eighteen inches before coming to a stop. He leaned over the table to retrieve them so she could try again. As he did so, his thigh brushed her hip, a brief, agonizing contact that sent him closer to the edge of reason.

He fought for equilibrium. "Use a bit more

force," he advised as he set the pair of billiard balls in front of her again, "but not so much that you send the ball flying off the table."

Even as he said those words, he did not understand how he was able to utter them in such a relaxed tone of voice. The shape of her hip was like an indelible brand against his body, burning him, dissolving his wits.

He needed a drink.

"Take a few practice shots." He walked away to pour himself a glass of port from one of the decanters in Dylan's liquor cabinet, reminding himself he had known this would happen. When he returned to her side of the room, he kept to the opposite end of the table, but even that was its own special torture, for every time she leaned over, he was given a splendid view of what was out of his reach. Her smile at him every time she managed to make a proper shot was like a touch that reached for him across the table. In a desperate attempt at distraction, he began explaining the basic rules of the game to her.

"So English billiards is a game of points," she said, when he had finished. She gestured to the table. "If I sink the red ball into the hole without letting my white ball go in with it, I can score three points?"

He nodded, and she leaned over the table. He focused on her face, watching as her dark brows furrowed in concentration. She caught her lower lip between her teeth, took aim, and made her shot.

Her cue ball sent the red one straight toward his corner of the table at a rapid clip, but instead of falling into the pocket, it ricocheted back toward her side of the table. It slowed down and slid right between the bumpers in front of her, stopping at the very edge of the pocket without going in.

"*Ma, no!*" Lucia leaned over the table, tilted her head, and blew on the ball, sending it that last fraction of an inch into the pocket. It was so outrageous and so in keeping with her nature that Ian burst out laughing.

"At last!" she cried and straightened. "I have at last made you laugh!" she told him, laughing, too. "I began to think perhaps you did not know how."

He was rather taken aback by that. "Of course I know how to laugh."

"I have never heard it until this moment, so I did not know. You have a nice laugh. I like it. It is deep and rich, as a man's laugh should be."

"Well, thank you." He gave her a bow. "Does this mean you have changed your opinion of me? Or am I still stuffy?"

She did not answer at once. Instead, she set the cue on the table and walked over to where he stood. When he faced her, she studied him for a long moment as if giving his question the most serious consideration. Then, without a word, she did something wholly unexpected. She reached up with both hands and slid her fingers into his hair, mussing it.

Ian froze at the touch of her hands. Sensuality seemed to radiate from her fingertips straight into his bloodstream, filling his body with all the heat of an Italian summer.

He could not move, he could not breathe, he could only stare at her upturned face as she played with his hair. Her attention was on her task, but his was on the impossible, erotic fantasies flashing through his mind. Fantasies of pulling her down to the floor, of pulling out pins and tumbling her long black hair down around his face, of sliding his hands under her skirts and feeling her soft, hot skin against his palms.

"Not so stuffy now," she murmured, smiling at her handiwork, but she did not lower her hands. Instead, she continued to toy with his hair, the insides of her wrists brushing against his face, as he stood stock-still and rock-hard on the edge of a cliff.

There was no one here to see him fall off.

The door was closed. It was late. Dylan and Grace were out. The servants were in bed. There was no one to watch his honor crumble into dust. No one to know but her, and she would annihilate a saint's resolve and revel in his downfall.

Ian was not a saint. The thick heaviness of lust began to overtake him, threatening to make him forget that he was a gentleman. It was what he had always been; he did not know how to be any other way.

Yet, even as he grasped at the honor that had dictated his actions throughout his life, it was like grasping at thin air. For at this moment, he yearned to be someone else, someone wild and reckless—like her, like Dylan, like all the people who did what they pleased and took what they wanted, who enjoyed the pleasures of life and did not care about the consequences.

If only he could be like that. The dark, secret wish that had always been in his soul whispered to him now in time with the thud of his heartbeats. If only . . . if only . . .

He bent his head a fraction, inhaling the scent of her hair, feeling the silky texture of her wrists against his face. He stirred, moved even closer, so close that her breasts brushed his chest. The contact sent exquisite pleasure shimmering through his body, tempting him beyond what any man should have to bear, and he bent his head to touch her lips with his. Her mouth opened at once, soft and cherry sweet. Forbidden fruit was the sweetest kind, and hungry for more, he deepened the kiss. If only . . .

It was a hungry wish, and a futile one.

He grasped her wrists, pulled her hands down, and pushed her firmly away from him. "God," he ground out, furious with himself for wanting what he could not have, furious with her for evoking it, "you are the most relentless woman alive. Devil take you for a flirt and a tease!"

He turned his back and strode to the desk, where he yanked his evening coat off the back of his chair and put it on, trying not to look at her. If he did, if he caught one glimpse of that gorgeous mouth of hers, his honor and her virtue would both be gone.

His back to her, he straightened his cuffs, smoothed his coat sleeves, and combed his hair back into place with his fingers, striving for order amid the chaos of lust that stormed through his body. "Forgive me," he said when he felt enough in control to speak again, "but I must go. I am expected at my club."

Ian turned and strode past her out of the room. He left the house without waiting for his carriage to be called and walked down the sidewalk in the warm July night, drawing in deep breaths of air.

He walked to Brooks's, intending to drink a glass of port, eat a joint of beef, and read the *Times*. But even at his club, surrounded by all the trappings of the honorable British gentleman, he still longed for the forbidden fruit; he still hungered for the hot, sweet kisses of an Italian girl.

Chapter 10

❧❧❧

I f Ian hoped that his club would take his mind off Lucia Valenti, it did not take long for that hope to be dashed. He managed to eat his meal in peace, but he had barely settled himself in his favorite chair of Brooks's reading room with a copy of the *Times* and a glass of port before the onslaught began, and Miss Valenti became the bane of his existence yet again.

"Sir Ian?"

He looked up to find Lord Montrose beside his chair. "Montrose," he greeted without enthusiasm and stood up to give a polite bow. He then immediately sat back down.

"Mind if I join you?" Without waiting for an answer, the other man pulled another chair forward and sat down opposite him. Smoothing his ornate brocade waistcoat, he said, "It is so fortunate that I find you alone, for I have been meaning to talk with you, and this provides me with the perfect opportunity."

"I was just about to read the *Times*." He picked up the newspaper from the table beside him, but this clear desire to be alone was lost on Montrose.

"Sir Ian, when you first called upon me with the desire to introduce me to Miss Valenti, I was not particularly enthused to make her acquaintance, for though she is a prince's acknowledged daughter, her illegitimacy places her true social position well below my own. But that day at Lady Kettering's concert, I became so enamored with her that I have been unable to keep my mind on any other matter. I can think of nothing but her."

Ian had made an entire career out of saying all the right things, so he resisted the impulse to tell Montrose to bugger off.

"As you may know," the baron continued, "I have called upon Miss Valenti numerous times and have always found her manner toward me to be most amiable."

"Miss Valenti is a very amiable young lady," Ian said, striving to keep his expression impassive, even as he remembered just how amiable Lucia could be. Her luscious kiss was still quite vivid in his mind, despite all his efforts this evening to eradicate the memory.

"She is enchanting." Montrose's face lit up with

the unmistakable and ridiculous rapture of an infatuated man. "And such an original."

"She is unique."

The baron did not appear to notice the terseness of Ian's tone. "But she is so unpredictable in her moods that I find it impossible to gauge the true depth of her feelings for me." He leaned forward in his chair with sudden eagerness. "Have I any chance with her, do you think?"

None. She thinks you are a peacock.

The acidic words hovered on the tip of Ian's tongue, but he did not say them. Instead, he took a sip of port and made a safe, innocuous reply. "It is not my place to give an opinion. For an answer to that, you will have to ask the lady."

"I intend to. If she is willing to accept me, can I count upon you to present me to her father as your choice?"

"Absolutely," he said with fervor. "Now, if you will pardon me," he went on, and rose to his feet, "I must return to my reading. So important for a man in my position to remain *au courant*, you know."

"Of course, of course. Thank you, Sir Ian. I appreciate your support."

The two men bowed to one another, and Montrose wandered off, but Ian had barely opened his newspaper before he was once again interrupted.

"Sir Ian?"

Smothering an oath, he reminded himself that Lord Walford was not a man to be snubbed. The fellow was a viscount, after all. Ian closed his newspaper and stood up. "Good evening," he greeted with scrupulous politeness. "Out about town this evening, are you, Walford?"

"Yes, yes. Just come in for a drink."

"I came to read the paper." Ian sat back down, but like Montrose, Walford was oblivious to hints. He took the seat recently vacated by his rival and began to wax poetic about the charms of Miss Valenti and complain in bewilderment of her capricious Italian temperament.

As Walford rambled on, Ian remembered what Dylan had said about her suitors and how they had been accosting him in Brooks's. At the time, Ian had thought little of the matter, deeming it nothing more than his brother's wicked sense of humor at work, but now he understood that Dylan's words had been the plain, unvarnished truth. Ian wished he'd paid greater heed to what his brother had told him. If he had, he never would have come here tonight. He'd bloody well have gone to some obscure East End pub instead.

"Hard lines," Walford was saying. "Don't you think so?"

"Quite," Ian said, forcing his attention back to the man before him. He rested his elbows on the arms of his chair, intertwined his fingers, and pressed his forefingers to his lips in his best diplomatic manner, hoping he appeared the sincere and sympathetic listener, wondering how to get rid of Walford as quickly as possible. "Quite so."

"But every time I call to pay my respects,"

Walford went on, "her beauty and her lively demeanor leave me stunned. My heart leaps in my chest, and I stammer like a schoolboy."

Ian looked at Walford with pity. The viscount wasn't a bad sort. He was, in truth, a good, kindly man, no match for a temperamental Italian tornado. If Walford married her, he'd probably die of a heart attack on the wedding night.

"When I am with her," Walford went on, "I cannot think what to say to make conversation. I would welcome your advice."

Ian decided to save the poor fellow from an untimely death. With a straight face, he said, "Rose pollination."

"I beg your pardon?"

"Yes." He gave a decisive nod. "I believe your discussion with her about your hobby made quite a vivid impression. I should advise you to discuss the topic with her at every possible opportunity."

"Indeed?" Walford's face took on a beatific expression, as if he had just been handed heaven. "It is true that at Lady Kettering's, she seemed quite impressed by my efforts to breed a blue rose."

"Well, there you are." Ian stood up, smiling, hoping this conversation was at an end. He held out his hand.

"Thank you, Sir Ian." Walford grasped his hand and shook it with gratitude, never knowing how close he had come to dying young.

The viscount walked away, and Ian sat back down. He opened his paper and tried to interest himself in the news that the Grand National

Consolidated Trades Union was on the verge of collapsing.

"Sir Ian?"

Christ, have mercy.

He looked up. "Haye," he greeted and rose, feeling like a child's toy jack-in-the-box. Resigning himself to the inevitable, Ian did not even mention his newspaper. Instead, he folded it and set it aside, then gestured to the chair across from him. "Have a seat?"

"Thank you."

Ian opened conversation, hoping to postpone another tale of Miss Valenti's charm, beauty, and fickle heart for at least a few minutes. "I hear your uncle has returned from Paris."

"Yes. He has seen my youngest sister settled in finishing school there, and he arrived back in town this afternoon, but I have not yet had the opportunity to see him."

"Give him my best regards."

"When I call on him tomorrow, I shall." Haye paused, took a sip of his claret, and said, "I must also tell him that my hopes regarding Miss Valenti are coming to fruition."

Ian's throat was suddenly dry, and he reached for his glass. "Really?"

"Yes. With your approval, Miss Valenti shall soon become the Countess of Haye."

Not a chance, Ian thought, planting a congenial smile firmly in place. *She hates your chin.*

"You see," Haye continued, "I have asked for her hand in marriage, and she has accepted me."

Ian almost dropped his port. "What?"

The earl nodded in complete earnest. "Earlier this evening at Tremore's water party."

There had to be some sort of mistake. "Haye, I am all astonishment," he managed to say. "I saw Miss Valenti earlier this evening when she returned from that party, and she said nothing about this."

"I am not surprised. I am sure she wished to keep our engagement to herself until I had the opportunity to consult with you. Since you act as the representative of her father's interests in this matter, I realize I should have made my feelings and intentions known to you before I made them known to her, but sometimes one must seize the moment, as it were. Her beauty, the romance of sunset—"

"Yes, yes," Ian hastily cut him off. "I understand."

"Since it was you who first approached me, I think I can safely assume I shall have your endorsement. Though it may not be necessary, I shall obtain her father's formal consent when he arrives next month. Then we can discuss the arrangements of the wedding, the dowry, and such."

Ian still did not believe it. Lucia would not have flirted with him over a billiard table or put her hands in his hair or kissed him if she had agreed to marry Haye. Would she?

She might. At that grim acknowledgment, his anger flared. She could play hell with any man, and this ridiculous parade of her tormented suitors was living proof. Even he was not immune. Two hours ago, the sound of her laughter and the scent of her hair and the taste of her mouth had threatened to destroy any shred of good sense he possessed.

He closed his eyes for a moment, smothering his anger, reminding himself that particular emotion was hardly useful right now. It was imperative that he ascertain the real facts, but before he could begin to do so, another voice intruded on the conversation.

"She cannot have agreed to marry you! It is not possible."

Both men turned in their seats to find Lord Montrose standing nearby, glowering at Haye from behind a tall, wing chair.

"I saw Miss Valenti only two nights ago at an assembly," he continued, "and she danced with me three times." He held up his fingers in an emphatic flourish. "Three! That is proof, I think, that the lady has not yet made up her mind."

Haye spoke before Ian had the opportunity. "Despite your rudeness in eavesdropping, I shall respond. I assure you, Montrose, the lady has made her choice. She accepted my proposal of marriage only a few hours ago. I know you had an interest in Miss Valenti, but her affections lie elsewhere. With me."

"I do not believe it."

"Are you calling me a liar?"

"If the shoe fits." Montrose came around from behind the chair.

Haye rose and stepped forward. "By God, you go too far."

Ian jumped to his feet and moved to stand between the two men. "Gentlemen, please. We are in Brooks's. Let us remain civil."

He was ignored.

"Montrose," Haye said, his face white with anger at the insult he had just been given, "I have the proof of her affection for me in her consent to marry me."

The baron shook his head. "You must be mistaken."

"A man cannot mistake a woman's affection when she boldly gives him a kiss!"

"What?" Both Ian and Montrose said at once.

Haye gave the baron a triumphant smile. "You see? Only the deepest affection could induce a lady to be so forward."

"You bastard." Montrose moved to take a swing at Haye. Without thinking, Ian tried to stop him. He realized his mistake when Montrose's fist slammed into his cheek.

Lucia could not sleep. Instead, she lay in the dark, feeling bemused, baffled, and quite unappreciated.

Ian Moore was a statue after all, she decided, sat up, and punched her pillow with her fist. He was inhuman, just as she'd thought. She punched her pillow again. She'd practically thrown herself at him, and one short kiss was all she'd gotten for her trouble. Proper, stuffy, thick-witted Englishman.

Her frustration only somewhat relieved by her abuse of her pillow, Lucia lay back down. *The man is impossible,* she thought, aggrieved. *Does he have to be so damned honorable all the time?*

Ian's kiss had easily vanquished all memory of Lord Haye's insipid mouth. Those few brief moments of Ian's mouth on hers had made her ache with a strange, tingly warmth, a wonderful feeling that had enveloped her whole body from her head to her toes. Unlike Haye, Ian knew how to kiss.

Lucia closed her eyes and pressed her fingers to her lips, that warmth flooding through her again as she remembered that kiss and how it had made her feel. As if she were floating and melting and—

"Maria Santissima!" she moaned and sat up, realizing the awful truth.

She liked him.

Why she liked him was an inexplicable mystery. He *was* stuffy. No doubt about that. He was also haughty, autocratic, and far too concerned with the proprieties. Sometimes, like tonight, she found him so infuriating, she didn't know whether to hurl heavy objects at his head or wrap her arms around his neck and keep him there until he kissed her properly. But earlier in the evening when she'd made him laugh, her heart had felt a sweet, queer piercing sort of joy like nothing she'd ever experienced before. He had great cares, she knew, great responsibilities, but when he laughed, those tiny worry lines between his brows disappeared.

And what had she gotten for easing his cares? One little kiss, just enough to leave her wanting more. Then, if that wasn't bad enough, the ungrateful man had snubbed her. Called her a flirt and a tease.

Which she was, sort of. But really, she thought with justified outrage, it was hardly her fault he was the only man on earth who didn't appreciate flirtation and teasing.

Lucia sighed, admitting another truth as awful as the first.

He didn't like her.

A little knot formed in the pit of her stomach at that admission. Men usually liked her. Men *liked* being flirted with and teased and made to laugh, but not Ian. She might have made him laugh tonight, but that didn't mean anything. He didn't like her.

A wave of loneliness swept over her. She wished there was someone here she could talk to, but there was no one. Grace was a lovely, warm person, but Lucia did not know her well enough to confide in her, and anyway, she could hardly talk to Ian's sister-in-law about her confused feelings. Oh, how she wished Elena were here. Or, better yet, her mother.

Mamma.

That was who she needed. Lucia had always

been able to talk to her mother about anything, and somehow, no matter what the situation, Mamma always managed to help her settle things right in her mind. And besides, Mamma knew everything there was to know about men, especially Englishmen, since she had lived here so long. Mamma would be able to advise her.

Lucia shoved back the counterpane and got out of bed. There were several hours until dawn, plenty of time to pay her mother a visit, and Mamma wouldn't care if she arrived in the middle of the night.

She dressed in dark clothes, then slung a midnight blue cloak around her shoulders and pulled its hood up to cover her hair and shadow her face. She left her room and started down the stairs. Someone had left a lamp burning beside the front door for Ian when he came home, and that light enabled her to see her way as she turned on the landing, came down the last flight of stairs, and crossed the foyer toward the front door.

At that moment, the door opened.

Lucia froze and glanced around, but she was standing in the midst of the foyer, and there was no time to hide.

"Going somewhere?" Ian asked as he came into the house and closed the door behind him.

Of all the bad timing. Lucia pushed back the hood of her cloak and looked at him, readying herself for a battle royal over the obvious fact that she was sneaking out to visit her mother, but when she caught sight of his face, her own predicament was forgotten.

She stepped closer to him and gasped. *"Ma insomma!"* Without thinking, she reached up and touched her fingertips gingerly to the dark purple blotch beneath his eye. "Oh, Ian, someone has hit you."

"Thank you for pointing that out, but my memory of the past hour is perfectly clear." He caught her wrist and yanked her hand away from his face, but he did not let her go.

"What happened?" she asked.

"I made the mistake of stepping between Lord Haye's face and Lord Montrose's fist."

"What?"

"Yes. And it is all thanks to you."

"Me? What do you mean?"

His hand tightened its grip on her wrist. "You seem dressed to go out. Where were you headed? To tell your mother the good news?"

His question puzzled her, but the tone of his voice did not. She could hear the tightly leashed anger within it, anger she knew was directed at her. "What good news?"

"Your engagement to Lord Haye, of course."

"What?" Lucia was astounded. "What are you talking about?"

"Poor Haye." He released her. "I hope he's a damn fine shot because duels will clearly be a necessary part of his married life."

"Did Montrose knock something loose inside your brain when he hit you?" she asked, staring at him dubiously. "I am not marrying Lord Haye."

"No? Haye thinks you are."

She opened her mouth to dispute such an absurdity, but Ian gave her no chance. "Lord Montrose," he continued, "who was eavesdropping while Haye gave me the happy news of your engagement, took exception to the idea. He felt that because you danced with him three times at the last assembly, your attachment and regard were for him, not for Haye. An argument ensued, at which point, Haye trumped us all by pronouncing that because you gave him a very bold kiss at Tremore's yachting party, you must love him very much indeed."

Lucia groaned and put her face in her hands. "What a mess."

"Needless to say," he went on, his voice rising, "this was rather a surprise to me, since only about two hours earlier you were making every possible attempt to kiss me!"

"What?" Lucia lifted her head, determined to set things straight on that score at least. "I did not kiss you! You kissed me. As for Montrose, yes, I danced with him several times. He makes me laugh. I like men who make me laugh."

"If you had bothered to read any etiquette books during those years in finishing school, you would have known that dancing with the same man more than twice in one evening is cause for speculation that an engagement is in the offing."

"I have three weeks left in which to find a

husband, and I do not have time for the niceties of etiquette!" she answered with asperity. "I should be able to dance with those men I enjoy dancing with so that I may get to know them better. What people gossip about is not my concern."

"Nor do Montrose's feelings seem of much concern to you. Those dances gave him ample reason to hope for your affections."

She pressed her lips together, feeling a hint of regret. "If that is true," she said after a moment, "then I am sorry for it. I simply wanted to get to know him better because I liked him."

"You seem to like whichever man you happen to be with."

That stung, especially since she had started to have a very strong liking for him. At least until now. "Well, I am a woman," she reminded him. "Liking men is quite normal for those of my sex."

"It's clear the men like you as well. In fact, three of them are deeply infatuated with you at the moment. And those are the ones I know of. I shudder to think how many more tormented men there might be out there."

"Infatuation is not love!" she said, becoming exasperated. "I told you, I will only marry a man who loves me. Lord Montrose and Lord Haye are infatuated with me, perhaps, but they certainly do not love me."

"They damn well care enough about you to engage in brawling at a gentleman's club!" Ian roared. "And I'm the one who ended up with a black eye!"

"*Santo cielo!*" she cried, her own frustration rising in the face of his. As always, when her temper was roused, Lucia found English inadequate to express her feelings and lapsed into her own language. "Men fight over women all the time," she said in Italian. "The same way boys fight over toys."

"I think it is Lord Haye and Lord Montrose who are the toys here," he answered, also in Italian. "Your toys."

"That is not fair!"

"No? Haye thinks you are going to marry him."

"I never agreed to his proposal!"

He glared at her, hands on hips. "Then, for the love of God, what were you doing kissing him?"

"He asked me to marry him, and I know I have to marry somebody, so I thought I should at least consider his offer of marriage. But of course I couldn't agree to marry a man without knowing how he kisses."

"Of course not!"

"So I had to kiss him and find out if I could ever grow to love him. But no, after that kiss, I knew I could not marry him."

Ian was staring at her in disbelief. "You mean, you only kissed him as some sort of henwitted experiment?"

"Would you marry a woman without kissing her first?" She shook her head, looking at him with sadness. "If so, I fear there is no hope for you, Englishman."

Ian raked a hand through his hair. "I don't

suppose you could just go ahead and marry him anyway?" he asked, a hint of desperation entering his voice. "Then I could go handle some *easy* diplomatic problem. Like the Turks and the Greeks. I mean, you could teach the poor sod how to kiss, couldn't you?"

She was appalled. Just the thought of enduring Haye's wet, fishlike mouth until the end of her days made her a bit queasy. Her feelings must have shown on her face, for Ian gave a deep sigh. "Never mind," he muttered. "I knew it was too much to hope for."

"I deserve a man who knows how to kiss," she said stubbornly.

"So this is what I am to expect for the next three weeks? Do you intend to investigate the kissing skills of every bachelor in London?"

Those words made Lucia's frustration flare into outright anger. "I did not ask for any of this!" she cried. "I did not decree that I had to get married and that six weeks was plenty of time in which to find a husband! My father did."

"That is a fact that cannot be helped. And it is also a fact that you brought a great deal of that situation about by your own past conduct."

She was not appeased by his facts or the disapproval with which he uttered them. "We are talking about my life, my future, and I seem to be the only one who thinks it is important enough to warrant serious consideration!" With each word she spoke, Lucia became more frustrated and more angry at the entire impossible situation in which she had been placed. Her temper unraveled.

Lucia glanced around and caught sight of the flowers reposing in a vase on the foyer table beside the calling-card tray, a dozen red carnations that had come the day before from Lord Walford. She yanked the bouquet out of the vase and brandished it at Ian. "You present men to me as if they are hats in a milliner's shop," she said as she struck him in the shoulder with the dripping-wet bouquet, "so you cannot blame me for treating them as such and trying them on. Shall I take this one? No, he does not fit me. Perhaps that one? No, I do not like him. What about that one? No, his kiss I do not like."

As she spoke, she punctuated her words with more whacks to his head and shoulders. "My father gives the money," she went on furiously, "and you bring the men for me to buy. I do not want to buy a man as if he is a hat!"

Ian swatted at the bouquet with which she was attacking him as if it were a troublesome fly. "Damnation, woman, cease batting me with that idiotic thing. I have already been struck enough this evening, thanks to you."

She landed her best blow yet, bashing the flowers right over his head, wishing it capable of smashing his thick masculine skull. She drew back for another strike, "Right now, I wish I could really hurt you, Englishman."

"Hurt me?" He eyed the pathetic, broken stems in her hand with scorn. "If that is your intent,

Miss Valenti, then have the good sense to use something more effective than a bunch of carnations."

She ignored that. "My father does not care what I want. You do not care what I want. I am the only one who can look out for my own interests, and that is just what I intend to do!"

"Interests? You seemed very interested in Montrose a few days ago. Then you thought you might have wanted Haye. I think you may even have wanted me for a moment there, but obviously, I was just another kissing experiment!"

"What kiss?" she shot back, and hit him again. "Was that a kiss? It was so quick, I wasn't sure."

He yanked the bouquet out of her hands. "Unlike your lovesick suitors, I don't like being played like a Spanish guitar," he said, crushing carnations in his fingers, "and I don't like listening to these men moon over you like pathetic schoolboys. And I really don't like having fists put through my face!"

"That is not my fault!"

"Like hell it's not!" His eyes flashed fire and he threw the carnations aside. He stepped closer, closing the short distance between them, his Italian words flying fast and furious. "You play with men, and you have no idea what you play with. These are intelligent, ordinarily rational British gentlemen, and you've got them so worked up, they are making utter fools of themselves over you, while you don't care one whit for any of them."

Faced with a blaze of such hot, splendid fury, even Lucia was forced to retreat. She took a few steps back, then stopped and lifted her chin a notch. She swallowed hard and faced him down. "I deserve to find a man who truly loves me," she said, mustering her dignity and controlling her own anger in the face of his. "I see no reason to settle for less, and if you and my father expect me to do so, you can both go to hell. As I said, Haye does not love me. He wants me, perhaps, but he does not love me. Lord Montrose does not love me either."

"They gave everyone at Brooks's a fine imitation of it when they proceeded to beat each other to a bloody pulp! They were both thrown out into the street. They may even lose their memberships over this."

"When the man comes along who truly loves me," she continued as if he hadn't spoken, "I will know it in my heart."

"Well, tell your heart to damn well get on with it, so I can get on with my life!"

"What on earth is going on here?" Grace's shocked voice entered the conversation. Both Lucia and Ian turned toward the stairs at the opposite end of the foyer to find they had gathered a crowd of amazed spectators. Not only had their quarrel awakened Grace, but also Dylan, Isabel, and a handful of servants.

"Good heavens!" Grace gasped as she looked at Ian's face. "What happened to your eye?"

Before he could answer, Dylan spoke up,

sounding both astonished and thoroughly amused. "You got in a fight? You, my disciplined, dignified big brother? Ye gods, I can scarce believe it. The last time I saw you like this, I was thirteen and put poison oak in your drawers. You gave me a damn fine whacking for it, too, if I recall."

"I did not get in a fight," Ian said through clenched teeth, speaking in English this time. He glared at Lucia. "I tried to prevent one, and this is what I got for my trouble."

His brother started to ask more questions, but Ian held up his hand to stop him. Still looking at Lucia, he resumed speaking in Italian. "Tomorrow," he said, "you will face Lord Haye. You will tell him that this was all a mistake, and you will apologize *profusely* for any misunderstanding you caused by your behavior. You will make it clear to him that, as wonderful as he is, you cannot in good conscience marry him. Since you have so much charm, I leave it to you to come up with a reason that will not hurt the fellow too badly."

Ian turned and strode toward the front door. Opening it, he went on, still in Italian, "Everyone at Brooks's knows about the fight, the kiss, and Haye's proposal, by the way. So in addition to already being London's most determined flirt, you will soon be its most famous jilt. Congratulations."

With that, he walked out and slammed the door behind him.

Chapter 11

Ian slept at a hotel. Not that sleeping had a whole lot to do with it. He spent most of the early-morning hours staring at the ceiling of his suite, trying to cool his temper, an ice-cold, unopened bottle of the Clarendon's best champagne pressed to his bruised eye. By midmorning, he was doing exactly what the cause of his fury had told him he needed to do more often. He let off steam in the only manner acceptable for gentlemen. He went to Gentleman Jackson's.

Stripped to the waist, he stood in one of the gymnasium's pugilist-training rooms with a hard, grain-filled sack hanging in front of him. He thought of Montrose, his own throbbing head, and slammed his bare fist into the center of the

sack, imagining it was Montrose's *handsome* face.
There was such satisfaction in that move that he
did it again. And again. And again.

He thought of Haye. How could any man think
a kiss was acceptance of a marriage proposal?
Slam. Addlepated ass. And what was the man
doing alone with Lucia in the first place, getting
kissed by her? Slam. Slam. Slam.

And what about himself? Wanting what he
couldn't have. Wanting that luscious mouth on
his mouth, wanting that amazing, voluptuous
body under his, craving it so badly he ached and
couldn't sleep and couldn't work. Couldn't even
think straight, God, he was threatening to become as much a blithering idiot as Walford. What
a nauseating thought. Slam.

Damn him for the biggest fool alive if he ever
started stammering over a pretty girl as if he
were a boy in short pants. Double damn him for
thinking with his groin and not his head. Slam.
Slam. Slam.

He needed a petticoat cure, he decided. He
hadn't had a woman for so long, he couldn't remember. Eight months, ten. Something like that.
Slam.

No wonder he was going crazy. Tonight, he
decided, he'd go invade a seraglio, find some
feminine company to set his body right, and return his brains north where they belonged. In his
head. Slam. Slam. Slam.

For the next hour, Ian pummeled the training
sack with all the force of his frustration, won-

dering how many more Hayes and Montroses and Walfords were out there waiting to make his life hell.

Breathing hard, he drew back and wiped sweat from his forehead, scowling at the sack in front of him. Why were the Italians always so much trouble? Especially one particular Italian, one who had a smile like the sun and the body of a goddess. She also had the soul of a house cat. She wanted to be pampered and spoiled, petted and adored. Until she didn't.

Ian readied himself for another round, then hesitated for no reason at all. With a curse, he turned and walked away. He supposed he'd let off enough steam for one day.

There were times when being an accomplished actress came in very useful. Lady Hewitt's rout that evening proved to be one of those times.

"Miss Valenti, I understand you are engaged to Lord Haye. Let me offer my congratulations."

Lucia pasted on a smile for Lady Westburn, amazed by how many congratulatory sentiments one woman could get in only a few hours. "*Grazie*, Contessa, but nothing is decided until my father gives his permission," she replied, thinking if she had to say those words one more time, she was going home.

"Of course, of course, but surely Prince Cesare cannot object to Lord Haye. Like yourself, Haye is a Catholic."

Lucia ignored the other woman's belittling tone.

She merely shrugged her shoulders. "My father is sometimes difficult to understand. There is no predicting what he will say. We shall have to see."

After a few minutes of polite conversation in which the countess tried to gain more information and Lucia delicately avoided giving it, Lady Westburn moved on.

Lucia leaned closer to Grace. "I wish I could simply tell everyone there is no engagement," she murmured in exasperation.

"You cannot refute it to others until you have clarified the misunderstanding with Haye himself," Grace replied for perhaps the tenth time since they had arrived at the party.

"I know, I know." Lucia sighed, wishing Haye had been able to call on her that afternoon. Wanting to clear up this mess as quickly as possible, she had sent him a note first thing this morning, requesting he pay a call on her. Haye, however, had replied with regret that his day was fully occupied with matters he could not set aside. Given the earl's feelings for her, such a reply was rather odd, but Haye had assured her he would call upon her the following day, and she had been forced to resign herself to twenty-four hours of pretending for others that she and the earl were intent on marriage.

"Miss Valenti, congratulations on your engagement to Lord Haye."

Lucia smiled at Lady Kettering and gave her little speech yet again.

The marchioness smiled back at her. "When I

introduced you to Haye at my little amateur concert, I had the feeling you two would suit. It
seems I was right."

Lucia widened her smile and laughed a little,
but as soon as the marchioness walked away, she
set her strawberry ice aside, half-eaten, and gave
Grace a pleading look. "I have a terrible headache. Is there any way I could go home?"

"Of course we'll go home if you wish." Grace
set down her ice and glanced around. "Let's
see if we can find Dylan and have him send for
the carriage."

The two women made their way through the
throng of people crowding Lady Hewitt's drawing room, then moved into her music room, but
there was no sign of Dylan in either place. They
did, however, encounter the Duke and Duchess
of Tremore at the bottom of the stairs.

"Has either of you seen Dylan?" Grace asked
them. "Lucia has a headache and wants to go
home."

"We saw him a moment ago," Tremore answered. "He said he was going outside to get
some fresh air." The duke glanced at Lucia. "I
understand you and Lord Haye are to be married, Miss Valenti?"

Lucia gave a groan.

Daphne nudged her husband in the ribs, and
he gave her a surprised glance in return. "What?"
he asked, clearly ignorant of the circumstances.
"The news is all over town. White's was buzzing
about it earlier. Is it not true?"

"Well—" Daphne hesitated and glanced at Lucia. "May I tell him?"

Lucia, who had already explained the entire mess to the duchess in whispers an hour earlier, said to Tremore, "Haye thinks we are engaged, but we are not."

The duke raised an eyebrow. "I see," he said in the tone of one who clearly didn't.

"It's complicated," Lucia said, giving him an unhappy look. "I leave it to the duchess to explain, if you do not mind. My head is aching, and I just want to go home."

"That's why we were trying to find Dylan," Grace said. "To send for the carriage."

"We are waiting for our carriage as well," Daphne said. "We've been waiting quite some time, so it should be here at any moment. This party is such a crush, if you wait for Dylan to send for his carriage from the mews, you'll be here another half hour at least. We would be happy to escort you back to Portman Square, Lucia. That way, Grace and Dylan can go home at their leisure, and you can rest your head."

Lucia looked at the duchess with gratitude, and a short time later, she was back at Portman Square. Dylan's cook, Mrs. March, insisted on giving her a cup of foul-tasting herb tea that worked like magic. By the time Lucia crawled into bed, her headache was gone.

She drifted off, but her sleep was not peaceful. She dreamed that her father was insisting she marry Haye. Ian was there, too, agreeing with

Cesare, saying that just because the poor sod couldn't kiss was no reason for Lucia to refuse him. Then, she was in a church with Haye, the vows were spoken, and though she kept trying to scream, "No, no, it's all a mistake," no words would come out of her mouth. Then she and Haye were in a carriage, husband and wife, and the earl was kissing her with that fish mouth. It was so awful that Lucia woke herself up.

She sat bolt upright in bed, gasping with relief as she realized it was only a dream. She lay down again, but the dream was still so vivid in her mind that she could not fall back to sleep.

She knew that dream could become reality. She could be forced to marry Haye, or if not him, some other man whose kisses were equally unappetizing. She had only three weeks left to find a husband. What if August came, and she had not found him?

She had been introduced to many men since arriving in England, but only one intrigued her. Only one captivated her. Only one had the passion she craved.

Lucia thought of the night before, of how Ian had looked standing there in the foyer, blazing with fury. She had wondered what would happen if his control ever slipped and his passions were unleashed. Now she knew. And even though his anger had been directed at her, it had been an impressive sight. Ian Moore was quite a man.

Not that it mattered. She couldn't marry Ian even if she wanted to. Lucia rolled onto her side and wrapped her arms around her pillow. Three weeks seemed a woefully insufficient amount of time in which to find a husband. What was she going to do?

That horrible dream came back to her, and worry began to gnaw at her insides. Though she tried to go back to sleep, it was useless. Finally, after tossing and turning a few more minutes, she pushed back the counterpane and got out of bed. Thinking perhaps a book would take her mind off her troubles, she slipped a robe over her nightgown and went downstairs.

As she approached the open door of the library, she realized Ian must be home, for she heard his voice and that of another man. Her first thought was that Dylan and Grace had also come home from the party early, but when she got closer to the library, she realized that the person with Ian was not his brother.

"It is insupportable!" an irritated male voice was saying. "Insupportable."

Haye.

Lucia stopped several feet away from the door, frowning in puzzlement. What was Haye doing here?

Ian said her name and something else she didn't quite catch. Lucia took a step closer.

"Sir Ian, she was carrying on a love affair! And with a blacksmith!"

Lucia caught her breath. They were talking about Armand. She heard Ian speak again, and she strained to listen.

"A most alarming rumor indeed," he was saying, "but with no basis in fact. The girl is—"

"No basis in fact?" Haye's voice held cold contempt. "Madame Tornay, as matron of this academy for young ladies, is a woman of scrupulous honesty. If she were not, I would never have placed my sister in her care. She would not impart such a tale to my uncle unless it was the absolute truth."

"So you condemn Miss Valenti based on stories imparted by others."

"Madame Tornay was quite clear in her account of the episode. Miss Valenti carried on this liaison with a blacksmith named Armand Bouget for months. It was well-known among her friends there, and Madame Tornay got wind of it. Miss Valenti—Miss Pelissaro, as she was then, for this was prior to her father's acknowledgment and she was actually living under her mother's name, of all the unconventional things! I did not even know Francesca's surname was Pelissaro until my uncle informed me today. Anyway, to return to the point, Miss Valenti would creep out of her room in the dark of night for clandestine meetings with this Bouget fellow."

"Perhaps they merely talked."

"Sir Ian, really! We are men of the world, you and I. We both know such conduct cannot be innocent."

Ian started to speak again, but Haye interrupted. "When you and I first discussed the matter of Miss Valenti's situation, I was hesitant even to consent to an introduction, given her mother's profession. But against my better judgment, I agreed to meet her."

Lucia bristled at that, highly indignant.

"When I did meet her," Haye continued, "she captured my heart at once, and I chose to overlook the matter of her mother and her illegitimacy. I became willing to forgive her misfortunes of birth as matters outside her control."

Lucia's hands balled into fists. She took a step closer to the door, thinking to interrupt and tell Haye what he could do with his forgiveness. She'd tell him what he could do with his kissing skills, too, while she had the chance. But then Haye spoke again, and she halted, curiosity overcoming her outrage.

"But Armand Bouget is a different matter. I had thought that the forward manner in which Miss Valenti kissed me indicated her affection for me. But now I discover that her affection has also been given to at least one other man, and probably her virtue as well. It seems she takes after her mother more than I would have liked to believe."

"Haye," Ian began, but the earl cut him off.

"My uncle and I, being gentlemen of discretion, will keep this knowledge to ourselves, but it does impel me to withdraw from this engagement. Miss Valenti is soiled goods. I cannot marry soiled goods."

Lucia wrapped her arms tightly around herself and closed her eyes. Whatever reply Ian might have made, she did not hear it, for it was his past words that echoed through her mind.

It will be difficult enough for me to find you a suitable husband in the short time we are allowed . . . you brought a great deal of this situation about by your own past conduct . . . I have no desire to clean the Augean stables . . .

Until this moment, she had not taken his words all that seriously, but now she began to appreciate the fragility of a woman's reputation, how her own past might come back to haunt her. Lucia's outrage dissolved into dismay.

All this time, she had been concentrating on finding a husband to love her. She'd been so fixed on that emotion, it had never occurred to her that her past might prevent her from finding a man who respected her. It was not fair, but it might very well happen. She didn't care what Haye thought, but what would another man think of her?

What did Ian think?

That question deepened her dismay into dread. Did Ian think she was soiled goods? He must. With his exacting standards of propriety, how could he think otherwise?

Pain squeezed her chest at the notion that he might think ill of her, and she realized she cared what he thought. His good opinion was hard to earn, but she wanted it. To think she did not have it, that he regarded her with the same disparagement Haye did, hurt more than she would have believed possible.

Memories of her past flashed across her mind. Did she regret her past? She thought about Armand, about that Carnival night in Bolgheri, and about all the rebellious, defiant things she'd done. The nuns had always called her sinful and wicked, and perhaps it was true, for she couldn't find it in her heart to regret any of the things she'd done. She had loved Armand. She'd given Elena a night of freedom the other girl would never forget. She'd had some wild times—smoking, drinking, gambling, sneaking out—and she'd enjoyed them all. Truth be told, she'd enjoyed rubbing her father's face in it most of all. Ian wouldn't understand that, she supposed. He certainly wouldn't approve of it.

In all honesty, Lucia had no regrets about her past, but when she thought of Ian, of how she would never have his respect or his good opinion, her lack of regrets wasn't much comfort.

Chapter 12

❧

Throwing an earl through a window would probably ruin his diplomatic career. Ian took a deep breath and rose to his feet, thinking if he didn't get Haye out of his sight in very short order, he'd do it anyway and be forced to find himself a new profession.

"I quite understand why you would come to these conclusions," he said through clenched teeth as he ushered Haye to the door. "I will give Miss Valenti your letter breaking the engagement. I am sure she will feel as you do, that ending it is for the best."

"I hope so," Haye answered. "Despite her past conduct, I fear hurting her feelings, but it cannot be helped."

"I am sure she will survive the disappointment." The ironic inflection of his voice was lost on the earl, who nodded in agreement.

Ian walked with Haye as far as the corridor, but he could not stomach giving him the courtesy of showing him out, and he was relieved that Haye was too preoccupied to notice. The earl went down the stairs, and Ian waited until he had passed the landing and disappeared from view, then he turned around to return to the library. The moment he did so, he froze.

Lucia was standing by the library door.

She was dressed as if for bed, her hair tumbled down around her shoulders and her bare feet peeping out from beneath the hem of her lacy white nightgown and wrapper.

Ian looked at her face, and he knew she had heard at least part of his conversation with Haye. She pressed her lips together as if in pain, and his chest tightened, for he remembered what she had overheard.

The silence grew, compelling him to say something. "I thought you were at Lady Hewitt's rout with Dylan and Grace."

"I was," she answered. "I came home early because I was tired and had a headache. The Duke and Duchess of Tremore brought me home in their carriage. I went to bed, but I had a bad dream and could not fall back to sleep."

She paused and drew a deep breath. "I wanted a book. Something dull, to make me sleepy." She lifted a hand to the library door. "I didn't mean to eavesdrop, but you know how it is. One hears one's name and—" She paused again, lifted her chin, and shook back her long hair. "Hell," she said, and walked into the library.

He followed her. "Lucia," he began, but she cut him off.

"You were right about my past, Sir Ian. It has come back to haunt me." She tried to smile, but it seemed a brittle one. "Your job just became more difficult. If word of Armand gets out, it will become much harder to find me a husband."

"Haye has given his word to be discreet. He is an honorable man. A prig, but honorable. He will keep his word."

"Word might still leak out, and then Cesare will have to increase the dowry." She gave a cynical laugh that hurt him. "If he expects me to be engaged within the next three weeks, that is."

"You could ask your father for more time."

Her expression took on a hardness he had never seen before. Her eyes narrowed. "I would crawl to the devil," she said in a low voice filled with loathing, "before I would ever ask my father for anything."

"Would you like me to ask Prince Cesare on your behalf?"

She thought about that for a moment, then she said, "Do you think he would agree?"

"Under the circumstances, with the Carnival incident sure to leak out, and now, with the possibility that your indiscretion with Bouget might also become known—" He paused, but he could not lie to her. "No. It is my opinion he would not give you more time. As you said, he would raise the dowry high enough that some impoverished peer would surely step forward."

Ian watched as she walked over to the table where a decanter of Dylan's favorite brandy sat on a tray. She poured a hefty amount into a crystal snifter and downed the contents in one swallow.

Having indulged in alcoholic excess a time or two himself, Ian pointed out the truth nobody in pain ever wanted to face. "That isn't going to help matters," he said in a gentle voice, and walked to her side.

"I know." She poured herself another drink, then turned toward him, decanter in one hand, glass in the other. "I suppose I'm now going to get the lecture about how proper young ladies aren't supposed to get drunk. I don't think we're even allowed to drink spirits, are we?"

"I'm afraid not. A glass or two of wine is all young ladies are supposed to be allowed."

She took a gulp of brandy and gave him a defiant look. "Too bad."

Ian studied her without replying. There was something raw and painful behind the defiance in her face, something that hurt him, that made him want to go throttle Haye. He reached out to take the bottle from her instead.

She pulled her arm back, keeping the decanter out of his reach. "I'll get drunk if I want to," she said in irritation. "What are you now? My chaperone?"

"Actually, I was going to pour one for myself."

"Oh." She eyed him with skepticism. "You were?"

"Yes." After listening to Haye's idiocy for half an hour anyone would need a drink.

She handed over the decanter, and he poured a brandy for himself, then took both the decanter and his glass over to his desk. He sat down and leaned back in his chair.

She followed him, sitting in her favorite place on his desk. He must be getting used to it, because he didn't even care that she had plopped herself down on top of the letter he was composing to send to the Russian viceroy. The Russian viceroy was an even more pompous prig than Haye.

"My first impression of Haye was right," she said. "He *does* have a weak chin. It fits a spineless character."

"Hear, hear," he concurred, leaning forward and lifting his glass for a toast to those sentiments. "We'll find someone worthy of you."

She nodded and touched her glass to his, but she did not meet his gaze. She drank her brandy and refilled her glass. She didn't speak. The silence between them grew, lengthened into minutes, as she stared moodily into her glass, her countenance troubled.

She seemed disinclined to talk, an odd thing for her, and after a quarter hour had gone by without a word from her, he began to be concerned. "Are you all right?" he asked, breaking the silence.

"*Si*." She still didn't look at him. She kept her gaze lowered.

He swallowed the last of his brandy. "You're not pining after the fellow, are you, and putting on a show for my benefit?" Even as he asked the question, he knew the answer.

She shook her head. "No. I told you, I want a man who knows how to kiss, and Haye has a kiss most horrible." She shuddered and took another drink. "It was like kissing a fish."

Ian gave a shout of laughter. "Really?"

His laughter seemed to please her. She looked up, smiling. "Fishhh," she repeated decidedly, slurring the word, a clear indication she was feeling the effects of her brandy. She gestured to him with her glass in an accusing manner. "You tried to persuade me to marry him anyway and teach him how to kiss." She pressed her lips together and blew air between them to express her derision.

He grinned and poured himself another drink. "Forgive me. I don't know what I was thinking to suggest such a thing."

"Neither do I. You see, I kissed him because I knew that would decide my mind about marrying him, and it did. I knew in that instant he was not the right man for me. And tonight, he proved my sense . . . my impression . . . ah—" She broke off with a sound of exasperation. "My first feelings, thoughts—how do you say it?"

"Instincts?"

"*Si*. My instincts were right." She leaned closer

to Ian in a confiding way as if to impart a secret. "If he had been the right man for me, if he had loved me and respected me, I would have given him my heart and made him a good wife. I'd have been faithful, and given him sons, so many sons, he wouldn't have known what to do with them all. I'd have made him glad his whole life he married me."

Ian wanted to kill the earl for rejecting her. He wanted to thank him. He looked away, lifted his glass, and drank until it was empty. "Haye is an ass," he muttered, his voice raspy from the liquor. He reached for the decanter, only to find they had emptied it. He walked to the liquor cabinet and fetched another bottle. He opened it, brought it to the desk, and refilled his glass.

"Sir Ian?"

He looked at her again as he sat down. "Hmm?"

"You were right about me, you know," she said in a low voice. "You were right."

"In what respect?"

She gave him a tipsy smile that made him suck in his breath. "I am a flirt and a tease."

Ian glanced down at her pretty feet peeping from beneath the hem of her nightgown. He indulged in a long look upward, torturing himself with imaginings of what was underneath two thin layers of muslin fabric. He paused, his gaze riveted to where a few tiny pearl buttons had popped free of satiny loops to reveal the inner curves of her breasts. His throat went dry, and he opened his mouth to agree with her.

She reached out, pressing her fingers to his lips, making heat curl in his belly. "Don't be all polite and gentlemanlike right now and apologize and say you didn't mean it. You said I'm a flirt and a tease, and that I manipulate men to get my way, and you are absolutely right. I like having my way, and I use what I have. I have teased men, and kissed men, and made them want me."

"Poor devils," he muttered against her fingers in acute self-pity.

Lucia pulled her hand back, much to his relief. "But since I was a girl of seventeen, I have known the truth about myself. All I want, all I have ever wanted, is one man. Just one. To love me just as I am, without being ashamed of me or wanting to change me. Is there anything wrong with that?"

Before he could answer, she spoke again. "I have much feeling in me, you see." She looked past him, her dark eyes all dreamy—from female romanticism or alcoholic haze, he couldn't be sure. "I have much to give, saved up all my life. I have passion and laughter and love and—" She paused to take a drink. "And myself," she went on in a soft, confiding voice. "I know what Haye thinks, but he's wrong about me."

Ian had once regarded the earl as a decent fellow, a man of good character, but now he could not think of him with any opinion other than utter contempt. Soiled goods, he'd called her.

God, the idiot couldn't see something luscious right in front of his nose.

And she was luscious. Of course, she was also an exasperating, unpredictable femme fatale who was making some of England's most well-bred gentlemen brawl like ruffians, and Ian didn't know if he was going to live long enough to get her married off. "I told you, Haye is an ass."

She bent her head, and coffee-black curls tumbled over her face. "I've done a lot of wicked things, you know. I've gambled at Parisian gaming hells, and I've smoked tobacco and eaten hashish and gotten drunk." Without looking at him, she lifted her glass in a wobbly salute to her past escapades, then lowered it again and continued, "At the convent, I used to sneak into the kitchens and steal food—they gave us so little, and I was always hungry. They thought going without food would make me good." She gave a little hiccup. "It didn't."

Ian smiled at that. No surprise there.

"Sometimes," she went on, "I stole vinegar or olive oil the nuns made, and I would go into the village to sell it so I could buy tobacco to smoke. Whenever the nuns caught me stealing, they used a rod to beat me, and I shouted curses at them and spat at them."

Ian felt another spark of rage, and his hand tightened around his glass. "Perfectly understandable of you, to my mind," he murmured, thinking anyone who put a rod anywhere near Lucia's pretty backside ought to be horsewhipped in return.

"When Cesare banished me and sent me to

my cousins in Genoa," she went on, "I stole two gold plates, sold them to a pawnbroker, and boarded a ship for London. I wanted to see my mother. Cesare hadn't let me see her since the convent."

"I've wondered how you'd managed to get yourself to England."

"Yes, I've done a lot of bad things," she said with a nod, her head bent, her voice low and contemplative. "Once or twice, I've even let a man I really liked touch me, but no more."

Damn it all, he already knew she was a virgin. Did he have to listen to this?

"I've never done . . . I've never given a man *that*," she went on. "Not even Armand."

Ian felt himself coming apart. He wasn't her priest, and he jolly well didn't want to hear her confession. He set down his glass, stood up, and grabbed her chin. He lifted her face, intending to kiss her and shut her up.

"He wanted me to," she said before Ian could carry out his intent. "But I wouldn't. I've saved myself for one special man who loves me, and I'm going to be the best wife in the world for him."

Christ. Ian yanked his hand away and sat back down. He wanted to go pound his head into a wall. Instead, he took another drink.

"I used to sneak out and meet Armand at night because I loved him. He didn't love me though. If he had, he'd have told my father to go to the devil and he'd have taken off with me somewhere and married me. Five thousand sous and a merchant's

daughter were more tempting than I was. But—"
She shoved hair out of her face and looked at Ian.
Her big brown eyes began to glisten. "I'm not
soiled goods."

Those words ignited something inside him,
something he'd never felt before, something primal and savage, something he could not control.
Before he knew it, his glass was out of his hand
and flying across the room toward the fireplace
where Haye had been standing earlier in the evening. It hit the marble mantel and shattered into
bits.

He looked at Lucia and found her watching
him, her eyes wide with shock at what he'd done,
her fingers pressed to her mouth.

"You're not soiled goods, damn it all," he told
her, "and it wouldn't matter if you'd been with a
man or not." He stood up. "I think we've both
had enough brandy. It's time to go to bed."

He took her glass and set it on the table, then
seized her hands and hauled her off the desk.
The moment her feet touched the floor and he let
her go, she started sinking.

He wrapped an arm around her shoulders and
hooked the other behind her knees, lifting her.
She curled an arm around his neck, gave another
hiccup, and nestled into his shoulder. As he carried her out of the room, she nuzzled her face
against his throat, and a shudder of pleasure
rocked his body, pleasure so intense he almost
dropped her on her gorgeous, shapely bum. With
an oath he kept on, valiantly carrying her up two

flights of stairs, thinking with every step that if he didn't get her married off soon, he was going to go mad. Stark, raving mad.

He paused before her room, and it took him several seconds of maneuvering the handle before he could get the door open. When he succeeded, he used his shoulder to nudge the door wide. A maid had left a lamp burning, and Ian was able to see his way to the bed. Once there, he dropped Lucia onto the counterpane and started to turn away, but she grabbed for him, snagging one tail of his evening coat in her fist. "Sir Ian?"

He paused with a long-suffering sigh and turned toward her again, but he didn't look at her. Instead, he stared at the wall. A stronger man might have been able to risk a glance at the bed and the delicious dollop of heaven in a lacy white nightgown who was lying there holding on to his coat. Ian was not a strong enough man to chance it. "What?"

"I want to tell you something."

"Can't it wait?"

"No, no. I'll forget."

No doubt of that. She was so sloshed, she probably wouldn't remember any of this tomorrow. She tugged at him again, more insistent this time. Telling himself he didn't want her to tear his favorite evening coat, he sank to his knees beside the bed and reminded himself of stupid things like duty and honor. "What do you want to tell me?"

"I—" She shook her head, frowning with the effort of concentration. "Ooh, I feel dizzy."

"I'll just bet you do. Put one foot on the floor. It'll help."

She complied, her nightgown hiking up in the effort, and one long, shapely leg brushed against his belly. He stared at her bare thigh, feeling her skin burning him through the fabric of his clothes. He began to imagine what he'd be looking at if that nightdress had ridden up just a few inches higher.

Stark. Raving. Mad.

He forced himself to look back into her face. "What do you want to tell me?" he asked again, his voice harsh to his own ears.

"You'd better find me a husband who loves me."

Aye, he'd better. Soon. "I shall do my best."

"I know." She smiled, and he wondered why whenever she smiled at him, it felt like a kick in the stomach. "I think you're a wonderful chaperone."

He wanted to tear her nightgown off. "Thank you."

"You're welcome." Her eyes closed and her hand fell to her side. She was out cold.

He studied her in the lamplight, knowing he should leave, but he could not move. There was no reason to stay, but he could not stand up. *In a minute*, he promised himself. *I'll leave in a minute.*

He glanced at the bare leg against his chest. *Maybe two minutes.*

He leaned in, the movement pressing her thigh to the side of the mattress. Before he could stop himself, he reached out and touched her cheek, brushing back the tendrils of hair that had fallen over her face. He tucked them behind her ear. "Foolish, foolish Lucia," he chided in a voice too low to wake her. "You're going to feel like hell tomorrow."

He moved closer, and his lips brushed the skin of her earlobe. It was like kissing velvet. She smelled of apple blossoms and brandy and warm, sweet woman, and Ian knew that at some point in his life he must have done something truly heinous to deserve being saddled with her. Or he'd done something wonderful. He could never seem to decide which hand fate had dealt him.

Lucia Valenti was a menace to male sanity, a blight on heaven and earth. Even so, she could sin her whole life long, and when she got to the pearly gates, she'd have St. Peter on his knees begging her to come inside. She was manipulative and vulnerable and a pain in the arse, and she looked so damned beautiful that he wanted to move those few short inches closer and take another taste of her mouth—a long, long taste this time. He wanted to pull that nightgown the rest of the way apart, run his hands over the lush, exquisite curves she'd been flaunting in his face for weeks. He wanted to kiss her and caress her and take what could never be his. He wanted to sate the aching need that flared up every time she deigned to give him so much as a smile. He wanted those things more than he'd ever wanted anything in his life.

But there were rules about this sort of woman and this sort of situation, and Ian had always been a man who played by the rules.

He took a deep, long breath and stood up. "There's nothing wrong with wanting to be loved, Lucia," he murmured. "Not a damned thing."

He turned out the lamp and left the room, his body in agony. Sometimes, it was absolute hell to be a gentleman.

Chapter 13

❧

The only time Ian had ever stolen anything, he'd been five years old, and the consequences of eating the cook's entire plum pudding two days before Christmas had been a four-day bellyache and a month of imprisonment in the nursery. When he was twelve, he'd gotten caught kissing Mary Welton from down at the farm and had learned by his father's hand just how painful a riding crop could be. There was that trouble at Cambridge, of course, and Tess. It had taken him a year of intense study to make up for his failed examinations, and three years to get over his broken heart.

These, along with several similar events of his life, had taught Ian one important lesson.

Whenever he did something stupid, he paid for it.

This fact was brought home to him yet again the morning after getting drunk on brandy with Lucia. When he awoke, the shaft of sunlight that filtered between two closed draperies hit him right in the eyes and sent intense, shattering pain through his skull. He was paying now. In spades.

Ian groaned and rolled over with a curse worthy of a Portsmouth sailor. His head was aching fit to split, his stomach felt like lead, and he was sure that during the night someone had stuffed a wad of cotton wool into his mouth. Deciding a day in bed sounded like an excellent plan, Ian went back to sleep.

Sometime later, the clattering of tea things awakened him again. He cautiously opened one eye to find Harper standing by the bedside table pouring him a cup of tea. After stirring sugar into the tea, the servant set down the teacup and turned toward the window. Before Ian's dazed mind could appreciate his intent, Harper did the unthinkable. He opened the curtains.

"Hell's bells, shut those damn things!" Ian covered his face with a pillow, blocking out the light.

"Feeling a bit under the weather today, sir?"

He felt like death. His response was a grunt from beneath the pillow.

Harper seemed to understand that his answer was affirmative. "Miss Lucia said you might not be feeling quite the thing this morning, but she would like to see you as soon as you are able to come down. It's important, she said."

"Unless war has broken out between Bolgheri and England," he mumbled, "nothing could be that important."

He thought of the night before, of how much he'd had to drink. Lucia had consumed far more brandy than he, and if he felt this bad, she must be in dire condition. That thought cheered him somewhat.

She should feel bad, damn her. He remembered with vivid clarity the way she'd tormented him with that tipsy smile of hers and that half-opened nightgown, of how she'd sat there telling him about all the kissing she'd done in her life as if he was her goddamned priest. He thought of how she'd looked lying on that bed, all tousled and tempting, with that nightgown riding up her legs. He thought of how he'd done the honorable thing and walked away. It had nearly killed him. He hoped she felt wretched this morning. It would serve her right.

In fact, seeing Lucia in the misery of alcohol's aftereffects was such an appealing notion, Ian deemed it worth getting out of bed. He took a deep breath, tossed aside the pillow, and pushed back the bedclothes. Slowly, carefully, he got up.

With Harper's help, he managed to shave and dress. When he went downstairs, he found Lucia alone in the dining room having breakfast. As he came in, she glanced up, radiant and smiling in her butter-yellow dress, looking far too cheery for someone who by all rights should be suffering as much as he.

He sat down on the other side of the table from her. "Where is everyone this morning?"

"Isabel is upstairs with her governess doing her lessons. Grace is in the drawing room with the Duchess of Tremore, and Dylan just left for Covent Garden to supervise auditions for his new opera."

Ian nodded. Forgetting a lifetime of meticulous good manners, he plunked an elbow on the table and rubbed his tired eyes. When he lifted his head, he found her watching him.

Her smile was gone, and she was studying him with a grave expression. "You should have something to eat," she urged, pushing a plate in his direction and gesturing for a footman. "You'll feel better."

He caught a whiff of buttered toast and leaned back in his chair at once. The mere thought of eating anything ever again revolted him. "What did you need to see me about?" he asked tersely.

Before she could answer, the footman placed a plate in front of him. Ian closed his eyes and swallowed hard. "Jarvis," he said in a very quiet voice, "if you don't get that plate of bloody kidneys out of my sight this instant, I will kill you."

Jarvis hastily removed the plate.

"Amazing." Lucia shook her head and shoved a forkful of eggs into her mouth. "You drank less than I did, and I feel wonderful."

That obvious fact did not improve his temper.

In fact, it made him feel downright hostile. He scowled at her.

Not the least bit intimidated, she looked at him, pressing her lips together as if trying not to smile. After a moment, she said, "Dylan told me you never could drink very much without feeling awful the next day. He was right, I think."

"You told Dylan about last night?"

"No. He noticed the empty decanters in the library this morning and came to the conclusion that you'd gone on a drinking binge. He seemed quite concerned about it. He said it's not at all like you."

"It's not." Ian closed his eyes. "I'm going mad. That's what it is. I must be going mad."

Lucia appeared not to hear this pronouncement about his sanity. "Your brother asked me if there was anything wrong with you, but I assured him that nothing was amiss. We all do unpredictable things from time to time."

"I don't." He opened his eyes. "I never do unpredictable things. Never."

Lucia didn't point out that two empty brandy bottles proved him wrong. Instead, she gestured to a tall glass beside his place at the table. "Your brother left a remedy for you. It works wonders, he said. He invented it himself."

"Dylan would be the one to invent such a thing." He eyed the brownish red liquid with doubt. "What's in it?"

"Tomato juice," she said, munching on a slice of toast. "Lemon juice, spices, a tincture of willow bark, and some sort of Russian liquor—vodka, I think he said."

Ian's stomach wrenched painfully. "It sounds vile."

"There's some other ingredient I'm forgetting." She paused, frowning as she tried to remember what it was. "Ah!" she cried and gave him a look of triumph. "Clam juice."

Ian jerked to his feet. "I'm going back to bed."

He returned to his room, still shuddering at the thought of clam juice. He closed the curtains and stripped off his clothes, then crawled between cool cotton sheets, vowing that he was never, ever going to do anything stupid again. It just wasn't worth the pain.

"I think it's an angel."

Lucia studied the cloud Isabel was pointing to, then she shook her head. Blades of grass tickled the sides of her neck. "No, it's an elephant."

"No, it's an angel. She has wings. See them?" Isabel gestured with her finger in a sweeping motion. "There and there. And she even has a halo."

"I still don't see it." Lucia yawned, starting to feel sleepy in the afternoon sun. "I see an elephant."

"You are hopeless at cloud shaping," the child told her, and got up. "I'm going to go see what Mrs. March put in our picnic basket. Coming?"

Lucia shook her head. "In a little while."

Isabel walked away, and Lucia closed her eyes. She inhaled the scent of grass and savored the feel of the sun on her face. Despite all the brandy last night, she felt wonderful.

Ian didn't. Poor man. She'd wanted to tell him this morning that today was her birthday, hoping to wheedle out of him a visit with her mamma, but she'd taken one look at his face and changed her mind. She smiled, thinking of how he'd looked, so disreputable with his black eye, so wretchedly miserable in his condition, and so adorable when he'd glowered at her, that she'd just wanted to kiss him and make him feel better. If servants hadn't been in the room, she might have done it.

She thought of that kiss he'd given her two nights ago, and just the memory of it started her whole body tingling. If that was what he could do to her with one short kiss, what would a longer kiss from him be like?

Lucia wanted to find out. The idea of just wrapping her arms around his neck, planting her mouth on his mouth, and sending all his English proprieties to the wall was so tempting. He'd probably get angry. He'd call her a flirt and a tease again, and accuse her of toying with him. That man had anger hot enough to scorch a woman, but she'd wager his kiss was worth it.

Lucia snuggled deeper into the grass, thinking of the night before, of the feel of his arms around her as he'd carried her up the stairs. It couldn't have been easy, for she was not a small woman. Two flights of stairs, and it hadn't even winded him.

She remembered how he'd hurled that glass across the room and told her he didn't share Haye's opinion of her. Those words and the fierceness with which he'd said them had pierced her heart like a ray of sunlight, making her glow from the inside out. A woman could fall in love with a man who made her feel like that.

"Lucia?" Grace's voice called to her from across the lawn.

She rolled over in the grass onto her stomach and rested her weight on her forearms. She looked at Grace, who was seated with Daphne on a bench about twenty yards away. Isabel was with them, rummaging through the picnic basket. "Yes?"

"Are you certain you do not wish to go somewhere?" Grace asked her. "We should do something special today. After all, it is your birthday."

Lucia smiled and shook her head, refusing again the offer of the two women to take her somewhere. "No, I am content to stay here."

Daphne, who was holding her new baby daughter in her arms, looked up from the child and pushed her spectacles higher on the bridge of her nose. "What about taking our picnic to Hyde Park?" she asked Lucia. "That would be more amusing for you than the park here at Portman Square, surely?"

"Oh, yes!" Isabel cried. She came running over and dropped to her knees beside Lucia in the grass. "Let's go to Hyde Park. There's a good breeze. We could fly kites. Or we could rent a boat and go punting on the Serpentine."

Still smiling, Lucia rolled onto her back again and stared up at the sky. "Not yet."

"We could at least walk down to the confectioner's on the next corner and get comfits for your birthday, couldn't we? Chocolates. Or toffee. Or peppermint sticks."

Lucia was unmoved by these delights. "No, I shall stay here. I am waiting."

"Waiting for what?"

"My birthday present."

"Who is sending you a present? Lord Haye?"

"Not Lord Haye. It is my mamma who will send it." Lucia smiled with anticipation. "Mamma always sends me something wonderful for my birthday, and I am not leaving until it arrives."

Isabel heaved a sigh, gave up the fight, and fell into the grass beside her. "Your mother is a courtesan, isn't she?" Without waiting for an answer, she went on, "My mama was a courtesan, too. She died."

Lucia turned her face toward the child's. "I know," she said. "I am sorry. It would be the hardest thing to bear, to lose my mamma."

"I barely remember her now, so I don't mind so much. When I first came here, I didn't like Grace, but it was because of Papa. I wanted it to be just us two, and I was jealous of her. But then, I got to thinking about how Grace would be a nice mother to have, and she is. She is very strict, but I don't mind."

"My mamma is not strict at all."

The child frowned thoughtfully. "Is your mother a good courtesan?"

"Ma insomma!" she gasped, half-laughing, so astonished by the question, she didn't know what to say. "I don't know," she finally answered. "Why do you ask me that?"

"Because if she is a good courtesan, you will get a very expensive present."

Lucia couldn't help grinning at that. "True."

"I hope your present comes soon. Then can we go to the confectioner's?"

"Si. We shall get chocolates and go to Hyde Park and fly kites."

"Good-oh!" Isabel endorsed this plan with wholehearted delight, but the plan never became reality. By nightfall, Lucia had still not received a birthday present from her mother.

That evening, Ian felt much better. He'd slept most of the day, waking in the middle of the afternoon only long enough to gulp down a glass of Dylan's awful concoction. Around five o'clock, he'd woken much more refreshed. He had bathed, shaved again, and dressed in evening clothes. Then he had gone to his club, where he'd engaged three men of his acquaintance for a few rounds of whist, men who thankfully did not know Lucia. By these efforts, he was able to avoid any woeful bachelors who might feel the need to confide in him. After all, interrupting a man's whist game was the height of bad taste.

He returned to Portman Square about ten o'clock. Grace and Dylan were out, but Lucia was home. She was in the library, stretched out in the chaise longue, reading a book.

"Good evening," he greeted her as he came in. "Not gone out this evening?"

"No."

He walked around his desk and opened his dispatch case. "Wasn't there a dinner party at Lady Fitzhugh's?"

She turned a page. "Yes."

He began pulling out documents, but he continued to study her across the room. Gone was the radiant woman he'd seen at the breakfast table, and in her place was someone whose nose was suspiciously pink and whose cheeks were puffy. Ian's gaze moved to the wadded-up handkerchief beside her on the chaise longue. "What's happened?" he asked, returning his gaze to her face. "What's wrong?"

"Nothing," she said in that small voice women were wont to use when something was very wrong indeed.

"You've been crying," he accused.

She looked at him, eyes wide. "I think I have a cold." She bit her lip, then lowered her chin.

"Don't you know by now I can always tell when you're lying? Something is wrong, and I want to know what it is."

A small cough interrupted them before she could answer, and Ian looked up to find Osgoode standing in the doorway with a small, paper-wrapped package in his hands. Before the servant could say a word, Lucia gave a cry, tossed aside her book, and jumped to her feet. She ran to Osgoode, and by the time she reached the butler, she was laughing.

Ian blinked at this startling transformation. How did a woman go from melancholia to ecstasy in the space of a few seconds? he wondered, baffled.

"At last!" she cried. "It has come at last! *Grazie*, Osgoode, *grazie!*"

She took the parcel and placed a smacking kiss on its brown-paper surface. This purely Italian show of sentiment no doubt shocked poor Osgoode, but ever the impassive servant, the butler did not show it. He departed with a bow.

"What is it?" Ian came around the desk and leaned back against it, watching as she untied the strings wrapped around what was clearly a jeweler's box. "A gift from an admirer?" he guessed, knowing it had better not be anything of the kind. "If so, it must be returned. You cannot keep anything more significant than flowers. Otherwise, you'll have another poor fool thinking you're engaged to him."

"This is not from a man!" She shook her head as she tore off paper with all the impatient joy of a child. "It is from Mamma. For my birthday. She did not forget me!"

"Is today your birthday?" he asked in surprise.

She nodded. "I waited all the day, but nothing

came, and I began to think she had forgotten. But no." Lucia succeeded in getting the paper off at last. Triumphant and laughing, she opened the box. "Oh, Mamma!" she cried in amazement.

She lifted her hand, and Ian saw that twined in her fingers was a delicate bracelet of rubies set in platinum. It glittered like a ring of red fire in the lamplight.

"Very lovely." He looked into her face, expecting to see smiles of delight.

She was crying again.

He stared at her. A tear rolled down her cheek, and he felt the world sliding sideways. The only conclusion he could make about this was that her seesawing emotions were sending him over the edge at last. "What's wrong now?"

When she didn't answer, he straightened away from the desk and moved to stand in front of her. "Lucia, what the devil is the matter?"

"It is rubies," she said, as if that explained everything.

He folded his arms and tried, with sensible male logic, to determine the problem and effect a solution. "You don't like rubies?"

She shook her head as another tear spilled over and ran down her face. "I love rubies."

Desperate, Ian tried again. "You don't like bracelets?"

With a sniff, she wiped the back of her free hand over her cheek. "I love bracelets."

He pulled out his handkerchief and handed it to her, resigning himself to a game of Twenty

Questions. "Prefer gold over platinum, do you?"

Lucia gave a sob, and he couldn't take it anymore. "What is the damned problem?" he shouted.

She looked up into his face. "I miss my mother."

Ian drew in a sharp breath and realized he'd just been outmaneuvered. Sucker punched. Checkmated by a woman's tears, the one move no man could ever defend against.

Hell.

He grabbed her by the elbow. "Come on."

"Where are we going?" she asked, clutching her bracelet with one hand and blowing her nose into his handkerchief with the other as he propelled her toward the door.

"Don't say a word, Lucia," he ordered. "Quit while you're ahead."

He ordered Jarvis to go out and hail a hansom cab, giving the footman very specific instructions that when the cab arrived, the top was to be up, the windows and curtains closed, and no lamps lit in the interior of the coach. The last thing Lucia's reputation needed right now was for someone to catch sight of them. As they waited in the foyer for Jarvis to return with the hansom, Ian's sensible side tried to reassert itself, reminding him that his orders had been very specific, that violating those orders was stupid, and that whenever he did something stupid, he paid for it.

When the hansom arrived, he ushered Lucia into the vehicle, gave their destination to the driver, and stepped up into the carriage. Then he sat down and looked at the woman across from him.

The curtains behind him had not been completely closed, and the moonlight through the window was a slash across her astonished, tear-stained face. "You are taking me to see Mamma?"

His sensible side told him he was going to regret this. "Happy birthday."

Through her tears, she smiled at him as if he was king of the earth.

Ian told his sensible side to shut up.

Chapter 14

⁓◡⁓

"*M*ia bambina cara!*" Francesca crossed the drawing room, arms opened wide to enfold her daughter. "What are you doing here?"

"Oh, Mamma," she cried in Italian. "I have missed you terribly!" Those words were all Lucia could manage before her throat clogged up. Unable to say anything more, she hugged her mother tight, so happy to see her, she felt as if her heart would burst.

Francesca patted her back in affectionate, soothing motions. "I have missed you, too, daughter. So very much. But what's this?" She pulled back, lifted Lucia's face, and smiled. "Some things do not change. You are a woman now, not a little girl, yet you cry every time I see you. We say hullo, we say good-bye—it does not seem to matter. You cry both ways." She pressed her lips to Lucia's cheeks, kissing tears away. "Did you get your present?"

In answer, Lucia pulled back the edge of her cloak and lifted her wrist. "It is beautiful. But rubies, Mamma?" She began to laugh through her tears. "That is so wicked of you."

"You are a child of the House of Bolgheri, and you should have jewels of the House of Bolgheri. The fact that I was never married to your father should have nothing to do with it."

"Cesare has never allowed me to have rubies. You know that. He would be furious if he knew you had given me such a present."

Francesca made a careless gesture with her hand. "I care nothing for Cesare's fury. I never did. He rages, he shouts, he stomps his feet. He is like a bull, your father, so unreasonable. So stubborn. But what can he do to me? Nothing."

"So, if he is a bull, the rubies are the red cape you wave in his face?" Lucia asked, smiling.

"Not in his face, no. Only behind his back. Be sure you never wear the bracelet around him, Lucia, for he will take it away." Francesca glanced past her. "But who is this who has come with you?"

"Oh!" Lucia realized her mother had never met Ian, and she performed introductions in English. "Mamma, this is Sir Ian Moore. Sir Ian, my mother, Francesca Pelissaro."

"Excellency." If she was surprised by Ian's

presence in direct defiance of Cesare's orders, she gave no sign of it. She curtsied. "Thank you for bringing my daughter to visit me. I am most grateful."

"Not at all." Ian took off his hat and bowed, then turned toward the fireplace, causing Lucia to realize there was another person in the room. "Chesterfield," he said with a nod to the other man.

"Sir Ian." Lord Chesterfield bowed, then he crossed the room to greet Lucia, a smile on his round, rubicund face. "My dear child. It is good to see you."

She returned his smile with sincere affection. The baron had been quite kind to her during her stay at Cavendish Square, and he was very generous to Mamma. In fact, he had the good sense to be in love with her. "It is wonderful to see you, my lord. I hope I do not disarrange your evening by interrupting?"

He patted her arm. "Of course not. I shall leave you to a nice, long visit and adjourn to the study." He turned to the man by the door. "Join me, Sir Ian?"

"My pleasure." Ian glanced at Lucia. "We cannot stay long."

She nodded, and the two men left the room, closing the door behind them.

Francesca led her to the settee. "I heard that you might be engaged to Lord Haye?"

"Ugh!" Lucia flung off her cloak and tossed it onto a nearby chair, then she kicked off her slippers and curled up on one end of the settee. "No, I am not engaged to Haye. It was all a misunderstanding."

She explained the circumstances.

"Soiled goods?" her mother cried when she had finished. "My daughter? That is an outrage! I should like to walk up to Lord Haye and slap him for such an insult. I might do it!"

"No, no, there is no need for that. I do not love him, so it does not matter."

"Still—" Francesca broke off and made a sound of contempt that sounded rather like a cat sneezing. "If that is how he thinks, it is no surprise he kisses like a fish."

"It does explain it," Lucia agreed. "I feel as if I have had a most fortunate escape. Still, Cesare comes in less than three weeks. What am I to do?"

"Since Haye is not a possibility, what of the other gentlemen I have been hearing about? This Lord Montrose, for instance, who gave Sir Ian the black eye. What of him?"

She shook her head decisively. "No. Not Montrose."

"Perhaps you should kiss him," Francesca teased, "before you make up your mind."

"Mamma!" she said in exasperation. "You are not helping!"

"You are right. I am sorry." Chastened, Francesca tried to be serious. "What of Walford?"

Lucia stared at her, horrified.

"Good," Francesca said, noting her expression

with a nod. "I'm glad your heart does not lean in his direction, for he is rather a fool. You would never be happy with Lord Walford."

"I quite agree with you, Mamma. I don't even have enough interest in Walford to *want* to kiss him."

Francesca nodded in understanding. "A man's kiss is very important. You will always be able to tell by a man's kiss how you feel about him."

"Do you think so?" Lucia sat up a little straighter on the settee, struck by those words. "Is a kiss enough to know?"

"You kissed Haye, and you were certain that he was not right. With Armand, you kissed him, and you fell in love. It seems to always be so with you."

"Yes, but I was wrong about Armand. I loved him, and he broke my heart. He did not love me, Mamma."

"Stupid man! He had no sense."

"Yes, but—"

"Just be sure you only kiss men with good sense, and all will be well."

She looked at her mother's smiling face, and she couldn't help laughing. "Oh, Mamma, you are impossible! I want advice!"

"But what is it you want me to say?" Francesca leaned forward and patted her hand. "Lucia, I am not like most women. Although I know what it is like to be in love with a man, having a man's love and giving him mine for a lifetime has never mattered much to me. I have always seen romantic love as a transient thing, here today and gone to-morrow."

"Love does not last." Lucia's spirits began sinking. "Is that what you are trying to tell me?"

"I am saying that is how I feel about it. But then, I am perhaps too cynical. Too hard."

"Mamma, you are not hard at all! I think you are wonderful, and if Chesterfield had any brains, he would marry you."

"He has offered many times. I have refused."

"But why?"

"Oh, my darling!" Francesca lifted her hand to Lucia's face and caressed her cheek. "You are so different from me."

"In what way?"

"You have such an enormous capacity for love. It astonishes me. It always has. When the right man comes, you will be able to throw all of yourself into loving him—your body, your heart, your soul."

"Of course." She stared at her mother, still not comprehending. "What other way is there?"

Francesca smiled a little, but it was a sad smile. "I envy you, Lucia. I loved one man, and that was all there was for me. Now, my body is the only part of myself I can truly give away to a man. That, and a bit of my affection. The rest, I hold back from him. I do not know why, but that is how I am. It is what I have become. It is what a courtesan must be."

Lucia did not know what to say. She had never thought of her mother in this light before. She said the only thing she could think of. "I love you, Mamma."

"I love you, too, my beautiful girl. More than I can say." She leaned back against the arm of the settee. "So it is advice you want of your mamma? Very well. As I said before, you need to fall in love with a man of good sense, enough good sense to love you in return."

"In three weeks? I am beginning to think it is impossible."

"Ask Sir Ian to persuade your father to give you more time."

"He offered to do so, but he did not think Cesare would consent. I am afraid he is right."

"Sir Ian offered to go to your father on your behalf?" She clapped her hands together with a laugh. "So you have succeeded in charming him, just as I suggested."

Lucia gave her a rueful look. "Most of the time, Mamma, he does not even like me."

"Nonsense. He brought you here in defiance of Cesare's orders, did he not?"

"Only because I got your present, and I missed you so much I started crying. He felt sorry for me."

"Men never do things for women because they feel sorry for us. Never. No, you have succeeded in charming him."

"He didn't seem very charmed after he got that black eye the other night," Lucia said and began to laugh. "Oh, he was so angry with me! If dragons were real, Mamma, that man would be one, for when he is angry, his eyes flash like dragon fire. It is extraordinary."

"Like a dragon, is he?" Her mother sounded amused.

Lucia scarcely noticed. She leaned forward on the settee. "Mamma, do you really think a kiss tells a woman what she needs to know?"

"I think it tells *you* what you need to know, Lucia. It is not so for all women, but for you, I think, yes."

"But—" Lucia bit her lip, wavering, uncertain. She wanted Ian's kiss more than she'd wanted anything in her life. On the other hand, she now had his good opinion and she didn't want to lose it. If she kissed him, it would confirm his original assessment of her as a flirt and a tease.

Her mind flitted back briefly over other men she had kissed. Some had been like Haye, a true disappointment. Some had inspired in her a sort of mild interest, but nothing more.

Then she had met Armand. She thought of him and their nights together in the dark. So lonely she had been then, and he had been the antidote. They had talked and laughed and held hands. There had been anticipation and secret plans and the ache of longing. There had been kisses, many sweet kisses. He had always wanted more. He had wanted to touch her in forbidden places, and she had always stopped him. He had wanted her to lie down with him in the grass. She never had. As much as she had loved him, never had she lost her head, never had she lost control. Always, she had held back, waiting for the declaration of love, waiting for the marriage proposal. Neither had ever come. Armand had wanted her, but he had not loved her.

She looked over at her mother, who was watching her with a little smile. "A kiss can never tell a woman how a man feels, can it, Mamma?"

Francesca's smile faded. "I'm afraid not, my darling. That is where a woman takes a leap of faith."

"I took that leap of faith with Armand, and I got a broken heart."

"But you still have utter faith in love. You want to love again, and you will." She paused, then said, "Perhaps that is the difference between us, Lucia. When I took that leap of faith as a girl, I ended up both ruined and devastated, and I could never find the courage to love again. You will find the courage. You are made that way."

The sound of the door opening interrupted her, and Ian walked in. He paused just inside the door, and Chesterfield stepped past him into the room.

"Forgive me." Ian looked at Lucia and donned his hat. "We must be going."

She did not try to argue, for she knew he had risked a great deal just to bring her here. She got to her feet, put on her slippers, and slipped her cloak around her shoulders. Then she took a deep breath and looked at her mother. "Another goodbye, Mamma."

"But there is always another hello, Lucia. Remember that, and do not be sad."

"I will try," she promised, kissed Francesca, and said farewell to Chesterfield. Ian beside her, she left the house without a backward glance. After assisting her to step into the carriage, Ian gave the driver instructions to return to Portman Square and followed her into the vehicle.

"Did you enjoy your visit with your mother?" he asked, settling himself in one corner of the carriage opposite her.

"Yes, I did." She pushed back the hood of her cloak and looked at him, but the carriage was so dark, she could not see him. "I know what it cost you to bring me here, and I—" She stopped, her heart so full of gratitude that she found it hard to speak. "Thank you. It was a wonderful birthday present."

"I am glad you enjoyed it."

She heard him rap his fist on the ceiling to tell the driver they were ready to leave. The carriage jerked into motion.

Lucia stared at the corner where he sat, wishing she could see him. Moonlight fell through an opening in the curtains of the window behind him, and though that slash of silver light illuminated part of her side of the coach, it left his side in darkness. She could make out his cravat, a ghostly glimmer of grayish-white, but that was all. She could not see his face, but even had she been able to discern his expression, it would have told her nothing. It never did. His eyes could sometimes tell her things, but in the darkness of the coach, she could not see them.

Never had she met a man like him. His unyielding sense of propriety baffled her. His control and his discipline fascinated her. His laughter enchanted her. His kiss delighted her. He was an intriguing, enigmatic mystery, and she wanted to understand him.

"There is something I want to know about you," she said, "something I have wondered ever since that night we played chess. How did you get the scar? And how did you break your nose? You must have been in a fight."

"Yes."

"What happened?"

"I lost my temper." He stirred in his seat. "I don't really like to talk about it."

"I understand. Because you are so controlled, so disciplined, you do not want to talk about the times when you are not."

"Yes."

She waited, not saying anything more, and her silence seemed to impel him to explain. "It was at Harrow. There was a fellow ragging me about my brother, and when he made a derogatory comment about Dylan's music, I just snapped. I went after him. He broke my nose, yes, and the ring on his hand gave me the scar, but I did far worse to him." He drew a deep breath. "I broke his jaw and three of his ribs before I was able to stop myself and walk away."

"Your own anger alarms you, does it not, when it flares up?"

"Yes." His mouth tightened for a moment. "It does."

"It should not. Because you *did* stop and walk away. That makes all the difference." She studied him for a moment. "The other night in your brother's house when I saw you so angry, I was very impressed. And when you threw the glass at the fireplace, that, too, impressed me."

"I cannot think why."

"It made me realize how much passion you have in you." She paused, then she slid forward until she was perched on the edge of her seat. Her knees brushed his leg, and he jerked as if she'd burned him. "Besides anger, what other passions do you possess, Englishman?"

He didn't answer.

Sensing her way in the dark, she leaned over his body. Half-crouching, she flattened her palm on the carriage seat beside his hip, bracing her weight on her arm. With her free hand, she pulled off his hat.

"Lucia, what are you doing?"

What she was doing was playing with fire. Dragon fire. She knew it, she couldn't help it. He drew her to him like a moth to flame, and she was determined to find out why. She was going to kiss him again, and she hoped that kiss would unlock the mystery of this enigmatic man and why he fascinated her so.

She tossed his hat over her shoulder, then she raked her hand through his hair. It was like silk in her fingers.

"Lucia, stop it."

"You are always so perfect, and it always

makes me want to muss you up," she murmured. "If I had my way, I would drag you into a pond and rub mud all over you."

He made a smothered sound. The first crack, perhaps, in the wall of his discipline.

Her eyes were becoming accustomed to the darkness, and she could see his face now. Lean, chiseled lines in the dim light, so implacable and hard he might have been a statue. The scar above his brow was a fine, white line. She touched her lips to it.

He closed his eyes and drew a sharp breath, but he did not move. She placed her free hand on his chest, feeling the wall of his muscles through the layers of his clothing. Excitement flooded through her. She lowered her head and kissed the scar on his chin, then the not-so-perfect line of his nose. Then she pressed her lips to one corner of his mouth.

"What is this?" His voice was harsh, his body unmoving beneath her. "Another of your kissing experiments?"

"Yes," she answered in a whisper. Her lips lightly brushed his cheek as she spoke. He needed to shave, she realized, for his skin was like sandpaper. "I want another kissing experiment with you, Englishman."

"God knows, you always do what you want."

"And you always do what is right." She kissed his ear and felt a tremor run through his body. Another crack. "This feels very right to me, Ian."

"Lucia, for God's sake—"

She trailed kisses back down his cheek, savoring the rough texture. She tilted her head and pressed one last kiss to the opposite corner of his mouth, then she drew back.

Her lips a few inches from his, she waited, hovering, hoping, knowing she had made her move. It was his turn now.

He remained utterly still.

Lucia continued to wait, so close to him that her breathing mingled with his. One second went by, then two. Three.

Uncertainty began to claw at her, blending with her excitement until she couldn't separate them. Never had a man done this to her, never had a man made her take the initiative, never had a man made her work like this. Wait like this. Always it had been the other way. Men wooed her, pleased her, waited for her, tried to kiss her. But Ian was not like any other man.

Kiss me.

Still she waited, but he did not move.

Disappointment pierced her. The wall was intact. There was nothing that would breach it. Lucia moved to withdraw.

Suddenly, he made a rough sound and his hands gripped her arms. He shoved her backward, and his body came over hers, his weight pinning her helplessly to the seat. He captured her mouth with his.

The kiss was hard, almost violent, bruising her lips. It shocked her. But she was not afraid. Her mouth opened beneath his with a wordless sound of accord.

He tasted deeply of her, his tongue in her mouth, his kiss driving all the air from her lungs. Never before had she been kissed this way. It was raw and powerful, dizzying and glorious, beyond his control or hers.

She slid one hand into his hair, and with the other, she caressed the back of his neck. She bent her knee, and her inner thigh brushed his hip.

He tore his mouth from hers long enough to mutter an oath under his breath, then he cupped her face in his hands and kissed her again, gentler this time, tasting her mouth in a soft, slow, drugging possession that spread aching warmth through her limbs.

Shoving aside the edge of her cloak, he pressed kisses along the column of her throat and across her collarbone, his breath hot on her skin. His body rocked against hers, and even through all the layers of clothing, she felt his hard shaft pressed against her. She moved her hips in a slow wriggle and felt him shudder in response. "Oh God," he whispered. "Oh, God."

He moved, sliding his body downward along hers. He spread his palm over her breast, shaping it through her clothing. She cupped his head, pulling him closer, wanting more, and he gave it, kissing the top of her other breast above the neckline of her gown. The warmth inside of her began to burn hotter, and she writhed beneath him. The movement tore a groan from his throat.

"You're killing me," he told her, panting, his palms sliding down over her ribs to explore the rest of her shape—her waist, her hips, her thighs. "Killing me by inches." He lifted his body from hers enough to yank up her skirt. "But it's a damn fine way for a man to die."

Then she felt his hand move beneath her petticoats for further explorations, sliding up her leg, across her hipbone to the apex of her thighs. A vestige of feminine sanity returned, and Lucia reached for his wrist through layers of fabric.

"I want to touch you," he said. His hand spread over her most intimate place, while she kept her hand locked around his wrist. "Just let me touch you."

Other men had said such words, and never had she yielded. Always she had decided when and how to stop.

He eased his hand between her thighs. "Lucia."

Her name was a rasp torn from his lips, and the agonized sound of it conquered her in an instant. She released his wrist and let her hand fall away in complete surrender. She would give this man everything she had, including her heart, if he wanted it. "Love me, Ian," she whispered. "Love me."

He cupped her mound, and the pleasure was so intense that she jerked in response. "Oh!" she cried out, wrapping her arms around him and burying her face against his neck. She felt her whole body must be blushing from the hot, shameful excitement of it. "Oh!"

His fingers found the slit of her drawers and slipped inside to touch the most intimate place of her body, a place she had never allowed any man to touch.

"Sweet," he murmured, the tip of his finger sliding between the secret folds of her, making her blush even hotter. "So sweet."

He began to caress her then in the most amazing way, his hand strong and sure and yet gentle, each stroke of his finger making her shiver. Her hips writhed, arching into his hand, moving of their own volition. Her body was no longer in her control, but in his, and what he was doing to her was like nothing she'd ever felt before.

Lucia could hear her own voice saying things in Italian, incoherent, desperate things she had never said to any man in her life. "Please, oh, please, oh, touch me, yes, oh, please."

The excitement was building inside her, rising higher and higher, until words failed her, and she could only make odd, strangled little sounds. She needed . . . something, but she did not know what.

He knew.

"Yes," he coaxed against her ear, also in Italian. "Yes, yes, that's it. That's it. You're almost there. Come for me. Come."

She didn't understand what he meant, but her excitement was almost unbearable, and she thought she would die. Suddenly, with his next caress, everything inside her ignited, then exploded in a shattering array of sparks and dragon fire that made her cry out. His fingers continued to caress her, and waves of the most exquisite pleasure she'd ever felt washed over her, again and again and again.

He kissed her mouth, gave her one last caress, then pulled his hand from beneath her skirt. She could hear his breathing, hard and fast as if he'd been running. Still on top of her, he shifted his weight and began unfastening the buttons of his trousers.

The carriage jerked to a halt.

Ian lifted his head and his hand stilled. His whole body went rigid. "Christ," he muttered. "Christ almighty, what am I doing?"

He shoved himself violently away from her. She pulled her skirts down and struggled to sit up, her breath coming in gasps as she stared at him in shock.

"Stupid bastard," he mumbled and rubbed a hand over his face. "I am such a stupid bastard. Brains in my crotch, that's what I've got. Stupid, stupid. So goddamned stupid."

The carriage door opened. Neither of them moved.

Dazed, Lucia could only stare at him in wonder. Never had she imagined anything like this. What had he done to her with his hands? The way he had touched her and caressed her was like nothing she'd ever felt before. And then . . .

Santo cielo.

Such sweet pleasure. Waves and waves of it. Like falling, like magic, like dying . . . none of those descriptions were adequate to define what he had done to her. It was an experience beyond words.

Vaguely, she heard the clatter of something and realized the driver was rolling out the steps, but for the life of her, she could not find the strength to move from her seat. She pressed her fingers to her lips with a grimace. They felt puffy, swollen from the bruising of his mouth, and they burned from the friction of his beard-roughened face. Moments ago, she'd been on fire, but now, her body felt warm and languid, boneless. She wanted to weep. She wanted to laugh.

"Ian . . ." Her voice trailed off, for she could not remember what she'd been about to say. After that extraordinary experience, what could any woman say?

He was sitting across from her, his head bent, his face in his hands. "Ian?"

He lifted his head and looked at her. "Get out."

With those words, Lucia scrambled out of the carriage and headed toward the front door of the house. He did not follow her.

"Walk on," he ordered the coachman. "Anywhere. I don't care. For God's sake, just drive." With that, he pulled back and slammed the carriage door, leaving Lucia stunned and alone on the sidewalk.

She knew she should go inside, but instead, she just stood there, staring at the hansom cab as it turned the corner of the square and vanished from sight.

She had found out what she wanted to know. Ian Moore fascinated her because she was falling in love with him. Falling in love was supposed to make a woman happy, but Lucia did not feel any joy. The venom in his voice when he'd told her to get out of the carriage confirmed her worst fear. He still didn't like her. He couldn't possibly respect her. And he certainly wasn't falling in love with her.

Lucia began to wish she had never played with dragon fire.

Chapter 15

Every cell in Ian's body was in complete rebellion against what had just happened to him. His hands opened and closed into fists, and he wanted to crush something, mainly his own skull. Lust was pumping through him with each beat of his heart, and it was like anarchy inside him. Plague take that woman.

Closing his eyes, he leaned back against the seat. He tried to shut her out, but it was useless. All the self-discipline he possessed could not erase her from his mind, nor banish his need for her. After Tess, Ian had always limited his liaisons with women to discreet affairs. Mistresses, if his work permitted him to be in one place long enough for such an arrangement. If not, courtesans had sufficed. But no woman—no mistress, no courtesan, not even Tess—had ever made Ian feel this way, like a beggar, like a king, like a madman.

He stared at the seat across from him, seeing Lucia, beautiful and warm and willing. With each breath he took, he inhaled the fragrance of apple blossoms and her. Those scents were everywhere—on his hands, on his clothes. They permeated the coach, and he couldn't bear it. He reached for the curtains beside him and yanked them apart. He opened the window, breathing deeply of the sultry summer air, trying to clear his head, force down his arousal, make sense where there was none.

Please, oh, please, oh . . .

Even in the midst of London traffic, even amid the clatter of carriage wheels and horses' hooves, her soft moans and incoherent pleas called to him, teased him, beckoned him back.

The carriage slowed for crossing traffic, and Ian noticed a trio of women milling by a street lamp near a shadowy alley. Tarts, of course. He was now quite close to Seven Dials, and tarts were everywhere.

Ian reached up and slammed his fist sharply three times against the roof. His body was screaming for release, and he intended to have it. The hansom stopped, the driver pulled on the brake, and Ian got out.

"Wait here," he ordered, and walked back to the group of women. All three smiled at him as he approached, positioning themselves for his perusal. He beckoned to the one with blond hair. Her smile showed her teeth, no doubt because she had them all. Her complexion was clear, with no pockmarks, and she had a pretty shape to her. He'd always preferred blond women anyway, damn it all to hell.

She came forward, smile widening. "Want a toss, guv'nor?" she murmured, her hand splaying over his chest.

"Come on." He grasped her arm and headed for the alley. It was a dead-end one, with a gate leading into a mews. He led her toward a darkened corner.

"It's a bob for the usual," she told him. "Anything else, the price be dependin'."

"On what?"

She simpered in the silly, practiced way tarts were wont to do, fingering the silk of his cravat. "On what ye be wantin'."

The usual would suit him perfectly well. Had she said a hundred quid, he'd have paid it. He reached in his pocket, pulled out the required coin, and pressed it into her palm. She bent and tucked it into her shoe.

When she straightened, he caught her by the shoulder and pressed her back against the blackened brick wall of the alley. He kissed her. She tasted of gin. He didn't care.

With that gin-soaked kiss, all vestiges of his reason dissolved. Burying his face against the harlot's neck, he grasped a fistful of her skirt and tugged it upward. With his free hand, he began unbuttoning his trousers. Lucia's excited pleas echoing through his mind, he closed his eyes and tried to pretend it was she whose skin he kissed, but an odd, alien sound intruded on his fantasy. Ian turned his head and looked through the gate into the mews.

In the moonlight of the stable yard, a male dog was mounted on a female, humping her with frantic fervor, and the force of his thrusts was making her squeal.

Ian stared at them, suddenly paralyzed.

Years of work and discipline, years of restraint and reason, years of being an honorable British gentleman whose affairs were discreet and whose behavior was impeccable, and he was now reduced to the actions of a rutting dog.

He tore his gaze away from the animals and looked at the upturned face of the girl in front of him, for she was a girl, he realized. In the moonlight, with her eyes closed and her lips parted in a ludicrous imitation of passion, it was hard to tell her exact age. Seventeen, perhaps.

Self-loathing filled him. He was not a dog, and he could not fornicate in an alley like one.

"Never mind," he muttered, and for the second time tonight, he tore his agonized body away from a willing female with her skirts up. Proof positive he had indeed lost his sanity. He turned and strode away, buttoning his trousers as he went, leaving the whore behind, a whore who was no doubt delighted that she'd gotten a shilling for doing absolutely nothing.

Hard as stone and still angrier than a gentleman should ever allow himself to be, he left the alley and went back to the cab. He paid the driver, sent him on, and then he walked. He traversed London streets, grasping for his wits, working to rid himself of whatever spell Lucia had cast over him.

With each step, he tried to remember reality. He wanted Lucia, but he could not have her. She was not his to take. It was morally wrong to corrupt any young woman's innocence. In this case, it was suicide for his career, a career he'd spent fourteen years building.

Yet, no matter how many times he reminded himself of these facts, he still hungered for her with a ferocity that went beyond ordinary lust, and the savagery of his own carnal appetite was something he did not understand. Never had he felt this way, and it was making him do things, desperate things, things that made him a man he did not recognize, things that went against everything he had always believed about himself. Nonetheless, if she were here at this moment, he would throw his career and his honor away just to touch her again and hear her cry his name.

Ian walked and walked and walked, wishing he could walk right off the edge of the earth.

Ian did not come home that night. Lucia knew that because she'd lain awake until morning, listening for the sound of his footsteps to pass her door. Nor did he return the following day. He sent a note to Grace, saying he intended to stay near Whitehall for the sake of convenience. There were many preparations to make for Cesare's arrival, he'd explained, and there was no sense staying in Mayfair.

Lucia knew it was an excuse. He was avoiding her. Despite the knowledge that he did not want to be near her, she yearned to be near him. Even if she had tried to forget what he had done to her, it would have been impossible. She recalled every moment of that night over and over, relishing memories of his kiss and his touch. Her heart savored the anticipation of when she might see him again, even while her head reminded her he was not in love with her.

During the three days that followed, she did not leave Portman Square. On the chance he might come back and she might see him, Lucia remained at home. She flew kites in the park with Isabel, she read books, she did embroidery. She practiced guitar, accompanying Dylan or his daughter when they played piano in the music room, but she did not go to any parties or assemblies.

Word that Haye had broken their engagement spread, though not the reason why. True to his word, Haye and his uncle had exercised their discretion, and word of Armand did not leak out.

Their hope renewed, her most persistent suitors once again came calling. Lord Montrose, Lord Walford, and Lord Blair all visited Portman Square, but she had no desire to see any of them. There was only one man she wanted to see, but that desire went unfulfilled, for Ian did not return home.

On the third evening after that night in the hansom cab, the Duchess of Tremore came to call, and if Lucia harbored any hope that her feelings for Ian were reciprocated, the duchess's visit vanquished it.

"Now that Parliament has ended and the season is nearly over, Tremore and I are returning to our home in Hampshire tomorrow," the duchess explained as she sipped Madeira in the drawing room with Grace and Lucia. "Ian has asked if Miss Valenti might accompany us."

Lucia stiffened on the settee, and her heart pinched with pain. Not only was Ian avoiding her, he was sending her away. She was being shuffled off again somewhere out of the way, and for a brief, irrational moment, she felt like a lonely little girl again, the little girl nobody knew what to do with. Only pride forced her to keep a neutral expression when her nature wanted to rage and weep. "I am going to the country with you, Your Grace?"

"Yes. I hope that is agreeable to you." The duchess turned to Grace, who sat beside Lucia on the settee. "What are your plans?"

"We were intending to go to Devonshire in a

few days, as soon as Dylan is finished with the auditions for the new opera. Does Ian want you to take over the chaperoning of Miss Valenti?"

"Actually, we were hoping you could also come to Tremore Hall."

"I suppose I could," Grace answered. "Dylan can follow me when he finishes his work here. We can go on to Devonshire from there."

"Excellent." The duchess returned her attention to Lucia. "Have you given any thought to your situation? Ian has informed me that you have several serious suitors and that each of them has expressed to him the desire to marry you. He needs to know which one you prefer."

Lucia felt horribly cold all of a sudden. She did not answer.

"Forgive me for being forward and asking questions that would not in normal circumstances be my affair," the duchess said, misinterpreting her silence for reticence, "but your situation is an extraordinary one that demands haste. Your father arrives in three weeks, and if I understand correctly, the prince expects you to be engaged by his arrival and married by his departure. The only question is which man you will choose."

Lucia stared down at her hands clenched in her lap and did not answer.

"Sir Ian suspected that you might not have made up your mind," the duchess went on gently. "He has asked Tremore and me to hold a country house party for you, and we shall invite all three of your suitors so that you might spend more time with each of them before you make up your mind."

In that regard, time was not going to help. "I see." She managed to choke the words out past the lump in her throat.

"Once you have accepted the gentleman of your choice," the duchess went on, "Ian will give his formal approval, and we shall conclude the house party with a ball to celebrate the event. When your father arrives, Ian will be able to give him the happy news before he leaves for Anatolia."

Lucia looked up in shock. "Ian is going to Anatolia?"

"I believe that is his next assignment. He was supposed to stay through Cesare's entire visit, but I believe the situation there is worsening, and the Prime Minister is dispatching him there as soon as possible."

"What about the marriage settlements?" Grace asked. "Is Sir Ian not supposed to negotiate them?"

"Cesare and his ministers shall make the final arrangements with the groom and his family, and banns will be posted from Hampshire. Prince Cesare will come to Tremore. There is a Catholic church in our village of Wychwood, and the wedding will be held there. I hope all these arrangements are acceptable to you, Lucia."

"I do not want to marry any of them," she said, wretched. "I do not love any of them."

Grace put an arm around her shoulders. "Perhaps you could persuade your father to change his mind and give you more time to find a man you truly want to marry."

"I shall ask my father for nothing! Through most of my life, he has pretended I do not exist. I would not ask Cesare for food if I were starving!"

"Then it seems you must choose among the three suitors you have."

"How can I choose? How?" *How could I ever let any man but Ian touch me?*

Grace's arm tightened around her shoulder, but neither of the other women answered her question. After all, what could they say?

Lucia closed her eyes and swallowed hard, trying to swallow down the pain. She was falling in love with Ian, but it was plain that he did not feel the same. If Ian loved her, he would not be leaving for Anatolia. If he loved her, he would not be shoving her into the arms of some other man. If he loved her, he would have caught her up that night in the carriage and taken her away, married her, and damned the consequences. But like Armand before him, Ian did not love her.

Lucia could feel her face puckering up, and she ducked her head. Tears pricked her eyes, but she blinked them back. She would not cry for a man who did not love her. She had done that once as a lovesick girl. She would not do it again as a woman.

It was time to face reality. She didn't love any

of these men, but they all seemed to be in love
with her. None of them would shove her away,
shuttle her off, go to Anatolia, and forget about
her. It seemed she had gotten what she had
prayed for that day in Lady Kettering's garden.
God had answered her prayer three times over.
None of them were Ian, but Ian did not want her.
Lucia took a deep breath and looked up.

"Invite them all to this party, Your Grace. Let
these suitors compete for my hand, and at the
end of the week, I shall choose one." She got up.
"How do you English say it? May the best man
win."

During the two weeks that followed, Ian did
nothing but work. He spent every waking moment getting things ready for Prince Cesare's
arrival, taking charge of even the most mun-
dane details, telling himself that if he didn't do
these things himself, they would not get done
right.

The prince's envoy, Count Trevani, arrived to
assist with preparations, bringing with him lav-
ish gifts from Cesare for King William, Queen
Adelaide, and the Prime Minister. For Lucia,
there were rich fabrics, gold plate, and jewels that
would become part of her dowry. Even Ian received a gift, an exquisitely crafted silver sword.

Ian politely accepted the sword, and on behalf
of his government, he accepted the gifts for the
king, the queen, and the Prime Minister, inform-

ing Trevani that William IV was eager to meet His Highness and a state dinner had already been arranged. He explained the arrangements he had made with the Duchess of Tremore, a plan Trevani found quite acceptable.

Ian also took charge of Lucia's gifts, promising to see that they reached her as soon as possible and expressing the opinion that she would be delighted and grateful to receive them. The jewels were a most generous gift for an illegitimate daughter, but Ian could not help noticing that among the pearls and diamonds, there was not a single ruby.

He remembered that conversation between Francesca and Lucia about the rubies. Not surprising, for he remembered every single thing about that night in excruciating detail. Over and over. He worked himself to exhaustion, but that did little good, for every task he was required to do brought Lucia to the forefront of his mind. Even sleep was no refuge, for he dreamed about her, waking with his body in the agonies of full arousal so often that he began to wonder if he had died without knowing it and gone to hell. Only hell could offer such torment.

For the seventeenth night in a row, Ian cursed her, raged at her, and tried to hate her, but he could not stop remembering that night in the carriage, he could not stop imagining her warm, willing body beneath him, he could not prevent her soft moans of pleasure from echoing through his mind. Though she haunted him every hour, he could not hate her, no matter how he tried.

Two weeks after Lucia's departure for Tremore Hall, he received a letter from the duchess, saying that preparations were under way for the country house party. Invitations had been sent, menus planned, and amusements arranged, culminating in a grand ball, at the end of which Lucia would make her choice.

Those words were a sharp reminder to Ian of the brutal truth. She would choose Montrose, Blair, or Walford. One of those men would be the one to kiss her, touch her, bed her, possess her. With that thought, Ian no longer had to wonder if he was in hell. He knew it for certain.

Ian folded the duchess's letter and put it in his dispatch case, reminding himself that his own private hell would not last long.

Prince Cesare was arriving in one week. Once that happened, there would be a fortnight of events to attend—diplomatic affairs to discuss with the prince and his ministers throughout the days, and state dinners and balls that would last through the nights. There would be plenty of activity to keep his mind occupied and hopefully put his body into such a state of exhaustion that even Lucia wouldn't be able to torment what little sleep he would get.

There would be a few days at Tremore Hall for the party, where Lucia would make her choice. He could endure that. Then there would be a wedding, but he wouldn't be there. Thank God Sir Gervase had messed up the Turkish situation so badly because it meant that by the time Lucia Valenti became the wife of some British peer, Ian would be on a ship for Anatolia. He would have his life back and, hopefully, his sanity.

Chapter 16

Tremore Hall was a vast estate and every bit as grand as Prince Cesare's palace in Bolgheri. The grounds and gardens were lovely, the interior of the immense house richly decorated, and the duke's conservatory filled with exotic plants from all over the world. The duke and duchess were thoughtful, gracious hosts, and did everything possible to make Lucia feel welcome. The food was excellent, there were plenty of amusing things to do, and Cesare's ministers had sent a slew of dressmakers from London to begin preparing her bridal trousseau. In such circumstances, most women would be ecstatically happy.

Lucia was miserable.

It was not in her nature to be sad for long, yet

she could not shake the gloom that hung over her. She put on a good show, for she did not want to hurt the feelings of the duke and duchess, or have them think she was ungrateful. She helped plan the entertainments and amusements for the upcoming house party, a party to which over one hundred guests had been invited. She learned to play croquet, archery, and whist. When the guests began to arrive, she was equally gracious to each of her three suitors. All of them were perfect gentlemen in return, even managing to be polite to each other. Lucia smiled, acted content, pretended to be happy. Inside, she felt as if she were dying.

She thought of running away. It wouldn't be the first time she had done such a thing. If she could get to her mother, Francesca would give her money. She could run, hide. But her father would eventually find her. He always did. She had run away from so many bad situations in her life. Had it ever solved anything?

Another option was to choose one of the men, get to the altar, and then scream, "No!" at the proper moment, in front of all the wedding guests. That idea held a bit more appeal than running away, for it would completely humiliate her father. But it would also humiliate the poor groom, who would have done nothing to deserve such treatment. In addition, Cesare would probably send her back into a convent, have her locked in a cell so she couldn't run away, and leave her there to rot.

During the week of the house party, she asked the duchess every day if Ian had arrived, but every day, the answer was no. Time was set aside for her to spend with each of her three suitors. She walked with each of them, talked with each of them, danced with each of them. She tried to forget the man who did not want her and tried to appreciate the qualities of the three men who did. She tried to consider each suitor on his own merits, tried to see herself married to him, having children with him, being content with him. Women married men they did not love every day, she told herself over and over, and many of those women managed to be happy.

By the night of the ball, Ian had still not arrived at Tremore, but it did not matter. The only reason he was coming was to know which man she had chosen, and she had not made that decision. How could she?

Lucia stood before a mirror in her room as one maid fastened all the tiny, fabric-covered buttons down the back of her pink silk ball gown and another dressed her hair with fresh pink rosebuds. Through it all, she studied herself in the mirror with an odd sort of detachment, as if she were looking at someone else, and she realized she was. This was a wraith, a shadow of herself. She no longer knew who she was. She felt as if she were lost in a mist, trying to find her way home. But she had no home, and without love, she never would.

When she was dressed and ready, she sent the

maids away and walked to the window. She looked out over the vast expanse of Tremore's lawn, where lanterns had been lit and carriages of local gentry invited to the ball clogged the drive.

She was out of time. She had to choose. Blair, Montrose, Walford. Which would it be? A sob escaped her and she pressed her white-gloved fingers to her mouth. It was an impossible choice, for she could not bear the thought of being kissed by any of those men. She could not bear to be touched by any of those men. Not now. Not ever. Not after Ian. The very thought of it sickened her.

"Pardon me, miss?"

Lucia turned to see one of her maids had reentered her room. "Sir Ian Moore has arrived, and he wishes to see you before the ball."

Her heart leapt in her breast, twisted with sweet, painful pleasure. Ian had come. "Where is he?"

"He said he would wait for you in His Grace's conservatory. Do you know where that is?"

"Yes, yes, thank you." Lucia reached for her fan and followed the maid out of the room. She went down the three flights of stairs to the ground floor, impossible hopes spinning through her mind. What if he had come to take her away? Hope quickened her steps, until she was running down the long corridor of crimson carpet and gold draperies that led to the conservatory. What if he had decided he loved her?

Ian's valet, Harper, was standing by the double doors at the end of the corridor, and he opened one for her. Lucia gave him a nod of greeting as she passed by. Once she was inside, Harper closed the door behind her.

The Duke of Tremore's famous conservatory was a glass-ceilinged room larger than the ballroom of her father's palace. It was filled with trees and plants from all over the globe and decorated with statues, fountains, and urns. Iron brackets set high in Roman columns held gas lamps and illuminated the room. Out of breath, she came to a halt, trying to find Ian amid the dense foliage, but she could not see him.

"Ian?" she called.

He stepped out from behind a thickly covered trellis of vines, and looking at him filled her with a joy so intense, she couldn't speak. She could only stare, drinking in the sight of him, hoping she was not dreaming.

He was dressed in formal attire for the ball. A fine jacket of black wool encased his wide shoulders, and matching black trousers sheathed his long legs. Not a single wrinkle dared to mar his waistcoat of gold-and-black figured silk. His linen was immaculate, of course, snowy white and perfectly pressed. He had not a hair out of place and not a speck of lint on his clothes. Even the black eye that had given him a sort of rakish air had faded to near invisibility. She had never seen a more splendid sight in her life. Her joy bubbled over and she began to laugh. "You really do have the most amazing valet," she said, still out of breath from her long run. "When you look like this, I always want to muss you up."

He did not laugh with her. His expression was composed, grave, inscrutable. His diplomat face.

Lucia felt her laughter fading away. "When did you arrive?" she asked.

"A few hours ago. I brought a gift for you from your father." He turned away, beckoning her. "Come with me."

She followed him behind the trellis of vines and saw a long, carved-marble table, where a vast array of orchids was displayed. Some of the orchids had been pushed aside to make room for a gold chest about eighteen inches square and six inches high.

He opened the chest, revealing a small but dazzling collection of jewels. "Your father felt you should have these. They will become part of your dowry."

She glanced at the diamonds and pearls on the red velvet interior, then she looked at him.

Not a flicker of emotion showed in his eyes. No flash of fire. His eyes were cool and impersonal, reminding her of the first time she had ever seen him. "This is only part of it," he said. "There is also gold plate, silver, and crystal. Service for thirty, I believe. I thought you might wish to wear some of the jewels tonight so I brought them with me. Everything else is in London."

She studied the chest and its contents. "Not only service for thirty, but jewels, too. Very generous of Cesare. No rubies, though, of course."

She forced a laugh, but it sounded hollow to her own ears. "I suppose it is a good thing that Cesare has not given me rubies. They would clash with my dress."

She set aside her fan and reached into the chest. She pulled out the tiara and put it on her head, setting it at an absurdly crooked angle. She turned to give him a whimsical smile, hoping it would make him laugh. "What do you think?"

He did not smile back. He did not straighten the tiara for her. Instead, he stepped back. "You must tell me whom you chose," he said, clasping his hands behind him in his most stiff and formal manner. "I have already received written approval from your father for any of the three, so I will be able to call the man of your choice aside during the evening and give him my formal acceptance. Then I will make the announcement."

Those words pierced her heart like an arrow, killing all the wild, crazy hopes she'd had while coming down the stairs. She ducked her head to hide her expression. Some of his rigid control must be rubbing off on her because pride would not allow her to let him see how she felt. Head bent, she toyed with the jewels. "I have not made my choice yet."

"I see." There was a long pause, then he gave a heavy sigh. "You must choose tonight, Lucia."

"Yes, I know." She pulled a diamond necklace from the chest and studied it. "I never gave you that rematch at chess."

"Forget about it."

"Don't you want to know if—" Her voice broke, and she held up the necklace, forcing another smile. "I want to wear this, but I cannot fasten the clasp with my gloves on."

He made a sound, impatience perhaps, and yanked the necklace out of her hands. "Turn around."

Lucia did, and felt the coolness of platinum against her collarbone as he wrapped the piece of jewelry around her neck. His knuckles brushed her nape as he hooked the clasp. Then his hands stilled, but he did not pull them away.

"I can hear the musicians tuning their instruments," he said. "The ball is about to begin."

"Yes." She didn't move. "Ian—"

"I had best take you there." His hands slid away, and Lucia felt as if he had just grasped at the arrow in her heart and twisted it.

"Of course," she murmured, picked up her fan, and turned to take his arm. He took up the chest with his free hand, and they left the conservatory.

His valet was still standing in the corridor. "Take this, Harper," he said, and handed over the chest, then he escorted Lucia to the ballroom at the other end of the long corridor. Neither of them spoke.

The music grew louder as they approached the ballroom. Its immense double doors had been flung back, and couples were beginning to take the floor. Standing just outside the doors was

Lord Blair. She had promised the first dance to him, and he was waiting to claim it.

Ian saw the other man as well and came to a halt. "Enjoy your evening," he murmured to her. "I'll be in the conservatory. When you've made your choice, have him come and find me so I can give my formal consent. I'll return here with him and make the announcement."

She watched him as he turned away. "You're not attending the ball?"

He paused. "No," he said over his shoulder without looking at her. Then he started down the corridor.

Lucia watched him as he walked away, and she thought of the prayer she'd made that day in Lady Kettering's garden. Every word of her prayer had come true. She had found the man she wanted to marry. She'd found the man who made her pulses race and her breath catch. She'd found the man she could talk to and laugh with and love for a lifetime. The problem was that man didn't love her in return, and she realized she had forgotten to ask God for that part. Lucia crossed her fingers, closed her eyes, and said another prayer. But when she opened her eyes, Ian was still walking away.

Dawn was breaking. Ian leaned back against the stone wall in Tremore's conservatory, staring at the place beside the table of orchids where he had stood with Lucia and given her the jewels from her father. He wondered when she would find the ruby. At his order, a London jeweler had removed one of the tiny baguette diamonds in her tiara and replaced it with a ruby. He'd had it placed at one end of the circlet, where it would be tucked into her hair, where Prince Cesare wouldn't be able to see it when she wore it to her wedding. But whom would she marry?

Ian lowered his gaze to his evening jacket, waistcoat, and cravat. They lay where he had tossed them hours ago, in a careless heap of black and white on the floor that would have horrified Harper. Ian stared at the garments. He'd meant to attend the ball. He'd been expected to attend, required to attend. It was terribly bad taste not to attend. Hell with it.

For the hundredth time, he wondered whom she'd chosen, and he forced himself to stop. It was not his concern. He would know her choice when that man came to him.

Only a few more hours, and he could leave. Only a few more days, after he'd seen her father, he would be done with this whole affair. Then he could be himself again. This hunger, this need, this madness that had been threatening to overtake him and ruin his life would pass. He could leave, put all of this behind him, and get on with things. Important things.

The Greeks and the Turks were about to go to war, and war would be catastrophic for British interests there. Within a week he'd be on a ship headed for Constantinople to try and find a diplomatic solution. That was the work he did. What he was meant to do. Strange that the trivial task of finding a husband for a beautiful, capricious, impossible, unpredictable tease of a woman was the hardest assignment he'd ever had.

In the distance, the music stopped. The ball was over. He waited, but no one came. He listened for the tap of some man's heels on the conservatory's stone floor, but none came.

As he waited, he closed his eyes and tried to concentrate on how he was going to prevent a war in Anatolia, but instead, he found himself imagining the nape of Lucia's neck, where dark wisps of her hair had come loose from the intricate knot at the back of her head. They had been like curls of silken thread against his fingers when he'd fastened that necklace.

He smiled, remembering how she'd put her tiara on crooked. Like a little girl playing dress-up, he thought, and he stopped smiling. In that moment, he'd seen her future—he'd seen what her daughters would be like. They'd be like her. Sweet, soft, beautiful, impossible girls with vulnerable, romantic hearts and smiles like warm Italian sunshine, girls who wanted to be loved and demanded to be adored, who would grow up to bedevil and enchant the next generation of honorable British gentlemen. The only question was who the father of those girls would be.

He heard footsteps. It was time. Ian drew a deep breath and opened his eyes.

Lucia stood there. Alone. With her tiara in her hand and a look of disbelief on her face that told him she'd found it.

"There is a ruby in my tiara." Her dark brows drew together in puzzlement. "Did you know about it?"

"Yes."

She held up the diamond-encrusted circlet, pointing to one end with her fan. "My father would not do this. It was you, Englishman. You put it there." She said it almost like an accusation.

"Yes," he admitted. "It seemed fitting. It seemed—" He paused an instant. "It seemed the right thing to do."

"It goes against my father's wishes." Suddenly she smiled, and sunshine radiated through the dawn-tinged room.

It hurt his eyes to look at her, and he turned his face away. "Like your mother said, just don't let Cesare see it."

"You did this for me?"

For her? No, his reason had been wholly selfish. He had done it because he had not been able to bear the idea that she might forget him.

He straightened away from the wall. He forced himself to look at her and ask the question. "Whom did you choose?"

She shifted her weight from one foot to the other. "I haven't decided yet."

"You must."

"I am finding this choice very difficult." She paused and cleared her throat. "I need you to advise me."

Oh, God. "I cannot."

Being Lucia, of course she ignored that. "Lord

Walford is a nice man," she said, tilting her head in consideration. "His love for me is deep and genuine, I think. It is true that he talks about his roses all the time, but a woman should develop an interest in her husband's hobbies, and I could learn to like rose breeding, I suppose. Walford reminds me a bit of one of your English sheepdogs. He would be loyal and faithful. It would be very easy to keep him happy. Should I pick Walford?"

"Lucia—"

"Of course, Lord Blair is also very cordial, very nice. Why such a pleasant man has such a horrid cousin, I cannot tell, but as you said, I would not be marrying his cousin."

Ian watched her as she gazed up and to the side. She tapped the tiara thoughtfully against her chin, and went on with exasperating persistence about Blair's attributes. "He is intelligent. Quiet, but not too shy, and he is very gentlemanlike. I pricked my finger on a thorn yesterday. It bled, and he wrapped my hand in his handkerchief. He was so considerate. But it was his perfect opportunity, and he missed it."

"Opportunity?" he choked out.

"Ian, he didn't even *try* to kiss me," she said, sounding indignant. "A man who wants to marry a girl ought to try and steal at least one kiss from her, don't you think?"

Ian made a smothered sound and turned his back on her, staring at a group of pink China roses. He forced himself to say something. "Blair was too nice, you said. Perhaps you were right."

"Perhaps. On the other hand, can a man be too nice? Most women do have a particular weakness for rakes, it is true, but I—" She paused, an odd wobble in her voice he did not understand. "But I think nice men make the best husbands. Blair is also handsome, and I do like men who are handsome, I confess it. Should he be the one?"

Ian closed his eyes, feeling the world caving in on him.

"Then there is Lord Montrose. He is the handsomest of all, tall and strong. He has wit, too, and makes me laugh. Laughter is important to happiness in marriage. What do you think? Should I choose Lord Montrose?"

His jaw was clenched so tight, it ached.

In the wake of his silence, she sighed behind him. She put a hand on his shoulder, and he drew in a sharp breath. He was hard in an instant, with one touch of her hand. He stood there, his back to her, hiding it, lost in lust and frustration as that horrible, desperate need for her engulfed him.

"I cannot choose," she said. "Which means there is only one thing to do. You must choose for me."

"What?" The word was a hoarse whisper that felt ripped from deep within his chest. He jerked his shoulders to shrug off her hand and turned in disbelief to find her watching him with a grave face. She meant it. His throat closed, and he could only look at her in mute agony.

She gave a slow nod in the wake of his silence. "You know what I want. I told you that night we played chess. Remember?"

Remember? Those words had been tormenting him for weeks. They were burned on his brain, and he doubted he would ever forget them.

"So, which man can give me what I want?" She leaned into him and her breasts brushed his chest. Her lips were close to his, so dangerously close. "Which man can love me and respect me and give me sons? Which one has a passion equal to my own?"

His hands curled into fists. He would not touch her. He would not.

"Which one?"

"Lucia, stop it." He cupped her face, breaking his vow that quickly, pressing his thumbs to her lips to stop the flow of words. "Damn you, stop it."

"Tell me what to do, Ian." Her lips whispered against his thumbs, sending the lust in him flowing to every nerve ending in his body. "Should I pick Walford? Blair? Montrose? You choose."

He thought of each of those men as she said their names, and then her little cries echoed through his mind. All that passion for a man who was not him.

Oh, please, oh yes, oh, touch me . . .

Like an oak struck by lightning, Ian shattered into splinters of fire. He lowered his hands and caught her by the arms, crushing the silk of those absurd puffy sleeves in his fingers as he shoved her backward. She hit the table behind her, and he bent his head, vanquishing the mention of any other man with a kiss.

She made a faint gasp against his mouth. Her tiara and fan clattered to the stone floor, and her gloved hands touched his face. Her sweet mouth yielded at once to his demand, and desire flamed in him as he tasted her. He told himself to stop, but he could not stop.

He let go of her arms and slid his hands between their bodies to cup her breasts, shaping them in his palms. They were perfect, so perfect. He wanted to touch them, kiss them. He wanted to lick her warm, satiny skin. He heard the rend of fabric, and he could not stop.

In the glittering morning sunlight, he could see what his force had exposed, the top of her breast—the luscious swell and the barest edge of her aureole. He traced it with his tongue, dampening her skin and the torn fabric. She arched against him, gasping his name. Her arms twined about his neck.

He heard pots breaking, and he realized he had broken them, sending a slew of Tremore's prized orchids crashing to the floor with a sweep of his arm. He caught Lucia's skirts in his fists, his frantic hands pulling up layers of silk and muslin in search of the warm, sweet woman beneath. He bunched her skirts between their bodies, and his hands fumbled for the eyelet hooks that held up her drawers. They came undone, and he slid the garment down her hips. His hands shaped her buttocks, cupped them. He lifted her onto the table. Then he was touching her in the sweetest place of all.

Just as in the carriage, she was hot and soft, slick against his fingers. He caressed her there, and her body jerked with the desperate awkwardness of need and inexperience. She clung to him, panting against his neck. He slid his finger inside her, and she cried out, her thighs squeezing convulsively around his invading hand. He eased in a bit deeper, savoring the virginal tightness of her. He wanted to tell her it was all right, that he wouldn't hurt her, that he would stop. But those words would be lies, and he could not say them. Because, God help him, he could not stop.

He yanked his hand from between her thighs and bent to completely remove her drawers, sliding them over the satin slippers on her feet. He tossed the lacy cambric garment aside, straightened, and freed his trousers. He cupped her buttocks again, pulling her toward him as he positioned himself between her thighs.

The tip of his penis touched her, then slid between her tight, wet folds. Ian nudged forward, pressing deeper into her until he touched her maidenhead. With that touch, all the primal desires he'd been fighting so hard to contain rose within him like a shout of triumph, and all he could think of was possession. Complete and total possession. He drew back, then with one hard thrust, he took it.

She sucked in her breath in a deep, shuddering

gasp. His entry had hurt her, he knew, and it shocked him that he could feel such exquisite enjoyment at the very moment he was causing her pain. But there was no way he could stop.

He pressed kisses to her face, her hair, her throat, anywhere he could reach. He heard his voice speaking to her, disjointed words meant to soothe her even as they fanned the lust inside him. "Beautiful Lucia, so soft . . . Lucia . . . oh, God, so good . . . dreamed of this . . . of you . . . for . . . so damn long."

She was breathing in little gasping sobs, and he tried to hold back, wait a little, give her time to adjust to his invasion, but it just wasn't possible. He tightened his grip, held her hips in his hands, and drove into her. Then he did it again, and then again, and then again.

With each stroke, he felt the rising thrill, thicker, hotter, taking him to the peak. With one last thrust, he climaxed in a flood of pleasure so intense that it nearly knocked him off his feet.

He buried his face against her hair, breathing hard, cradling her in his hands as the tidal rush of orgasm ebbed away into satiation. Her arms were still wrapped around him, her face pressed to his neck.

"Are you all right?" he whispered.

"I—" The sound was muffled against his throat. She shook her head. "I don't know."

Remorse nudged him, and a dark, shadowy guilt. He slid his hands out from beneath her hips and slipped his penis free of her.

"Oh!" she said, a little sound of surprise, as if until this very second, she still hadn't quite understood what had just happened.

She lifted her head and looked at his face, then her mouth puckered, and she looked down again at once. He wasn't sure what she had seen in his countenance, and he didn't want to know. He turned away to adjust his linen and button his trousers, then he looked down at the floor and found her drawers. Scooping them up in one hand, he knelt in front of her. He slid the cambric over the pink slippers on her feet and began pulling the garment up her legs.

He paused with her drawers just over her knees. Her skirts had fallen over her lap, and he could not see the dark curls at the apex of her thighs, but he could imagine the sight. That primal need flickered inside him, and he jerked to his feet. "Raise your hips," he said.

She flattened her palms on the table and did as he bid, enabling him to bring the drawers up around her waist. Billows of pink and white covered his hands, and he couldn't see what he was doing, but he'd dressed and undressed enough women in his life that he didn't have to see the tiny hooks of her drawers to fasten them back together.

As he dressed her, he tried not to think. He pulled down her skirts and smoothed them out, he adjusted the gold-and-pink net sash at her waist, he pulled a crushed rosebud out of her hair, keeping reality at bay a little longer by these tiny considerations, these mockeries of gentlemanly solicitude.

Her bodice was torn, he noticed, and the corset beneath it as well. He'd done that. Torn her dress and so much more.

Shame consumed him as he stared at her ruined gown and bent head. He reached up and tried to tuck the torn edges in somehow, to hide from himself what he had done, but there was no hiding it. Some things could not be hidden. Some things could not be mended. His hand stilled against her silk and linen, and he loathed himself.

He opened his mouth to say something. To apologize, when he wasn't sorry. To say it wouldn't happen again, when he knew if he had half a chance, it would. To tell her everything would be all right, when it wouldn't. He said nothing.

She lifted her head and gazed at him. Her eyes seemed huge, soft and brown like those of a doe, and he did not know if what he saw in their depths was fear or condemnation. Both, perhaps. If so, he deserved them, for despite all her kissing experiments, she had been a virgin. He, on the other hand, could make no claim of ignorance. He had known precisely what this was, what would happen, and what it would mean. She, even with all the girlish indiscretions of her past, hadn't had a clue. No one ever did until it happened. No one truly knew what innocence was until they lost it.

"I'm sorry," he said. "So damned sorry." He started to pull his hand away.

Staring at him, she lifted her hand and covered the back of his, keeping his palm against her breast.

Just that, and excitement flooded him, excitement, relief, and a queer, piercing feeling in his chest he couldn't quite define. Ian knew he was indeed a hopeless business, idiotic as well as skirt-smitten, if he could want her again only a few scarce minutes after ruining her and himself and everything he'd striven all his life to be.

A sound came to him, a faint gasp that wasn't Lucia. Ian glanced sideways and looked straight into the shocked blue eyes of Lady Sarah Monforth. Behind her, looking over her shoulder, stood her cousin, Lord Blair.

Chapter 17

Lucia lay on her side on top of her bed, huddled into a ball, staring at the pale blue willow wallpaper of her room. The pattern of blue and white kept blurring in front of her eyes, colors blending together into gray. She blinked, willing herself to keep back tears as she tried to make sense of what had happened.

She shouldn't feel like this, stupidly stunned and weepy. She was a courtesan's daughter. She knew about these things. Her mother had explained it to her once when she was twelve, with stern warnings not to let a man do what Ian had just done. She'd seen statues in Paris museums, she'd peeked into forbidden books, she and Armand had done some passionate kissing. But none of that information had prepared her for the complete reality.

It hurt, for one thing. That had been quite a shock, shattering all the wondrous feelings that had come before. She hadn't expected that. When Ian had helped her dress, she'd seen her own blood on herself, and she knew well enough it wasn't her monthly courses. Lucia pressed her knees tighter to her chest and flinched. She was still sore, deep inside. But that wasn't what made her feel like crying.

Lady Sarah and Lord Blair had seen them. She had followed Ian's sideways glance to find them standing there. Even though it had only taken Ian the blink of an eye to move in front of her and shield her, he had not been quick enough. Lucia had seen them, and they had seen her.

Lord Blair and Lady Sarah had been tactful enough to leave without a word, and Ian had taken her up a little-used servants' staircase near the conservatory. He had somehow managed to get her back to her room without anyone else seeing her, but she had no illusions that this would remain a secret. Lady Sarah was not like Lord Haye, whose discretion had kept the story of Armand Bouget from leaking out. No, Sarah's malicious tongue would be quite busy. By the end of the day, everyone at Tremore would know what she had seen, and in lurid detail. If Lucia hadn't been soiled goods before, she certainly would be now. But even that was not what made her stare dazedly at the wall on the verge of tears.

It was the look she'd seen on Ian's face afterward, a terrible look of shame and self-loathing he hadn't been able to hide as he'd touched her gown and realized just what he had done.

Lucia straightened a bit on the bed and looked down at the shredded edge of her dress and corset, two flaps of fabric that hung in a disproportionate triangle over her left breast. She had seen his face, and she'd wanted to tell him it was all right, that she was to blame, not he. That she'd known, and she'd pushed him on purpose, using her words and her body as if they were matches and he a powder keg. The resulting explosion was her fault, not his, and he had nothing to reproach himself with. But the words to tell him all of that had failed her, and all she'd been able to do was touch his hand.

A knock sounded on her door, and Lucia sat up with a jolt. Grace slipped into the room, closing the door behind her, and Lucia reached for the torn edge of her dress in an instinctive move to cover herself, but then stilled as she saw Grace's face. She blinked back tears and gazed helplessly at the woman by the door. "You know? Already?"

Grace gave a gentle nod. "Yes. It's nearly eleven o'clock."

"So late?" She glanced at the sun pouring through the windows, wondering how time could have passed so fast. "Knowing Lady Sarah, even the scullery maids have heard by now." A shaky laugh came from her throat, the laugh turned into a sob, and she pressed a hand over her mouth.

"Oh, my dear." Grace came to sit on the edge of the bed and put an arm around her shoulders. "Daphne is dealing with Lady Sarah. She will be gone by dinnertime, and her cousin, too. All the guests are going today."

"I was right, then." She'd never meant anyone to know. *Oh, Ian.* She stared at her lap, her heart aching for him and what she had done to him. "Everybody knows."

Grace's arm tightened around her shoulders. "It's all right," she murmured, running her hand up and down Lucia's arm in a soothing motion. "It's all right."

She shook her head. "No, it is not all right. I looked at his face afterward. *Santo cielo!* The look on his face. I will never forgive myself. I didn't know. I didn't know." Her voice rose, she felt panicky. "I didn't understand."

"Hush," Grace murmured and lifted her hand to stroke Lucia's hair. "Hush."

She tried to get her emotions under control, but she felt so shaky inside. She shuddered, sucking air into her lungs in dry, gasping sobs.

"Lucia, Lucia." Grace hugged her, drawing her face into the curve of her shoulder. "It will be all right, I promise you. Ian will make everything all right."

The sound of a scratch on the door made her jump.

"I've ordered a bath for you." Grace stood up. "The maids have brought it."

Lucia swung herself off the bed and ran to the window, looking away from servants who surely must know by now what had happened. Her back to the room, she forced herself under some semblance of control. She waited, listening as maids moved about under Grace's soft instructions, pouring water into a bath, laying out towels and soap, lighting lamps. Only after the servants had gone did Lucia turn back around.

Grace moved to her side of the room. "There are fresh clothes on the bed for you," she said as she pulled curtains together. "And a pad such as you use for your monthly. You will need that."

No need to ask the reason. The soreness inside her and the blood she'd seen on her thighs told her. She nodded, and a strange numbness crept over her as she allowed Grace to lead her to the small copper bathtub.

The other woman unfastened the buttons down the back of her dress, handed her the jar of soap and a wet cloth, then patted her shoulder. Compassion shone in her green eyes, so much compassion that Lucia wanted to start weeping all over again. She looked down at the floor.

"I'll leave you to your bath," Grace said, "but first there are some things you must know." She paused, then said, "Lucia, did he hurt you?"

She could not look up. Her hand tightened around the small jar in her grasp. "Yes."

"Please believe me when I tell you that it only

hurts the first time. The discomfort will pass, and it will never hurt like that again."

That was a bit reassuring. She nodded, her head bent.

"There is something else you need to know," Grace went on. "This news will spread everywhere. Sarah and her friends will be delighted to tell everyone they meet. You must be prepared for that. Ian will marry you. He will take care of you. But both of you will pay a high price for this. Your father will want Ian's head, and one of you will have to convert to the other's religion."

"I will." Lucia knew that was the least she could do under the circumstances. Religion had never mattered much to her anyway. "I will convert."

"That blunts the damage to Ian somewhat, although I suspect the Prime Minister will terminate his ambassadorship. No doubt, the king will concur."

She jerked her head up, staring at Grace in horror. "Ian will lose his position?"

"Almost certainly."

"Oh, no," she moaned, feeling sick. "No, no, no. What have I done?"

"Listen to me, Lucia." Grace grasped her arms and gave her a little shake. "This is not all your fault. He is a man of thirty-five, and he knew what he was doing. He must accept responsibility."

"You don't understand." She shook off the other woman's grasp. "I have to see him."

"Of course. I will tell him you wish to speak with him. I hope he hasn't left already."

"Left?"

"He is going to London today as planned. When Prince Cesare arrives, he will meet with him and obtain consent to marry you. If you want to see him before he goes, I had best go find him." Grace started for the door. She paused before opening it. "Lucia, don't be afraid. Ian will do right by you. He will do the honorable thing."

Grace departed and Lucia stepped into the steaming water of the slipper bath. "I know he will marry me," she whispered to the closed door in abject misery. "That's why I did it."

"There's a most astonishing rumor going around this morning."

Ian's hands stilled in the act of smoothing down his cravat. He glanced from his own reflection to that of his brother, who stood framed by the doorway of his bedchamber. There was a look of disbelief on Dylan's face that demanded explanations, but Ian did not want to explain. He had spent the past few hours striving not to think, fighting not to feel, working to bury his emotions deep down until he felt nothing. It was the only way he knew to make what he had done bearable. Yet, when he returned his attention to his own reflection, the sight of his face almost demolished his carefully cultivated state of numbness, for everything he'd thought himself to be was gone, and he no longer recognized the man in the mirror.

"I heard this rumor from Tremore himself when we rode this morning," Dylan went on. "You're not going to believe it."

Ian turned to Harper, who stood beside him. "Leave us."

The valet gave a quiet nod and started for the door. Dylan waited until Harper had departed and the door was closed before he spoke again. "Lady Sarah started it, of course. That woman is the most vicious creature alive. I can't believe Tremore once thought of marrying her. She would say anything."

"Yes, she would," Ian agreed. He took a deep breath and met his brother's eyes. "Sometimes she even tells the truth."

"What?" Dylan gave a half laugh. "You mean—" He broke off and shook his head in denial and disbelief. "Sarah has been telling anyone who would listen that after the ball she and her cousin found you with Miss Valenti." He said it slowly, as if he thought perhaps Ian didn't understand just what rumor was circulating amid Tremore's guests. "She's been saying they saw the two of you in the conservatory. You were in a partial state of undress, she said."

Ian looked past his brother at the black evening suit and white linen on the bed. "Yes."

"Miss Valenti's dress was torn," Dylan said.

Ian closed his eyes, remembering the exact

moment when he'd torn it. He could still hear the fabric ripping. The memory of that sound could arouse him even now, even as it shamed him. He felt his numbness slip, and he fought hard to regain it. "Yes, I know."

"It must be a mistake. I *know* you. Sarah must be lying. Or she misunderstood what she saw."

Ian opened his eyes and returned his gaze to his brother's. He said nothing.

Dylan stared at his face. "It's true," he murmured, seeing past the careful diplomatic mask. "Ye gods, it's true. My brother caught in a compromising situation with a young lady. The planets are standing still."

"Lady Sarah saw the *end* of that compromising situation, not the beginning," he found himself saying, and it baffled him that he, the most taciturn and discreet of men, was feeling the need to make some sort of confession. Even more baffling, he was making that confession to his notorious younger brother, of all people. "The . . ." He swallowed hard, galled to say it out loud. "The damage had already been irreparably done."

"You mean you . . . that you and she . . . you did it?" Dylan, the shit, actually began to grin. "Well, well, well," he murmured. "How are the mighty fallen."

"I am in no mood for your wit," Ian snapped, almost at the end of his tether. "By God, if you say one more sardonic word, I will make what I did to you when you were thirteen seem like a little girl's game of patty-cake."

Dylan held up his hand in a gesture of truce, and any hint of his amusement vanished. "Sorry, sorry. It's just that you have to understand how astonished I am. You never do anything wrong. You never make mistakes. You are always so damn perfect. You always were. I find the fact that you are human an extraordinary revelation."

You are human after all.

Lucia's words echoed through his mind. "Of course I'm human." Wishing he wasn't, he rubbed a hand over his face in irritation. "God, why does everyone think I'm not?"

"Well, I've always been inclined to doubt it. When we were boys, our tutors always made comparisons, and I always came out on the losing end of those, let me tell you. Your assignments never had errors. Your handwriting was like copperplate. You knew the answer to every question. It was nauseating. By the time I was seven, I knew I could never live up to you, so I didn't try. But, oh, how I resented you."

Ian's anger evaporated. "This is ironic," he said. "All the while you were resenting me, I resented you. When we were growing up, you could do anything you wanted. I vow, Dylan, if it was wicked, or naughty, or forbidden, or just plain stupid, you did it and always got by with it. I always got caught. I always got punished. *That*, little brother, was nauseating."

"You were our father's favorite."

"You were our mother's."

"Because of music. Mother and I could share that. You and Father had the estate, I suppose. As for my getting away with things . . ." He paused, then said, "Ian, there's something I've been meaning to tell you for years. Maybe now is the time." He sat on the edge of Ian's bed.

Curious, Ian also sat down, taking the chair by the fireplace. He could tell from Dylan's voice that this wasn't one of his jokes, and he was glad of the diversion from his own situation. "Tell me what?"

"My ears ring. It almost drove me mad."

"I beg your pardon?"

His reaction made Dylan shake his head in amazement. "God, Ian, does nothing rattle you?"

He gave his brother a wry look. "You mean besides Lucia Valenti?"

Dylan laughed at that. "My brother has a sense of humor. And in these circumstances, too. How extraordinary." His laughter faded, and he said, "Remember that riding accident years ago when I hit my head on a rock? You were in India or Egypt or some other remote place."

"I remember. I was in St. Petersburg." He frowned, trying to understand. "So, because you hit your head, your ears ring? Doctors cannot cure it?"

"No. I have this noise in my head all the time. It's an unwavering whine, like a tuning fork not quite on pitch. I can't sleep sometimes. I get headaches. I used to take opium and smoke hashish to blunt it, but it never went away. For five years,

I couldn't compose. I kept publishing old pieces. Things I had already written. I thought I'd never write music again. It was hell."

He knew what music meant to Dylan. It was his lifeblood. It was everything. "I see."

"I almost killed myself. I put a pistol under my chin and cocked the hammer."

Ian sat up straight in his chair. "God, Dylan!"

"Rattled you at last, I see. But it's the truth."

"What stopped you?"

"Grace." He smiled, his face lighting up as it always did when he mentioned his wife. "She saved my life. Literally and figuratively. When I first saw her, I heard music, and I was so surprised because I hadn't heard music in years. I thought she was my muse. I lowered the gun, and she took it out of my hand, telling me I had no business killing myself." He paused. "I think I fell in love with her the moment I saw her. Heaven knows, I needed her. I still do. I need her every single day."

Ian was beginning to know all about need. "So, you can no longer compose because of this noise?"

"I have learned to work around it. Isabel helps me. She has so much talent, Ian, more talent than I, really. Music comes so easily to her, as it used to do for me. Composing will never be easy for me again, but at least I am once again able to do it."

"I'm glad, and I'm glad you told me about this, that you finally felt you could." He leaned back in his chair. "Well, this explains a lot. You've always been wild, God knows, but your behavior became so erratic, I knew something was very wrong. I just didn't know what it was. Why didn't you tell me sooner?"

"I don't know. I suppose—" He paused, frowning. "I suppose I thought you wouldn't understand. You are such a disciplined person, I feared you would tell me to just get over it and stop feeling sorry for myself. Which is, of course, what I was doing, but I dreaded hearing it, especially from you."

"I would not have said that." His brother's disbelieving look impelled him to add, "I might have thought it, but I would not have said it. I am the diplomat, after all. The man of tact and discretion who always says and does the right thing." He laughed, but there was no humor in it.

Dylan leaned forward, forearms on his knees. "What's going to happen now? You'll have to marry the girl, obviously."

"Obviously."

"Will you lose your position over this?"

Ian pressed two fingers to his forehead. He did not want to believe everything he'd worked for was now in ruins, but he could not deny the truth. "Of course. The Prime Minister doesn't take kindly to scandals. This is the Age of Reform, you know."

"I'm sorry, Ian. I know your work means as much to you as mine does to me, and I know what it's like to lose it."

Ian lowered his hand and stood up. "I have no one to blame but myself," he said, his dishonor a bitter taste in his mouth. "Knowing Prince Cesare, I shall be fortunate if he does not send the *carbinieri* after me and have me shot."

Grace arranged for Ian to come to her that afternoon in a little-used writing room that overlooked the front of the house. As she waited, Lucia stood by the windows, watching guests climb into their carriages and depart. Thankfully, most of them had chosen to leave that afternoon, rather than linger another day in the stifling awkwardness of the situation.

Lucia watched them go, sipping the Madeira Grace had given her for her nerves. It wasn't helping much in that regard, but when Ian entered the room, she took one glance at his face and downed all the sweet liquor in a gulp. For what she had to say, she needed all the fortification she could get.

"We'll be married in three weeks," he said before she could speak. His words were brusque, his face unreadable. "Grace tells me you are willing to become Anglican, which simplifies matters. After I have talked with your father, banns will be posted. We'll have the wedding in the ducal chapel here at Tremore."

Though there was no tenderness in his voice, relief flooded through her at his words, such enormous relief that it made her weak in the knees. Even though she already knew his sense of honor, and even though Grace had told her his intent, she was so glad to hear him say it. "Thank you."

"I'm leaving for London today. You're staying here."

"Yes. Grace told me."

"Your father arrives in two days, and I have to tell him what happened. For your sake and, I must confess, for mine, I would prefer to avoid it." His face twisted, his composure faltered a little. "I have faced many difficult meetings in my life, but truth be told, I do not know how to look a man in the eye and tell him I violated his daughter."

"Don't!" she cried. "Do not berate yourself this way!"

"Why not?" The diplomat returned, grave, cool, and distant. "It is no less than I deserve. But," he went on before she could make another protest, "Prince Cesare's requirements for the man you marry make me a wholly unsuitable candidate. And your departure from the Catholic faith will enrage him. Unless he is told the exact circumstances, he will never give his consent."

"Yes," she said with a hint of irony she knew he did not understand. "I know."

"Good." He turned to leave. "My carriage is waiting."

"Don't go yet, please," she said, her words stopping him. "Before you leave, there is something I must tell you. Something you must know about . . . about what happened between us."

"I think I have a pretty clear recollection of what happened between us, thank you."

"Ian, this is very difficult for me to say. Please do not make it more so."

His face grew taut. "What do you want to tell me?"

She clasped her hands, drew them to her mouth, and prayed for composure. This was the hardest thing she'd ever had to do because she knew he would hate her for it, but she had to tell him. She lowered her hands, lifted her head, and looked at him. "I had to make a choice," she said simply. "And I made it. That's why this happened."

"What do you mean? You didn't have the choice. I took the choice away from you."

"No, Ian. You did not."

"Lucia, don't you understand, even now, what I did? I could not stop." He exhaled a sharp breath. "God help me, I could not stop myself."

"I understand perfectly." Her voice shook, and she forced herself to steady it. "As I said, I made my choice. I chose *you*. I said the things I said in the conservatory because I knew what would happen. I knew you wanted me, and I knew I could—" She stopped and swallowed hard. "I knew I could break you, Ian. So I did."

He stared at her, comprehension dawning in his face. "You wanted me to do it? In heaven's name, why?"

"So that you would marry me. I knew—" She paused, fighting not to shrink from the condemnation hardening his face. At least now he would blame her fully, and not condemn himself. "I knew you would insist upon marrying me, and that when my father learned what you did, he would have no choice but to give his consent. So you see, I chose you."

The silence was terrible. It seemed endless.

When he spoke, his voice was low, calm and deadly. "You pushed me on purpose, hoping I would . . ." A muscle worked in his jaw. "You intended this outcome?"

"Yes."

"I don't suppose it occurred to you to consult me on the matter beforehand and find out what my wishes might have been about marrying you?"

"No." She watched his eyes take on the frost of arctic lakes. They were so cold, she shivered inside. "I was afraid you would refuse. Even though the ruby told me you might have . . . have some regard for me, I know you do not want to marry. And even if you . . ." She faltered, and tried again. "Even if you cared enough for me to agree, I knew my father would never consent because you are not Catholic, and because you have no title. So I pushed you over the edge, I impelled you to do what you did. Now my father has to accept you as my choice because I am ruined and I might be carrying a child. Your . . . your child."

"You manipulated me."

The quiet accusation was like the lash of a whip, but she did not flinch. "Yes."

"I will lose my ambassadorship."

"I did not know that would happen." She began to shake, the emotions of the day threatening to overwhelm her. "I am so sorry."

His eyes narrowed. "And Lady Sarah and Lord Blair? I suppose they were there to bear witness?"

She stared at him as the implication of his question hit her. *"Ma insomma!"* she breathed. "You think I . . . that I had them come . . . you think I *arranged* for them to see us?"

Emotionless gray eyes assessed her. "Did you?"

She pressed her shaking hand to her mouth, dismayed. That he would think such a thing had not occurred to her, but she could hardly blame him for it. "No," she answered, knowing even as she said it that he did not believe her. Why should he? The tears that had been threatening all day to fall began spilling down her cheeks, and she wished she possessed even a fraction of his sangfroid.

His lips pressed into a tight line. He turned away, reaching for his hat. "My duty is clear. You're getting me for a bridegroom, which is what you wanted." He slapped the hat against his palm. "But then, you always get what you want in the end, don't you?"

The bitter tinge of his voice was unmistakable. He turned away and walked out of the room, closing the door behind him. Lucia ran to the window and watched through a blurry haze as he got into his carriage.

"I'm sorry, Ian," she whispered, finally saying the most important part as the carriage drove away. "I'm so sorry. But I couldn't choose anyone else. I couldn't bear to give another man the right to touch me the way you did."

Chapter 18

⟨◦∞◦⟩

The wedding of Sir Ian Moore and Miss Lucia Valenti took place early on a rainy September morning at Tremore Hall's ducal chapel. The bride wore a silk gown of the palest magnolia pink, embroidered with pink and white seed pearls. In the tradition of her home country, a veil covered her face. The groom wore an impeccable morning suit of midnight blue. The mother of the bride did not attend, which was appropriate. The father of the bride was also absent, which was understandable. The Duke of Tremore escorted the bride to the altar. As for the bride herself, she was of trying hard not to throw up.

Three weeks had not done much to put Ian in a more forgiving frame of mind, or if it had, Lucia wouldn't know it, for she had not heard from him at all. Grace had received one brief letter confirming the worst: Though they had not stripped Ian of his knighthood, they had taken away his ambassadorship. He had gone to Plumfield, his estate in Devonshire, to make things ready there, arriving back at Tremore late the night before the wedding. Now, as she started up the aisle on the duke's arm, Lucia saw Ian's face for the first time in three weeks, and she found it just as hard and implacable as it had been when he'd left.

As she made her way toward him, her stomach in knots, she could read nothing in his face. As they spoke their vows, his voice was grave and composed. When he lifted her veil, she smiled at him, but he did not smile back.

Now husband and wife, they left the chapel together and led the way to Tremore's dining room for the wedding breakfast. As they walked side by side, Ian did not say a word, and Lucia tried to reassure herself with the phrases she'd been repeating for days. Everything would be all right. He would come to understand the reasons for what she'd done. She would make him a good wife. He would become content and not regret the loss of his career. He would learn to love her. She loved him. That, at least, was true. The rest sounded a lot like wishful thinking.

Because it was a ten-hour journey to Plumfield that Ian wanted to make without stopping overnight along the way, the newly married couple departed right after the wedding breakfast. Lucia was glad of it, for the breakfast seemed to be an incredibly awkward affair. The customary toast to their health was made by Ian's groomsman, a certain Lord Stanton, whose scrutiny of her whenever she chanced to look at him was rather unnerving. The guests amounted to a dozen in all, and though Daphne was a superb hostess, conversation was stilted at best. After all, what was there to say?

Her husband seemed to share this view. As the carriage taking them to Devonshire rolled through the countryside, the silence was like a wall between them. Lucia knew she had to find a way to break down that wall. She began with conversation.

"So, our home is called Plumfield. Do we grow plums, then?"

"Yes. Plums, pears, apples. And there are tenant farms, of course." He leaned down, slid a traveling case from beneath the seat, pulled out a newspaper, and slid the case back. He opened the newspaper in front of his face, visible evidence of the wall. As if she needed any.

She tried again. "What does Devonshire look like?" She glanced at the rain-washed countryside. "Is it like this? All green and pretty?"

"Some of it, yes."

"What is our house like?"

"You'll see it when we get there."

Silence fell again, lengthened from seconds

into minutes. Clearly, conversation was not working. She changed tactics.

"Ian?"

"Yes, Lucia?"

She yawned. "I'm very sleepy."

He turned a page. "Take a nap."

"I don't have a pillow."

There was a heavy sigh from the other side of the *Times*. He slid the paper down and looked at her. She looked at him, waiting, hoping he would take the hint.

He did, though he looked less than happy about it. He shoved himself away from his side of the carriage and moved to her side, settling beside her to offer his shoulder.

"Thank you," she said, curled an arm around his waist, and lapsed into silence. As they made the journey into Devonshire, he read his newspaper, and she made no further attempts at conversation. Instead, she savored the solid strength of his shoulder beneath her cheek, telling herself that even stone walls could be chipped away, bit by bit.

She loved him. That love and a place to call home were enough for her, but she knew they weren't enough for him. She was determined to find a way to change that.

Relentless, Ian had called her once. She supposed she was, because she was going to be relentless about making up for what she'd done to him. And there was a lot to make up for. She had ruined his career, the thing that mattered more to him than anything else. Even worse, she had caused him—the most honorable and discreet of men—to be the victim of public disgrace and humiliation. She had not done that part on purpose, but it had happened because of her.

She knew what it must have cost him to face her father, endure the gossip, give up his livelihood. It might take her the rest of her life, but Lucia vowed that she was going to make him happy. She was going to make him glad he had married her. Tonight, she decided as she fell asleep against his shoulder, would be a perfect time to start.

It was intolerable. There was no way a man could read a newspaper in peace when his wife was using his shoulder for a pillow and her arm was curled around his waist. It was too distracting. Even now, after everything that had happened, her touch could arouse him in an instant.

His wife. A wife, he reminded himself, who had cost him dearly.

Ian closed his eyes and leaned his head back against the padded back of the coach. Cesare's fury had been a sight to behold. If there had been a pistol or knife anywhere in the prince's vicinity as he'd heard the explanations of just what the compromising situation had been, Ian knew he'd be dead right now. As it was, the prince who had once regarded him as a trusted friend had looked at him with contempt and called him an animal. And he was. The prince had demanded that the British government revoke Ian's ambassadorship. And they had.

Now, he was thoroughly at loose ends. Deprived of the one thing that had given his life meaning, he did not know what he was going to do with his time. As he contemplated the life that stretched before him, his heart felt leaden. After over a decade in the diplomatic corps, Ian could not help regarding the life of a country squire as an empty and purposeless existence, filled with endless rounds of race meetings and foxhunts, county balls and London seasons.

He opened his eyes and fingered the folded edge of the newspaper. He always read the important English and European papers every day, no matter where he was. Not doing so was as unthinkable to him as wearing limp linen or going to a dinner party without a fresh shave. Even now, when his world had narrowed to a small slice of the Devonshire countryside, he still cared about world affairs. He did not know how to accept that he was no longer a part of them.

Lucia stirred in her sleep beside him, and he glanced at her. She was curled up on the seat in a most awkward way, and her head was jammed against the side of his shoulder. If she stayed in that position, she would have a crick in her neck, sore muscles, and probably a headache, too, when she woke up.

Ian sighed and tossed the *Times* onto the opposite seat. Carefully, so as not to wake her, he eased her onto his lap and put an arm around her shoulders to support her back. She gave a sigh, stretched out her legs along the seat, and snuggled her face against the dent of his shoulder. As she slept, Ian stared out the window at a stretch of wet English meadow. He inhaled the scent of apple blossoms in his wife's hair and tried not to care what was going on in Constantinople.

Lucia hoped that her wedding night would provide her with the opportunity to begin making Ian happy, but she found her plan dashed in very short order. They arrived at Plumfield around eleven o'clock in the evening. After a quick introduction to the upper servants and a late supper, Ian showed her to her room. He commented that she must be very tired after the journey, said he'd see her in the morning, gave her a kiss good night—on the forehead—and went next door to sleep in his own room.

It seemed she was going to spend her wedding night alone.

Lucia stood in her bedchamber, feeling surprised, dismayed, and rather aggrieved. Their marriage had gotten off to a bad start, but during the three weeks leading up to this day, the one thing she hadn't had doubts about was Ian's desire for her. She stared at the connecting door between their rooms, and she was tempted just to march on through it, throw him down, and kiss him until he couldn't resist her anymore.

A scratch sounded on her door, and a maid

entered carrying a kettle of steaming water, fresh towels, and soap. "If you please, ma'am," the woman about her own age said with a curtsy, "the master sent me to wait on you. My name is Nan Jones."

The maid crossed the room and poured water into a white porcelain bowl on the oak dressing table, placed a plate of soaps beside it, and turned to her. "I hope you like your room," she said, a little shyly. "Mrs. Wells, the housekeeper—you met her earlier, ma'am—picked all the fabrics and things. She and I did the room up."

Lucia looked around. Lamps had been lit, throwing a soft glow over walls of creamy yellow. A carved oak bed, dressed in ivory linens and pillows, was topped by a crown-shaped canopy of golden-yellow velvet and flanked by two night tables. The bed draperies were tied back against the canopy's four supporting posts with ivory silk ribbon. In front of the bed was a chaise longue of gold-and-white stripes. The room was a large one, and possessed not only a closet, but also a pair of immense armoires, their panels painted in the Italian style. Two comfortable chairs of yellow-patterned floral chintz stood in front of the Siena marble fireplace. The floor was covered in a carpet of soft browns, golden yellow, and deep red.

"It's lovely," she said, smiling. "I wouldn't change a thing."

"Oh, Mrs. Wells will be ever so glad! The master told us when he came home three weeks ago that he was getting married, and you could've knocked us over with a feather, we was that surprised. With the master gone so much, we'd given up ever seeing a mistress here at Plumfield. The master said as yellow was your favorite color, he wanted your room done up that way before he brought you home."

"Ian had the room redone for me?" Pleasure and hope warmed her deep inside.

"Yes, ma'am. It was blue before." She walked to the armoires and opened one of them. "Would you like to change into nightclothes, then have a wash before bed?"

"Yes, thank you, Nan." The other woman assisted her out of her clothes, then helped her don one of the soft, lacy nightdresses of her bridal trousseau. As the other woman fastened the buttons, Lucia asked, "Are you going to be my permanent maid?"

The question flustered the servant. "Oh, ma'am, I'm just first parlormaid. I've never been a lady's maid. There hasn't been a lady's maid at Plumfield since the master's mother died, and that was well before my time. The master sent me to do for you, but he thought you'd be wanting to choose your own maid later on."

Lucia studied her for a moment. "Would you like to do for me permanently, Nan?"

"Oh, yes! Thank you, ma'am. I'd like that ever so much." Her face shone with such pleasure that Lucia laughed.

As Nan gathered up her traveling clothes to be

laundered, Lucia walked over to the dressing table. She wetted her face, then began lathering soap and caught the scent of apple blossoms. Her favorite. "Did my husband give instructions about the soap, too?" she asked.

"Yes, ma'am." Nan laughed. "We make apple blossom soap here, so there's plenty of it. We also make pear oil soap, but he said no pear, only apple. He was very firm about that."

With those words, Lucia's spirits rose another notch. She looked in the mirror and stared at the reflection of the closed door between her chamber and Ian's, and she abandoned her previous plan. Though she hadn't planned on spending her wedding night alone, such a circumstance might serve her better in the long run.

Nothing whetted the appetite better than anticipation and imagination. Lucia decided she was going to start whetting her husband's appetite for her first thing tomorrow.

Ian was by nature an early riser, and he had a set routine for himself and his household when he was in residence at Plumfield. He always rose at seven, took a horseback ride, then breakfasted at nine and read the morning post.

By the time he returned from his morning ride, Lucia was up and about. He found her in the writing room, a small study beside the drawing room where the mistresses of Plumfield always wrote their letters in the mornings. With her were Atherton, his butler, Mrs. Richards, his cook, and Mrs. Wells, his housekeeper. She looked up from the writing desk when he came in and turned one of her beaming smiles on him. "Ian! Good morning."

The servants turned to him with bows and curtsies. "Morning, sir," they said in unison.

He nodded to them, then looked at Lucia. "Going over the household routine?"

"Yes. I hope you do not mind?"

"Not at all. I would expect you to do so. You are mistress here, and the house is your domain," he added, with a meaningful glance at the three upper servants just on the off chance they didn't fully appreciate that fact. "Feel free to make any changes you like."

"I was just telling Mrs. Wells that one thing I am not going to change is my room," she said. "It is perfect in every way, and it even has my favorite soap. Thank you, Ian."

A pleasurable warmth washed over him, and it took him a moment to think of something to say. He lifted his fist to his mouth, cleared his throat, and in the most ordinary possible tone he could manage, he said, "Glad you like it, my dear. Now, if you will pardon me, I must meet with my steward. I shall leave you to contemplations of the household routine." He bowed and started to leave, but she called him back.

"Ian? Do you have plans this afternoon? I hoped you might give me a tour of the estate."

"Of course. One o'clock?"

"Oh, that will be just right!" she cried. "Then we can take a picnic."

The idea of a picnic had never occurred to him. Sitting on the ground to eat had never been something he particularly favored, and he couldn't remember the last time he'd gone on a picnic. But he looked at the pleasure shining in Lucia's face at the idea, and he found himself saying, "A picnic it is. You'll prepare something, Mrs. Richards?"

"Yes, sir," Richards said, sounding astonished.

"Very good." With that, he bowed and departed for his study to meet with Coverly. He had a lot of estate business still to do, and if he was going to while away his afternoon on something frivolous like a picnic, he'd better get to it.

"It is larger than I imagined it." At the edge of the south gardens, Lucia stopped and turned around to study the four-story structure of the house.

Ian paused beside her and set down the laden picnic basket. "Plumfield was built in 1690. The two wings were added by my grandfather. Which is fortunate, because he also added several water closets. And there is a plunge bath, too, just for the master chambers. It's across from our suite of rooms and down a private staircase."

"Yes, I saw the bath when Atherton showed me over the house this morning. It is enormous." She paused. "Big enough for two."

Wild, erotic images of the two of them in that bathtub flashed across his mind, and he sucked in a sharp breath.

She didn't seem to notice. "I like the brick on the outside of the house," she said, and gave a nod of approval. "And the stone accents are nice. It is a very English house, is it not?"

He forced erotic fantasies aside before what he felt became obvious. "Yes, I suppose it is."

"The grounds are very English, too," she went on, glancing around. "At home, and in France as well, it is all formal knot gardens and potagers. Your English gardens are different. More natural. All these lawns. And the flowers and herbs and shrubs are all mixed up together. There are not quite so many fountains here, but more lakes and ponds, and"—she paused to point at the sunken ditch near their feet—"little streams like this."

"Ha-ha," he corrected.

She looked at him, puzzlement puckering her forehead. "Did I say something to make you laugh?"

He did laugh then. "No, no. These ditches are called ha-has. They are there to keep the deer and cattle out of the gardens."

"We have deer and cattle?"

"Yes, of course. Plumfield is four thousand acres. Orchards, tenant farms, some park and woodland, too, of course. And cattle." He pointed to the distance. "Dylan's estate, Nightingale's Gate, is ten miles south of us. On the sea."

"So near? That is wonderful. We can see them often, then, can't we?"

"Any time you like. It's an hour's drive at most."

That seemed to please her. She smiled at him, and he wondered what it was about her smile that always made him feel so topsy-turvy that he wasn't ever quite sure if he was on his heels or his head. That thought had barely gone through his mind when suddenly there were tears sliding down her face, mingling with the smile and confirming that with Lucia as his wife, everything in his world was going to be topsy-turvy, upside down, and inside out from now on, especially him. "Why are you crying, in heaven's name?" he demanded. "What's wrong?"

"Nothing." Lucia wiped her fingers across her cheeks. "Ian, I cry all the time," she reminded him with a sniff. "You should know that by now."

Yes, he probably should. "Well, I wish you wouldn't," he said, and jerked a handkerchief out of his pocket. "I really hate it when you start getting all weepy."

"I know you do." She took his handkerchief and dabbed at her face. "But I can't help it. I look around me, and I see our house and our gardens, and I am happy. That is why I am crying."

He gave her a dubious glance. "You're crying because you're happy?"

"*Si.*"

"Is it the brick or the boxwood that has inspired all this joy?"

She shook her head and gestured to their surroundings. "How can I explain? All my life I have been shuttled from place to place. Schools, convents, the houses of relatives, Cesare's palace, Mamma's house, your brother's house, Tremore Hall." Her hand curled in a fist around his handkerchief, and she pressed it to her heart. "But here, I look around, and I know I am home."

Tightness squeezed his chest, and he looked away, staring out over the fruit orchards in the valley below them, feeling deuced awkward, and yet, strangely pleased. "I'm glad you like it."

"It's beautiful. How could I not like it?" Giving one final sniff, she folded up his handkerchief and put it in her pocket. Then she wrapped her arms around his neck, stood up on her toes and pressed a quick kiss to his mouth. "I am home," she said, and kissed his chin. Then his jaw. "Thank you, husband. Thank you."

"Lucia." He cast an uncomfortable glance past her toward the gardeners working nearby. He reached for her wrists. "People can see us."

She ignored that and kissed him again. "Are you embarrassed?"

"No." His hands closed over her wrists, but he liked the feel of her arms around his neck more than he minded being watched, and any thought of pulling her hands down went out of his head.

She kissed him again. "Is it that you are shy?"

He liked it when she kissed him, too. He caressed the insides of her wrists with his thumbs. "No, I am not shy," he corrected. "I am discreet.

I am . . ." He paused, then said, "I have never been a demonstrative person."

"If you kiss me back just once," she teased against his mouth, "I'll stop."

That made him smile. "So that's the plan, is it?" he murmured, his body starting to burn. "Get a man all worked up, then stop. Why am I not surprised?"

Her expression became serious. Her hands slid into his hair, and it didn't even occur to him to object. "Are you?" she asked.

He frowned at the question, trying to think, finding it a bit difficult at this moment. "Am I what?"

She pressed her body against his, and even trying to think went to the wall. "Are you all worked up, Ian?" she whispered.

"God, yes." The thick heaviness of lust was fast overtaking him. "And you know it, too, I suspect."

He tightened his grip on her wrists and stepped back, pulling her with him until they were behind the tall boxwood hedge of the maze. Shielded from curious gazes, he let go of her wrists, cupped her face, and kissed her. It was a long, lush kiss that made him ache and brought back memories of that night in the carriage and her body beneath his. At this moment, he didn't care what it had cost him to have her, and he didn't care what part she might have played in his downfall. He tasted his wife's mouth and began to think that doing the gentlemanly thing last night and leaving her alone to rest after their long trip had been truly stupid. He lowered one hand to caress the side of her neck.

She broke the kiss and pulled out of his grasp before he could collect his wits enough to prevent it. When he tried to grab her, she darted away, laughing, and stepped back around the hedge where they could be seen. "I promised I'd stop," she reminded him as she turned and started down the hill. "I always keep my promises."

"You are driving me mad," he said as he picked up the picnic basket to follow her.

She paused and flashed him that gorgeous smile over one shoulder. "I hope so, Englishman. I certainly hope so." Laughing, she turned away, caught up her skirts in her hands, and began running down the hill.

The sight brought him to a halt. His mind flashed back to the first time he had ever seen her, and how he'd imagined her this way, running through knee-high grass, laughing, with her hair flying behind her. He'd never been a fanciful man, but even then, in that first moment, he'd sensed that his fate was intertwined with hers. For so long, he'd thought his feelings for her to be just an overpowering physical desire, but now, at this moment, he understood that it was something deeper. Something that compelled him to turn toward her again and again, when reason and good sense had always told him to turn away.

"Ian, what are you still doing up there?"

Her voice, breathless and laughing, brought him out of his reverie. "Hmm? What?"

"What are you doing? You are standing on the side of that hill as if frozen in place."

He wasn't frozen. Not anymore. Not since he'd met her. He stared at the woman who was smiling up at him in the bright autumn afternoon, the rays of the sun glinting on the silver comb in her hair.

Luce, he thought, the Italian word for light. And she was. That was what always drew him to her, kept him turning toward her again and again, the way a plant in a window insisted on turning toward the sun. He needed her, needed her so much he'd been willing to throw away everything else that had ever mattered to him. That was a frightening thing, for never in his whole life had he needed anyone.

"Ian, are you all right? You have the strangest look on your face."

He started down the hill and forced himself to say something. "I was thinking of the first time I ever saw you."

She glanced about her, then back at him. "You mean that day in Mamma's drawing room?"

"Yes."

She gave him a dubious look, as if he wasn't quite right in the head. "Sometimes, Englishman, I do not understand you. I love you, but I do not always understand you."

She turned and started across the meadow. He remained where he was and watched her walk away, with her skirts in her hand and the sun on her hair.

"I love you, too," he said, but only after she was too far away to hear. "I always have."

Chapter 19

⁓◦◦⁓

They had their picnic on a stretch of green turf beside the millpond, partaking of cold ham, cheese, bread, and fruit from the basket Mrs. Richards had packed. Lucia studied her husband as they ate, smiling as she thought of how he'd pulled her behind that hedge so the gardeners wouldn't see him kiss her. He really was adorable. So proper on the surface, and so fiery underneath. She intended to spend the entire day stoking that fire inside him until both of them were burning hot.

Now was a perfect time to start.

"It's a lovely day," she commented, "but it's so warm." With that, she leaned forward on the blanket and slipped off her shoes. She hitched up the hem of her skirt just enough to give him a view of her calves. She removed the garters at her knees and began to peel off her stockings. She did it slowly, allowing him a long, lingering look before she tugged her skirts back down and tossed her stockings aside. She stretched out her legs, leaving only her bare feet showing, and leaned back on her arms with a contented sigh. Then, she looked into his eyes and saw that look she loved.

"You are staring at me," she said.

"Wasn't that the idea?" His voice was wry.

"Yes," she admitted. "I like it when you look at me. Shall I tell you why?" Without waiting for an answer, she went on, "When I first met you, I thought you were haughty and proper, even cold. But then I realized something about you."

"What's that?"

She crossed her ankles, and her bare foot brushed his hip. She felt his body tense.

"I can almost never tell by your face what you are thinking, but sometimes when you look at me, there is something in your eyes, something hot that makes me catch my breath. Even when you are very angry with me—and you have an anger most powerful, husband—even then, I know you want me. You are looking at me that way now." Her words and his eyes were starting to have an effect on her, for she was beginning to feel a warmth that had nothing to do with the weather.

"Lucia." He moved toward her and rose on his knees. He leaned over her, resting his weight on his arms. He bent his head to kiss her.

"Ian, don't." She pressed her fingers to his mouth. "You mustn't."

"Why not?"

She smiled and glanced past him. "Because we are not alone."

Ian turned to look over his shoulder and saw two little girls sitting on the bridge over the stream about eighty yards away. The pair were watching them, heads together, and it was clear they were the topic of the children's discussion. He returned his gaze to her. "Lucia, you did that on purpose!"

"You deserve it," she answered at once, slid out from beneath him, and got to her feet. "No bride should spend her wedding night alone. Today, I am taking my revenge."

She walked away, but of course, she didn't get the last word. "Enjoy your revenge now," he muttered behind her. "Because tonight, I intend to take mine."

After their picnic, Ian showed her some of the estate. He thought that made him safe from her tantalizing form of revenge since they were surrounded by people for the remainder of the day, but he should have known better. When he took her to the mill where the soaps were made, she commented oh-so-innocently how pretty a bowl of the pale green soaps would be on the travertine tiles of the plunge bath.

At the cider house, where the apples and pears were fermented, the way she slowly licked sticky drops of cider off her lips and her fingers was such a sin, she'd have given a Methodist minister a heart attack.

He took her to one of the farms and gave her an extremely dry lecture about how tenant farming worked, but of course, it didn't help him keep his thoughts away from ravishing her. Oh, no. For when Mrs. Trent, the farmer's wife, offered her a glass of buttermilk, Lucia just had to mention that buttermilk lotion was the most excellent way for a woman to keep her skin soft and white.

After a tour of the stables and kennels, they returned to the house, but even then he wasn't safe. She made the mere eating of dinner so sensual, that afterward, Ian was forced to use that plunge bath for a dunk in cold water.

It was a good thing he did. An entire afternoon of her provocative comments and quick kisses had left him aching for her just as badly as she'd intended. Though she might have enjoyed bedeviling him all day, tonight he would make her pay for it.

That thought made him smile. Yes, she was going to get a dose of what she'd been dishing out, and he was going to love every minute of it. He intended to make sure she loved it, too. Ian tightened the sash of his dressing gown, opened the door, and entered her room.

She was seated at her dressing table. Nan Jones, the maid he'd sent to do for her, stood behind her, brushing her hair. Both of them turned as he came in and closed the door behind him.

Jones immediately bobbed a curtsy, then looked at Lucia. She nodded, and Jones put down the brush. She left the room, smothering a giggle as she went out the door.

Ian moved to stand behind his wife. She smiled at him in the mirror and picked up her hairbrush. She leaned sideways and began to brush the hair on the right side of her face. He leaned down and kissed the left side of her neck above her cream-colored dressing robe.

The brush faltered for only a moment, then she resumed her task. *Tease*, he thought, laughing to himself. She didn't know what she was in for. Tilting his head, he tasted her skin with his tongue and felt her shiver. "Cold?" he asked.

"No."

"You're shivering."

"Am I?"

"Yes." Smiling, he lifted his head and his eyes met hers in the mirror. His hands reached for the thin strip of brown-satin ribbon at her throat. He untied it. His fingers slipped inside and began to caress her skin just above her collarbone.

She stirred on her seat, and the hairbrush hit the floor with a thud. She arched her neck to give him better access, and he trailed kisses along the side of her throat. "Like that, do you?"

Her breathing quickened, and her hand lifted to touch his hair. "Yes," she answered.

He straightened. His hands curled around her arms, urging her to her feet. When she was standing, he kicked the seat out of the way and turned her around. "You have been toying with me all day," he murmured. "Now it's my turn to toy with you."

His mouth came down on hers before she could reply, and as always, her lips parted freely beneath his, telling him how much she loved his kiss. He slid his hands into her hair and deepened it, reveling in the taste of her and the feel of her.

Already, with just one kiss, he was fully aroused, but he had no intention of losing his control. Not this time. He tore his lips from hers and pressed brief kisses over her face as he banked the fires inside himself. But when he put his hands on her waist, the fires flared up again, for there were no corsets, no petticoats to get in his way. Just two loose layers of ivory silk between his hands and her soft skin. His hands moved up and down her torso, from her ribs to her waist down to the flare of her hips and back again.

"Do you want me to put out the light?" he asked, hoping she'd say no.

"Remember the night we played chess?" She looked up at him, tilting her head to one side, black hair spilling across her shoulder. "That night, I wondered what you looked like under your clothes."

That stunned him rather, but he merely raised an eyebrow, and a smile curved one side of his mouth. "Indeed? I was thinking the same thing about you at the time."

She reached up and began to unbutton his

shirt. "Why don't we both satisfy our curiosity and leave the light on?"

"Hear, hear." He untied the sash of his dressing gown and pulled it off. Then he unbuttoned his cuffs and pulled off his shirt. It joined his dressing gown on the floor at their feet.

He moved to begin unfastening the ties of her night robe, but she stopped him. "Wait," she said, her hands flattening against his bare chest. "Let me look at you first."

That wasn't quite in keeping with his plans, but it was a temptation he couldn't resist. He let his hands fall. She began to caress him in slow circles, her hands gliding over his pectoral muscles, along his shoulders, down his arms, and over his abdomen.

As she touched him, she began pressing kisses over his chest. At first, they were light, her lips touching him like the brush of butterfly wings. But then, the kisses became lush explorations as she tasted his skin with her tongue. Under this slow assault, his body shuddered with pure pleasure. He tilted his head back with a groan. The seducer had become the seduced. He closed his eyes, suffering the delightful torture as long as he could.

He tangled his hands in her hair and tilted her head up, stopping her. "That's enough," he said and kissed her. "I told you, it's my turn tonight."

He slid his hands to the front of her robe. He grasped the ends of the second bow and untied it. Then the third. Then the fourth. He pulled bows apart one by one, slowly working his way down her body to her thighs. When all the bows were undone, he hooked his thumbs beneath the edges of her robe and pulled the garment off her shoulders. It fell to the floor behind her in a heap.

Under the silk peignoir, she wore a matching nightgown, and through the fabric of that garment, he could see the round, full shape of her breasts. He brushed his fingertips lightly over them. She inhaled a sharp breath, and her nipples hardened. The sight of them jutting out against the pale silk and the feel of them against his fingertips almost sent his lust careening out of control, but he wasn't going to give in to his own desires. Not yet. This time was not going to be like last time.

She lifted her hands, held his wrists in her grip, stilled his caress. "Ian, I didn't arrange for Lady Sarah to see us."

"I know." He tilted his head and kissed her.

"How do you know?"

"I told you, I always know when you're lying. You open your eyes very wide and tell your lie, then you bite your lip."

She stared at him. "I do not do any such thing."

He kissed her nose. "Yes, you do. It gives you away every time."

"Someday, Englishman," she murmured, "I'll have the upper hand with you."

"Like hell you will. Now where were we?" He

opened his hands over her breasts and made a sound of appreciation at the luscious full shape of them. "Ah, yes."

"Ian, I have to tell you something."

It appeared they were going to have a conversation. He stilled his hands, striving to keep himself in check. "Yes, Lucia?"

She pressed her hands over his just as she had done in the conservatory. "This was why I did what I did," she whispered. "I looked at those men at the ball, and I thought of that night in the carriage when you touched me, and I knew I could never let any of them touch me." She tilted her head back and closed her eyes, pressing his hands to her breasts. "Only you."

God, she was beautiful. He felt that tightening in his chest again, pushing air from his lungs, squeezing his heart. He drew a profound, shaky breath and bent his head. He opened his mouth over her nipple and suckled her ever so gently through the silk of her nightgown. She gasped and arched into him. Her hands lowered to curl over the edge of the dressing table on either side of her hips.

As he suckled one of her nipples through her gown, he brought his free hand up to toy with the other, his teasing as slow and provocative as his own tightly leashed desire would allow. She began to gasp and shiver, and he played with her, relishing the way she moved and the soft, agitated sounds of excitement she made. This was revenge for all the times she'd driven him mad, and it was sweet. So sweet.

It was also very short. He could feel his control slipping, and he knew that soon it would be gone. His hands slid to her hips. Bunching silk in his fists, he began pulling her nightgown up. The move met with unexpected resistance. He felt her tense.

"Lucia, I want to see you. I want to look at you." He lifted his head, kissed her mouth. "Lift your arms."

When she did, he pulled the gown up over her head and tossed it aside. Cool air rushed over her naked body, and she gave a nervous laugh. "I'm not sure I want the lamp on after all."

"I do," he said, and took a step back to gaze his fill.

She couldn't look at him. Instead, she stared at a shadowy corner beyond his shoulder. How odd, she thought, to be nervous now. Perhaps it was because of the merciless teasing she'd endured as a girl, but having him stare at her unclothed body made her long to cover herself up. Instead, she clenched the edge of the dressing table even more tightly in her fingers. "I'm very big," she blurted out, and his low chuckle made her realize just how inane that comment was.

"Yes," he agreed. "In all the right places." He cupped her naked breasts, shaping them in his palms. "You are so lovely," he murmured, caressing her. "Even more lovely than you've been in my imagination."

She stared at his face as he looked at her and touched her, and she realized in wonder that he had done this very thing many times in his mind. With that understanding, all the nervous tension went out of her, leaving nothing but her love and desire for him. When he opened his mouth over her nipple again, as he had done through her nightgown moments ago, the sensations that shot through her body were even more delicious than before.

He suckled her more strongly this time, tearing soft little moans from her throat. Raw heat was radiating throughout her body, and she couldn't stop herself from writhing against him in desperate need. "Touch me," she moaned. "Touch me like you did in the carriage."

He shook his head in refusal and sank to his knees. His hands grasped her hips, and then, before her dazed senses could figure out his intent, he leaned in and kissed her, his lips pressing to the curls that covered her secret place. The pleasure was so exquisite, her whole body jolted in response.

"Oh!" she gasped and squeezed her thighs tight together. "Oh, Ian, that's wicked!"

He breathed soft laughter against her, making her shiver. His fingers curved around her inner thighs, inexorably pulling them apart. Then he kissed her again, more deeply this time, his tongue sliding over her. The feeling was so carnal that she gave a startled cry and stirred in his grasp, trying to shy away.

He wouldn't let her. His hands tightened on her inner thighs, his wrists pressing her hips, keeping her open and imprisoned against the dressing table. "Let me," he whispered. "Let me do this."

"I can't!" she moaned, and then she did, clinging to the table behind her as his tongue moved up and down. With each gentle lash of his tongue, indescribable pleasure rose within her and she cried out, her body jerking helplessly against his mouth. The pleasure came in waves, each one carrying her to an even higher peak, until she felt faint and every breath was a pant, until her body was tightening in shuddering, exquisite explosions.

Then suddenly all the strength seemed to drain from her, and she collapsed back against the dressing table with a sigh of pure bliss.

He turned his face and kissed her thigh, then he rose and lifted her into his arms. He carried her to the bed and laid her in the center. He watched her as he unfastened the Cossack trousers and slid them off his hips.

He didn't look like any statue she'd ever seen. His sex was fully, flagrantly stiff, and she stared at him, appreciating for the first time just how this part of things was managed. No wonder it had hurt. She swallowed hard and tried to remember what Grace had told her. "Ian?"

The mattress dipped with his weight as he

moved to lie beside her on the bed. Leaning over her, his weight on one arm, he reached out his free hand to touch her face. "Don't be afraid," he said fiercely.

Lucia looked up at him. "I'm not," she said, and bit her lip.

He smiled a little, his fingertips grazed her cheek. "You are such a liar." He leaned down, and his mouth touched her ear. "If you don't like it, just tell me and I'll stop." He drew a deep breath. "I promise I'll stop."

She could feel his sex hard against her thigh. She lifted her hands to his shoulders and felt a tremor run through him, the effort of holding back. She slid her arms up around his neck, accepting whatever happened. "I love you," she murmured, and kissed him.

He moved on top of her, his knee pushing between hers. "Open for me."

Realizing what he meant, she parted her legs and he positioned his hips between her thighs. She closed her eyes, waiting, but he didn't enter her. Instead, his weight on his forearms, he pressed the tip of his stiffened penis against her, pushing into her soft folds, but not coming inside her.

He stroked her with himself, again and again, until his breathing was harsh and fast, and she was shivering all over.

"Want me?" he asked, pushing himself into her just a little bit, then pulling back out.

She was panting now, her arms tightening convulsively around his neck. She tried to speak, but she couldn't seem to get the words out.

"Was that a yes?" he asked, and pushed into her a little deeper. "Or a no?"

"Oh!" she gasped. "You tease!"

"Damn straight." He pulled back again, caressing her with the tip of his penis. He was breathing hard, and his eyes had that hot gleam like molten silver. "Want me, Lucia? Yes or no."

She nodded, frantic, her hips arching up against his hardness in a way that she was helpless to stop. She forced the words out the only way she could. *"Si, si, oh, si!"*

With a hoarse cry, he entered her, but it didn't hurt this time. It felt so good, she moaned in delighted surprise. He was thick and full inside her, and hot. Scorching hot.

She pressed her hands to his buttocks, urging him to continue, and the change in him was instant, the sudden urgency intense. "Lucia," he groaned, quickening the pace to plunge deep into her, then deeper still. "Oh, God. Oh, God."

She moved with his rhythm, and that queer tension escalated within her, building with each of his thrusts, and once again, the waves of pleasure came, taking her higher and higher. Again, she reached that intense peak and fell apart in that shattering bliss.

Her inner muscles tightened around him in clenching pulsations, and a shudder rocked him.

He groaned, thrust against her one more time, and was still. "Lucia," he said against her neck. "My wife."

Tenderness like she'd never felt before washed over her. Tenderness and an incredible, overpowering joy. She stroked his hair. After a moment, he stirred above her. "I must be getting heavy."

He pressed a kiss to her temple and rolled away from her. He sat up, reaching for the tangle of linens at their feet. He pulled the bedclothes over them both, stretched out his arm, and extinguished the lamp. Then he slid back down and took her in his arms. It was like a homecoming, and she curled up in the circle of his embrace, utterly content. Within moments, his breathing deepened into sleep.

"Good night, Ian," she whispered and smiled into the dark. "My husband."

Lucia was awakened from a deep and heavy sleep by the clatter of dishes. She opened her eyes and found a maid beside her with a tea tray on the bedside table. Turning her head, she saw that the place beside her was empty. Ian was already gone. She stared at his place, the rumpled pillow and sheets, and she felt a stab of disappointment. She wished he had stayed with her. Pushing hair out of her face, Lucia sat up.

"Good morning, ma'am," the maid greeted her in a friendly voice. "I'm Dulcie Sands, kitchen maid. "I've brought your tea. Would you like sugar and milk?"

"No, just plain, thank you. Where is my husband this morning?"

"Oh, the master always rises early when he's here, ma'am. He's up and about hours ago."

"Hours ago? What time is it?"

"Half past ten."

"So late?" No wonder Ian had left her.

"Yes, ma'am. You was sleeping like a baby when I brought early tea. I scraped the coal scuttle and started the fire, and you didn't even stir. The master said you must have been tired after all that walking the two of you did yesterday, so before he went riding, he said to let you sleep until the very last before we sent up your breakfast."

Lucia smiled at that. She suspected the reason she had been so tired had less to do with their tour of the estate and a great deal to with the far more delicious activities of last night. She also knew the routine of the estate from her conversation with the upper servants the day before, and though she had little experience with the running of country estates, she knew rising early was necessary to the daily routine. "From now on, I wish to rise when my husband does. If I am not awake when you bring early tea, please wake me up."

"Of course, if you wish." The maid handed her a steaming cup of tea and gestured to the tray. "Would you like your breakfast in bed?" When Lucia gave an affirmative nod, the maid set the tray on her lap. "Will there be anything else, ma'am?"

"Send for Nan, would you, please, so I can dress?"

"Very good, ma'am." The maid curtsied and departed.

An hour later, Lucia went downstairs. Inquiring of Atherton, she was told Ian was in his study, working, but when she went there, she found working wasn't exactly an accurate description of his activities. He was standing by one of the windows, in profile to her, head bent over the document in his hands. He did not notice her when she came to a halt in the doorway.

The room itself was in disarray, a complete contrast to its neat and tidy appearance the day before when she had toured the house. There were crates all around the room, half-filled with sheaves of documents, books and other such items. The doors of a huge mahogany cabinet against one wall were open, showing the cabinet had been emptied of its contents. The maps that had been hanging on the walls had been taken down and replaced with paintings from other parts of the house.

Lucia looked around, and she realized what this meant. He was packing up his old life.

She started to enter the room but stopped again, watching as his shoulders slumped, and he bent his head. The document fluttered to the floor.

She felt his pain. It shimmered to her across the room, and broke her heart. She backed silently out of the room, tiptoed down the corridor, then turned and tapped her feet decidedly on the wooden floor as if she was just arriving. By the time she entered the room, he was standing by his desk, filling a crate with books.

"Good morning." She looked around. "Redoing the study?"

"Yes."

She had to do something. She had to help him, but she did not know how. She did not know what to do. She walked over to him, put her hand on his arm.

"Ian, are you all right?" Such an inadequate question.

"I am perfectly well." He touched her cheek and smiled at her, but it was a diplomat's smile. It did not reach his eyes.

She put her arms around his waist and rested her cheek on his shoulder. "You'll find a new occupation," she said, willing it to be true. "You just need time."

He stirred, and when she pulled back, he turned away. "Time is something I seem to have plenty of, my dear." He started toward the French doors at the other end of the room. "I believe I shall go for a walk."

Lucia pressed her lips together, heartsick, as she watched him step out onto the terrace. He walked away without a backward glance.

Because of her, he was a man who did not know where he was going, who did not know what to do with his time. She had hoped somehow to fill the void her actions had caused, but she was beginning to realize she never could. She loved him, and that was enough for her, but she was afraid it would never be enough for him. To save herself, she had robbed him of his purpose in life, and she did not know how she could ever make up for that.

Turning away, she glanced at the floor and picked up the document he had been reading earlier. Lucia stood there for a long time, her tears falling onto a commendation from the Prime Minister to Sir Ian Moore for his excellent work in negotiating the Treaty of Bolgheri.

Chapter 20

During the two weeks that followed, Lucia did everything she could think of to make her husband happy. She distracted his mind whenever she could, she filled the holes in his day with her company. She tried to get him to talk about his feelings, but Ian was not the sort of man who talked about things like that. She made love with him, she made him smile, she sometimes made him laugh. But no matter what she did or tried to do, her guilt and his melancholy hung over their life like a gray cloud that grew larger, darker and heavier with each passing day.

At breakfast, she watched him read letters from his colleagues in the diplomatic corps, and she knew how much he missed his former life. She listened during the infrequent times he talked of diplomatic affairs, and she could hear the longing in his voice. He tried to pretend it didn't matter that he was no longer a part of those affairs, but she knew it did matter, and that knowledge tore her heart in half. He received newspapers from all over Europe by post, and he read them every day. Though by the time the ones from the Continent reached Devonshire, most of them were weeks old, Ian pored over them in minute detail, and watching him do so was almost unbearable.

When she had taken away his livelihood, she had not understood just how deep a wound her action would inflict, but she understood it now. She knew she had to make things right, but she did not know how. They had been married just over two weeks when she thought perhaps the opportunity she'd been waiting for had come.

"Your father's visit is nearly over," Ian told her at breakfast as he perused a letter from Lord Stanton. "He is going back to Bolgheri in a week."

Lucia stilled, knife and fork poised over her plate. "He leaves in a week?"

"Nine days from now, Stanton tells me."

With sudden clarity, Lucia knew just what she had to do. Right after breakfast, she wrote a letter to her father, went into Honiton on the pretext of shopping, and sent her letter by express. As the rider galloped away down Honiton's High Street to carry her letter to London, Lucia watched him go and did what she always did when she wanted something impossible. She crossed her fingers and said a prayer. "Let Cesare see me," she whispered, "and let him, for once in his life, behave like a father and not like a prince."

Three days later, the first part of Lucia's prayer was answered. Ian, however, threatened to ruin her plans before they could ever come to fruition.

"You're not seeing him," he said, setting down his knife and fork and glaring at her across the table at breakfast.

"He commands me to come," she answered, ducking her head so Ian wouldn't see her face. She pretended to read the letter in her hand. "Count Trevani says Cesare wants to see me one last time before he leaves."

"The only one who has any right to command you anywhere is your husband, and I say you're not going. Why should you, after the abominable way he has treated you?"

"I think I should see him," she said, choosing her words with care. "After all, I shall probably never see him again." She tapped the letter against her mouth, pretending to consider it, then she nodded. "Yes, I think I should go. I want to go."

"You do?" He stared at her askance. "Why, in heaven's name?"

She smiled, tried to be flippant. "It will enable me to thumb my nose at him one last time. That temptation is irresistible."

Her husband did not seem impressed by that argument, and she became serious. "Ian, I want to go," she said earnestly. "Truly. I want to see him."

"I cannot think why."

She gave him the most truthful answer she could. "I have a new life, and I want to put the old one behind me." She leaned forward and put her hand over his. "If I don't do this, I will always feel bad about it."

"It's that important to you?"

She looked at her husband, the man she still found a fascinating, intoxicating mystery, the man whose happiness she wanted more than anything, the man she loved. "Yes, Ian," she said quietly. "It's that important."

Ian arranged with Dylan for them to stay at the house in Portman Square. Four days after receiving Cesare's summons, they arrived in London, and the day following that, Ian escorted her to her audience with her father.

The prince and his entourage occupied an enormous suite of rooms located opposite Whitehall, where most royal guests of the British Crown were housed for state visits. Ian insisted upon accompanying her to the audience, and when they arrived, they were shown into a gold-and-white antechamber, where they were instructed to wait until her father's minister, Count Trevani, came to fetch her.

"There is no need for you to stay," she told Ian

as she sat down on a padded velvet bench. "Cesare won't allow you to be present during the audience, so you would be sitting out here for heaven knows how long. Why don't you go to your club? Or better yet, go see your colleagues at Whitehall. You will be able to hear all the latest news from them."

"Perhaps I will go across and see Stanton. He's probably in his offices at this time of day."

"Excellent idea. Leave me the carriage, and that way, you can visit with your friend as long as you like. I shall see you at Portman Square later."

Ian didn't need any further persuasion. Lucia watched him walk out the doors, and a bittersweet tenderness pierced her heart. How he loved to be involved in international affairs. Soon he would regain his place in the world, and he would be happy. That was enough for her. It had to be enough.

The doors into Cesare's private suite were flung back and Count Trevani came in, leaving Lucia no time to feel sorry for herself.

"His Serene Highness will see you now." The count offered his arm to her.

"*Grazie, Conte.*" She walked with him through the double doors into an enormous room of glittering gold and white, with a carpet of deep crimson. At the far end of the chamber, a tall, dark figure sat on an ornate receiving chair.

Trevani paused by the door, and Lucia walked toward her father alone. With each step, she prayed for the right words to accomplish her purpose.

Cesare was dressed in the full regalia of his rank, complete with a sash of purple draped across his chest and the Bolgheri crown of rubies on his head.

She studied him as she came closer. In appearance, they were so alike that no one who saw them together had ever doubted her paternity. Yet, there was no familial feeling in her heart when she looked at the man who bore such a striking resemblance to her. There was no respect in her heart for his royal rank. There was no admiration for his dark, still-handsome countenance. In fact, she felt nothing but a mild combination of pity and contempt. The pity was new. The contempt was not.

She couldn't afford to show either of those emotions. Lucia knew she had to be her most deferential, her most charming, her most persuasive. Whatever it took. Whatever would work.

She halted in front of him and gave her deepest curtsy. "Your Highness."

"Lady Moore."

He held out his hand, she kissed his ruby ring.

"Why do you wish to see me, madam?" he asked, speaking as if she were a stranger.

Humility, Lucia. Deference and humility.

"At this moment, Your Highness, I ask that you think of me not as a banished subject in exile and disgrace," she said softly, "though that is what I am. At this moment, I ask that you think of me only as your daughter. Your flesh and blood."

Cesare's mouth pressed into a thin, unforgiving line.

Lucia took a deep breath and said something she had never thought to say in her entire life. "Papa," she said, and she sank to her knees in front of him. "I have come to ask you for a favor."

"So, how is the world stage?"

Lord Stanton looked up from the stacks of work on his desk. "Ian," he greeted with a smile, and stood up. "I heard your wife had an audience with her father, and I thought you might come my way." He beckoned Ian to enter his office. "Come on in, man. Don't hover in the doorway like a stranger. Sit down."

Ian took the offered chair. He glanced at the documents spread across the desk as the other man resumed his seat, and the sight gave him a pang of wistful nostalgia. He shoved it aside. This wasn't his life any longer. He had to accept that. "Busy as usual, I see?"

"Of course. Let me tell you what's been happening in Anatolia. I know you'll be interested."

Ian listened, not at all surprised to learn Sir Gervase was still mucking things up in that region. The situation was still deteriorating, the Turks and Greeks were actually massing troops, and each side was demanding British assistance. Stanton was at his wits' end. "It's now a serious crisis," the earl told him. "As a diplomat, Sir Gervase is hopeless, and if it were up to me, he never would have been sent there, but he's married to the Prime Minister's second cousin, and you know how these things go."

He did know, and even though it was probably wrong to get any enjoyment from Sir Gervase's incompetence and the disastrous results, there was a part of him that did enjoy it. Enjoyed it quite a bit, in fact.

"It's amazing, really," Stanton said, "how sometimes things just fall perfectly into place."

This abrupt segue into the philosophical caught him by surprise, but before he could answer, Stanton went on, "For instance, it's perfect that you've come down to London just now because I wanted to talk with you. I was going to pay a call later if you didn't come by here this afternoon."

"Indeed?" Ian leaned back in his chair. "What's on your mind?"

"Peel's going to be the new Prime Minister."

"That seems a certainty. So?"

"He'll be forming a government, choosing new people." He met Ian's gaze across the desk. "Given the mess Sir Gervase has made of things, Peel will need someone truly skilled to get the Turks and the Greeks calmed down enough for talks. Care to recommend anyone for the job?"

Jubilation rose within him, but he stamped it down at once, telling himself not to jump to conclusions. "Does it matter who I would recommend?"

Stanton grinned. "Not really. Peel's already decided he wants you. He knows all about the brouhaha with Prince Cesare and you and your wife. He doesn't care. Cesare's leaving next week, and you've married the girl, so the scandal's bound to die down and be forgotten. When Peel is confirmed as Prime Minister, he's going to offer to give you back your ambassadorship and send you to Constantinople to patch things up. He's sure the king will agree to the appointment."

They wanted him back. Never in his professional career had Ian ever felt a sweeter moment of triumph than he did right now. He closed his eyes for a moment, savoring it, allowing the satisfaction of it to sink in.

Just then, a commotion was heard out in the corridor.

"Where is Sir Ian?" bellowed a deep, male, unmistakably Italian voice. "Is he with Lord Stanton? Are they in here?"

"Your Highness, if you will—"

"Out of my path." The door opened and Prince Cesare came striding into the room, followed by Stanton's clerk, a very embarrassed-looking Count Trevani, and a pair of Cesare's guards.

Ian and Stanton both rose at once and bowed.

"Your Highness," Ian greeted his father-in-law with cool civility and nothing more. He glanced past Cesare, Count Trevani, and the guards, but he did not see Lucia. "Have you finished your visit with my wife?"

"Visit?" Cesare spat the word at him. "Is that what you call it?"

By now, Ian figured he ought have some understanding of the Italians, but he didn't. They still had the power to confound him. "I beg your pardon?"

Cesare's face flushed with rage. "Never in her life has Lucia asked me for anything. Always when I see her, she puts her chin up, so, and looks ready to spit in my face. But not when she comes on your behalf. No! For you, she asks for favors. For you, she goes down on her knees. A daughter of my blood on her knees?" His voice rose to a shout. "It is unpardonable that you send her to beg for you!"

"What?" Ian did not need to feign his astonishment. Lucia on her knees to her father? It wasn't possible. "Your Highness, I have no idea what you are talking about. You summoned—"

"Hah!" Cesare raked his gaze over Ian with venom. "She wrote the letter asking to see me, but I am not fooled." He pointed an accusing finger at Ian. "You sent her to me. Get him back his profession, she says. Please, Papa, talk to his government, she says. I want him to be happy, she says! Happy?" Prince Cesare slapped the back of one hand against the palm of the other three times in rapid succession. "I ask her what right has he to be happy after what he did, and she says what happened was all her fault! What have you made her, Englishman, that she comes so to me and takes the blame for your dishonor? Did you make her say these things? She says no, but I think, yes!"

Ian stared at the prince, and as he understood just what had happened and what Lucia had done, he realized William was right. There were times when everything in life fell perfectly into place. The aimless lethargy that had been haunting him for weeks vanished, and in its place was something else. A feeling of coming home. He knew who he was and what he wanted and where he belonged. He stepped around Cesare and walked to the door.

"I am not finished!" Cesare roared, turning. "Where are you going?"

Ian paused and looked at Stanton. "Well, I'm bloody well not going to Anatolia." With that, he walked out the door, leaving William to the unenviable job of international diplomacy. He had far more important work to do.

Lucia went into the library at Portman Square and sat in her favorite place on the desk, remembering the times she and Ian had sat here talking in the wee small hours. She wondered how long it would be before they sent him to Constantinople, or some other place. He'd come home sometimes, she reminded herself, but that wasn't much consolation. The only thing that comforted her was knowing Ian would soon have his life back the way he wanted it.

At first, Cesare had refused to grant her request. She should have known even begging on her knees wouldn't move him. She had been forced to use blackmail, and she was relieved he had complied, for she couldn't really have written her memoirs for the scandal sheets. Ian wouldn't have liked it.

A home without a husband beside her wasn't what she had envisioned for herself, but that was the way it had to be. For her, a home and a family were enough for happiness, but she had fallen in love with a man for whom those things would never be enough. Perhaps that was because he did not love her in return. Though he had done the honorable thing and married her, love had not been his reason for doing so. Nonetheless, he had given her a home, a place in the world. Now, she had given him back his purpose, and he would be himself again. That was all she wanted.

She imagined him sitting in the chair as she had seen him so many times. The night he'd told her about his first love. How they'd gotten drunk, and she'd told him about her past.

"I love you," she said as if he was sitting there. "I hope the Turks don't give you too much trouble. Just—" She caught back a sob. "Just remember not to show your emotions, and you'll keep the upper hand."

"Don't cry."

She lifted her head and turned to see him standing in the doorway. Only when he blurred before her eyes did she realize what he'd said. "I'm not crying," she said, then immediately bit her lip and had to turn her face away.

"Liar."

She stared at his chair, blinking back tears. She'd hoped for more time before he came back from Whitehall. Time to compose herself. But it was too late. Now she was unraveling, and he'd see it. Being so honorable, he'd feel guilty about going away.

He walked around in front of her, put a hand under her chin, and tilted her head back to look at her. "Lucia, what have you done?"

He knew.

"I suppose Cesare told you." She scowled through tears. "I asked him not to, but I should have known he wouldn't listen. Damn him."

"He burst into Stanton's offices in a fury, shouting at the top of his lungs, blathering about how you came and begged him to help me get my job back." His hands slid down her arms. "Wife, I don't know whether to kiss you or shake you. When I think of what it must have cost you to go to him—" He broke off and his hands tightened on her arms. "Why did you do it? Why?"

"I love you. I had to give you back what I took from you."

He pulled her off the desk and kissed her hard. "Don't ever do anything like that again," he ordered. "I mean it. Don't ever sacrifice your pride for me or anyone else!"

"Well, it's done now." She swallowed hard and stared at the perfect knot of his cravat. "So when do you leave for Anatolia?"

"I'm not going to Anatolia."

"You're not?" She lifted her face. "Where are you going?"

Ian wrapped his arms around her waist. "Devonshire."

Lucia's heart gave a leap, and she was terribly afraid she'd misunderstood. "What do you mean?"

"I'm saying I turned them down. Told them no."

"You did? But why? Your work is everything to you. If you do not have your work, what will you do?"

He pretended to think it over. "Arrange marriages, perhaps? I'm getting rather good at that, I think." He tightened his arms around her waist. "By the way, I've been to see your mother."

Lucia blinked at the abrupt change of subject. "You went to see Mamma?"

"Yes. I called on her after I left Whitehall. It was a diplomatic assignment to arrange her marriage to Lord Chesterfield."

"What?" Lucia was becoming more astonished by the moment. "Mamma will never marry Chesterfield. She told me so."

Ian kissed her nose. "That's why I'm the diplomat, my dear, and you're not. I have gotten both parties to come to terms, and the wedding is in December. I had to do it, so I hope you don't mind. After all, I couldn't possibly stand for Parliament if my mother-in-law is a courtesan. I'd never get the votes."

"You're going to be in Parliament? You would rather do that than be an ambassador?"

"I told you I wouldn't drag a wife and children all over the world. Don't you remember?"

"You said it wouldn't be right," she choked. "But you didn't marry me by choice, so I thought—"

"So you thought I'd just go off and resume my old life without you?"

"I thought returning to your profession would make you happy. I thought it's want you wanted."

"You're what I want. How could leaving you ever make me happy?" He cupped her face in his hands. "Do you remember the day of our picnic, and how you said I had this strange look on my face?"

"Yes."

"That was the moment I realized how much I need you, need you more than anything else, including my career."

"Oh, Ian!" she cried, afraid to believe it. "I don't want you to ever regret that you married me."

He smiled, and his fingertips caressed her cheeks. "Regret it? How could I?" You are my passionate Italian wife. You are the woman who is going to give me children and whose bed I intend to sleep in every night. You're the reason I'll wake up every morning with a smile on my face. I love you, I will be in love with you every day of my life, and the only day I'm leaving you is the day they put me in the ground."

He loved her. He wasn't leaving. Joy welled up inside Lucia, flooding up and spilling over until she couldn't contain it. She began to laugh and cry at once.

"Here we go again." He pulled a handkerchief out of his pocket and handed it to her.

"You turned them down," she said, her voice muffled by his handkerchief. "For me."

"Damned right. Why should I settle for being a mere ambassador when I can be treated like a king? I believe that was what you promised your husband, wasn't it?"

"Yes." Lucia tossed his handkerchief aside and wrapped her arms around his neck. "Does that mean I'm truly royal now?"

"You? My dear, you may be Prince Cesare's daughter, but you're no princess. Most of the time, you're a blight on my sanity." His arms tightened around her. "By the way, there's one thing I want to know."

She raked a hand through his hair, messing it up with a sigh of pure contentment. "What?"

"Did you let me win that chess game on purpose?" He pulled back and looked at her. "Did you?"

Lucia opened her eyes very wide. "Of course," she said. Deliberately, she bit her lip.

He laughed, his arms tightening around her again. "I want a rematch."

"All right." She paused with a wicked smile. "On one condition."

"No. The condition was that I teach you to play billiards, and I did. No more conditions."

"You'll like this one."

"I liked the last one. Too much if I recall." His mouth curved up at one corner. "So what is this new condition I'm going to like?"

"That you take me upstairs right now and start treating me like a queen."

Ian didn't need to be told twice. "Yes, Your Highness," he said, lifted her into his arms, and headed for the door.

DISCOVER CONTEMPORARY ROMANCES *at their*
SIZZLING HOT BEST FROM AVON BOOKS

Avon Romantic Treasures

Unforgettable, enthralling love stories, sparkling with passion and adventure from Romance's bestselling authors